EMERALD VICES

KUZNETSOV BRATVA
BOOK 2

NICOLE FOX

Copyright © 2024 by Nicole Fox

All rights reserved.

No part of this book may be reproduced in any form or by any electronic or mechanical means, including information storage and retrieval systems, without written permission from the author, except for the use of brief quotations in a book review.

EMERALD VICES

I did a bad thing...

And the man I love is here to make me pay for it.

"You're coming with me," he snarls.

"There's zero percent chance THAT's happening," I fire back.

But I only get about two steps away before Andrey decides to take matters into his own hands.

Literally.

And it's me.

I'm "matters."

So now, I'm back where I started.

Stuck somewhere I don't belong with a dangerous man who hates me.

The difference between now and then?

This time around...

I'm pregnant with his twin babies.

EMERALD VICES is Book 2 of the Kuznetsov Bratva duet. The story begins in Book 1, EMERALD MALICE.

1

NATALIA

Everyone is staring.

The people I pass look at me as if they can see every single thing I've done. Like my sins are splayed across my face and written in blood on my hands for the world to see.

What? I want to scream at them. *Never seen a desperate woman before? Never seen a pregnant murderess?*

I didn't kill anyone, though. At least, I pray I didn't.

He can't be dead.

The moment I think of how Andrey sagged to his knees, the smell of gunsmoke still so strong and acrid it makes my eyes water, my stomach churns and my chest tightens until I have to stop walking.

But I can't stop. If I stop, they'll kill me.

If not Slavik, then Viktor.

If not Viktor, then Nikolai.

If not Nikolai, then… well, hell, if Andrey is alive, he probably wants to kill me, too.

The same way I wanted to kill him. Because that's the only reason I would've picked up that horrible, terrible, life-stopping, death-bringing instrument, isn't it? That's the only reason I would've pointed it at another human being, right?

All I see when I close my eyes is the nameless criminal with his gun pointed at my mother and then my father. All I can think about is how easily and carelessly he pulled the trigger.

I'm no better than him now.

Teetering off course, I stretch my hand out and grasp the closest object I can reach. I sag against a sign post, the only thing keeping me from collapsing in a puddle of tears.

People keep walking past me without bothering to stop and check in. I don't mind. No one needs an audience when they're spiraling into madness.

Until one man slows and pauses. "Excuse me… ma'am?"

I flinch at the voice, kind and concerned though it may be.

The man addressing me has a young face, but deep-set wrinkles around his eyes. He's wearing a navy jacket and a wool bucket hat that comes down to his eyebrows.

"Are you okay?"

I blink at him and he seems to think I can't understand him, because he repeats the question again.

"I'm fine," I mutter. "Just waiting for someone." The lie flows off my tongue so easily, so smoothly, that I'm impressed with my own presence of mind.

But I don't know this man. I don't know who he's working for or what he wants with me.

I can't stay here. I can't stop.

Picking up my feet, I force myself to walk away, moving farther down a road I don't know the end of.

I don't even know how I got out of the manor in the first place. All my mental and emotional bandwidth is focused on keeping me upright, keeping me functioning long enough to get somewhere "safe."

Then again, now that I've shot the man who practically runs this city… *is* there such thing as a safe place?

I eventually find a bench and drop down onto it. People still hurtle past in every direction, their features blurring, morphing into the next, and the next, and the next.

I think I see people I recognize in the crowd. Katya, Mila, Misha, Shura… but none of it is real. I'm surrounded by strangers. One after the next after the next.

As I sit there, growing numb, something cold weighs against my chest. I claw at it and feel the pendant Andrey gave me.

I curl my fingers over the interlinked cherries and bite back tears until I taste blood.

Please don't let him die.

I wish I could ask someone how he's doing. But I don't have a phone or a purse or money or hope. I'm a sitting duck. Waiting for retribution. For the cavalry. For the consequences I know I must face.

I tuck my knees to my chest.

For a moment, I close my eyes, but then I see Yelena's wide-open mouth as Andrey slashed her throat open. I shudder and tear my eyes open.

When I'm sick of sitting, I get to my feet and walk into the nearest restaurant. It's a small shop with faded pictures of pizza displayed in their greasy window.

Ignoring the gnawing hunger in my stomach, I approach the portly older woman behind the counter. She reminds me of Yelena. I shudder again.

"Can I help you, sweetheart?"

"Uh… I'm sorry—" I cringe at my own ineptitude. But maybe it can work in my favor. "I-I need help…"

The woman's smile falters.

"I was on my way to meet my husband." I place my hands on my pregnant belly and step away from the counter so she can really appreciate my predicament. "When I was mugged—"

The woman gasps. "You poor thing!"

I don't fight back my tears. They're real, though not quite for the reasons this woman might suspect. "H-he took everything," I stammer. "My purse, my phone. If you could just let me… let me c-call my husband?"

"Of course, *cara mia*. There's a phone in the back. Step behind the counter." She ushers me back with a raised arm. "That's right, come, come." She shows me to a phone in the kitchen and then backs away around a corner to give me privacy.

There are only two numbers I know by heart, but I can't call Aunt Annie. Especially not in her condition. So I call Katya instead.

When we were drunk and stumbling home, we swore we'd always be each other's emergency calls. If she needed bail, if I needed to bury a body—we're each other's person.

Problem is, that was before Katya got involved with Andrey's closest friend.

Funny how her romantic choices always come back to bite me in the ass. Although, that's precisely why she owes me.

I hate myself for even thinking it. But I'm a desperate woman with no options left. Punching in Katya's number, I pray to God that she's not with Shura when she picks up.

"Hello?"

"Kat…" I breathe, pressing my lips into the receiver as another waiter rushes past. "It's me."

"Nat!" she practically yells. "Oh, thank *fuck*! Where—"

"Are you alone?"

The urgency in my voice silences her. "I… Yes, I'm alone."

"Shura can't know I'm calling. No one can know, okay?"

"Nat, you don't sound good." I can tell she's straining to hear me. Hell, I'm straining to hear myself. "What's with all the noise? Where are you?"

"I'm at…" Looking up, I find a neon sign. "—Francesca's Pizzeria. I need your help, Kat. If you can get my phone and my wallet here, I swear I won't ask you for another thing for as long as I live."

"You're still planning on leaving? *Now?*"

I don't have time for her shock or her reservations. "Kat, please. I'm desperate and you're the only one I trust."

There are a few gaping seconds of silence. "Okay, Francesca's Pizzeria. I'll send you what you need. Don't move, do you hear me?"

Clutching the phone tighter still, I ask the one question that makes my heart want to burst right out of my chest. "Kat—" I take a deep breath, the words still coming out in a hitch. "I-is he okay?"

She doesn't pretend not to understand. "Shura's with him now. He's going to be fine."

Only with that assurance do I hang up.

2

ANDREY

"Easy there."

Misha squints at me, his color still ghostly pale. He attempts to raise his arm to shield his eyes from the chandelier directly above us, but he barely gets halfway before a hiss of pain escapes through his teeth.

"She—" I can't bring myself to say Yelena's name. "—really put a dent in your shoulder."

Clasping Misha's forearm, I reel him forward so that he can sit up a little better. He looks around and catches sight of Remi across the room. Still unconscious, still recovering.

"Wh…what happened?"

I prop a pillow behind him and sit back down. "You fainted. Picked an inconvenient place to fall, too. You whacked your head against the edge of the china cabinet. Dr. Abdulov said you might have a mild concussion."

Misha rubs the back of his head with his undamaged arm, and I feel the urge to pat his knee or clasp his shoulder. I want to do something, anything to wipe that scared, worried look off his face.

But I don't know what the fuck I'm doing.

This is Natalia's area of expertise. She was the one who knew how to comfort and coddle and reassure. She was the one who knew what to say and when to say it.

But Natalia isn't here.

My little bird took flight, leaving behind a broken dog, a traumatized boy, and a bloodstained bullet that I had to pry out of my arm.

"You'll be okay. The shoulder will take a few weeks to heal, though, so take it easy."

Misha looks around the room. I know what he's going to say before he even opens his mouth. "Where's Natalia?"

I dodge the question because I still don't have an answer. "You did great back there, Misha. If it weren't for you, we'd never have known what Yelena was really up to."

His cheeks brighten with pleasure.

"I owe you my gratitude. As do all my men. You single-handedly found the mole in our midst."

"It wasn't single-handed." Misha's forehead wrinkles, his lips turning down. "I wasn't the one to kill her."

There's no denying the bloodlust in his voice. I can relate, intimately. And yet hearing it thick in the voice of my fourteen-year-old ward is unsettling.

I know exactly what Natalia would say if she were here: *He's too young to feel so responsible for us.*

Then again, maybe I'm just fooling myself. Maybe I have no fucking clue what Natalia would say if she were here. She's already surprised me twice today.

"Andrey?" His voice is barely a whisper. "W-why did I faint?" There's shame driving the question.

"You were badly injured. Adrenaline was the only thing keeping you upright. That and the desire to protect Natalia."

"But Natalia..." He shakes his head as though he's trying to dislodge a memory. "It's all hazy... I don't remember all of it. But I do remember Yelena trying to attack Natalia."

"She tried," I acknowledge. "But she didn't succeed."

"She had a gun," Misha continues. "But she dropped it, and then... did... did Natalia pick it up?"

I don't say a word. It takes only a few more seconds before the memory clicks into place. Misha's eyes flare as he remembers.

He stares at my arm. At the bandage similar to the one wrapped around my torso. I've got a matching set.

"You killed Yelena," he wheezes. "And Natalia... she *shot* you."

"She was scared, Misha. I'd just killed an old woman—one that we knew and loved—in cold blood. I don't think she could process the brutality of it."

I've had ninety minutes to come to terms with what happened in the living room, including my role in it. I should've done it differently. I should've knocked Yelena out and killed her later, somewhere far from Natalia. I was a fool to think that whatever feelings she had for me would override her trauma.

Then again, I wasn't thinking at all when I took that knife to Yelena's throat. My instincts were simple: *Kill the bitch before she hurts my woman.*

Misha shakes his head. "But to actually shoot you…"

"I don't think she meant to shoot at all." I saw her face just before she pulled the trigger. She wanted me to stay away from her. When I didn't, she panicked. "It was an accident."

A single tear slides down Misha's cheek. "Where is she now?"

Great fucking question. In the chaos of the moment, she slipped through the cracks and out into the city. She could be anywhere, for all I know.

I settle on the only thing I know for sure. "We'll find her."

Misha looks skeptical, but he swallows and nods. I pat his good shoulder. "Dr. Abdulov will be in to check on you soon. Until then, get some rest. That's an order, soldier."

Misha's eyes spark with life. "Soldier?"

"You proved yourself today, Misha. If that doesn't make you part of the Bratva, I don't know what does."

Stepping out of the infirmary, I come face to face with Shura. His face is set in hard, grim lines. "Have you dealt with her body?"

"The old bitch has been taken care of," he snarls. "The living room has been stripped down and wiped clean. There's no sign she was ever there."

"Good. Now, we have to purge the whole damn manor of her."

I can tell by the dark look in Shura's eyes that he's taken

Yelena's betrayal just as personally as I have. "I'm on my way to her room now."

"No," I say. "I want to look through it myself first."

"We'll do it together. By the way, I—" He pauses for a split second. "I know it's not a good time but there's something else you should know."

Fuck. Already, this new information smells of Slavik. "What is it?"

"Vaska and Yuri sent in their daily report. The old man was just seen meeting with the Halcones."

"The fucking Halcones? He must be desperate."

"It might be a desperate move," Shura agrees. "But it could also prove to be an effective one. The Halcones have no code of honor. That makes them deadly."

"Spare me. I know the kind of scum they are. Let them come."

I brush past him. On any other day, this information would have demanded my full attention. Right now, it feels like a fly buzzing stubbornly around my ear.

The smell of gunpowder and bleach stings my nostrils as I pass the living room, but I keep moving.

"Andrey!" Shura grunts, rushing to keep pace with me. "I know you've got a lot on your mind right now, but we can't just ignore this. The Halcones are a dangerous new piece on the board."

I'm in full view of the pool house when I stop short. "Need I remind you that I'm the reason those scum retreated into their holes in the first place?"

Shura's jaw tightens. "They didn't have the backing of Slavik Kuznetsov back then."

Bzz-bzz, goes the fly. I swat it away. "Have you heard from Katya?"

He sighs. "I spoke to her half an hour ago. She's heard nothing."

Natalia's bags are still sitting in the living room. She has literally nothing on her—no ID, no money, no phone. She's untraceable, a needle in a city-sized haystack.

But at least she can't go far.

"She'll come back home, 'Drey," he promises in a measured voice. "She doesn't have anywhere else to go."

Just what I want to be: a last resort.

Before I can tell Shura to stick his reassurances where the sun doesn't shine, my phone rings. There's only one reason I can think of that Katya would contact me instead of Shura. Answering, I turn my back on Shura.

"Did she contact you?" I demand.

Katya's breathing is heavy on the other line. "Yes. She sounded strange… She wasn't herself."

The woman put a hole in my arm less than two hours ago. This is not new information. "Where is she?"

"Francesca's Pizzeria. She's expecting me to show up with her phone and purse."

She's not so far gone that she's scrapped her escape plan entirely. Unfortunately for her, *I* certainly have.

If the past few hours have taught me anything, it's that I can't let Natalia out of my sight.

Not now.

Maybe not ever.

3

NATALIA

As it turns out, one mozzarella stick is all I need to take the edge off my hunger. Either that or I'm positively stuffed with anxiety.

As soon as I hung up with Katya, I felt nauseous. *Will she actually come? Will she bring Shura with her? Or worse: Andrey? Will she help me leave or will she try to convince me to stay?*

As the minutes tick by, the restaurant clears out. Apart from me, there's an old man by the bar and a young couple canoodling at a table by the window. There are a million couples like that in a million restaurants across the world, but I can't stop watching this one.

It's easy. It's normal. It's human nature to touch and laugh and stare longingly.

And it'll never be mine.

The pang of seeing what I'll never have is enough to distract from the nausea, so at least I've got that going for me. But I'm so lost in someone else's life that I barely notice the sleek black Escalade drawing up outside the restaurant until the bell above the door dings.

He's beautiful as he enters, backlit by daylight and set into harsh relief by the red neon sign hanging on the wall.

Say what you will about Andrey Kuznetsov, but he's always been easy on the eyes.

Some part of me must have known he'd come for me, because I'm calm. Whatever he's here to do, I deserve it.

He sees me and pauses. Breathes. Those silver-gray eyes are as cold as the wind outside.

I'm going to kill Katya.

But a second later, as Andrey takes the seat next to me, all thoughts of my soon-to-be-dead best friend vanish. His silver eyes ripple with something—anger? Betrayal? Hurt?

"Are you with me, *lastochka*?"

I blink a couple of times before squeaking out a meek, "Yes."

His eyes flash again, and I finally understand what I saw the first time: *relief.*

Despite the fact that I… did what I did. And then ran away instead of staying put to see if he was alright.

I curdle with shame. "Are you going to punish me?" I blurt before my courage fails.

"No."

I draw in a sharp breath. "Kill me?"

"Jesus, little bird," he sighs. "Do you really think I would hurt you?"

"*I* hurt *you*."

"Do you plan on shooting me again?"

Startled, my eyes dart to his face. "Of course not."

"Then there's no reason to mention what happened, as far as I'm concerned." My gaze flits to his arm, but I can't tell how badly he's injured while he's wearing a trench coat.

"I shot you, Andrey. At the very least, you should be angry with me."

I think I see a flash of anger skyrocket across his eyes, but I blink once and it's gone. He looks calm as a glacier. "I'm not angry."

Frowning, I lean away from him. "Then there's a catch."

He leans forward all at once and takes my face in his hands. I freeze, unable to tear my gaze away from his. I feel his thumb drag a half-moon arch against my cheek as his eyes say something I don't understand, but that I feel in my soul.

Then he drops both hands and gets slowly to his feet. "Come now. It's time to get you home."

I stay seated. "Nothing's changed, Andrey."

He responds by extending his hand to me.

My body is aching. So is my head. Every part of me is spent. So when he says nothing and that hand stays outstretched, I do the only thing I can do: I take it.

We drive back to the manor in silence. He doesn't mention Yelena and neither do I. But her ghost lurks between us, taking up space and oxygen, reminding me that she's not leaving anytime soon.

A few lone stars twinkle above me as I get out of the Escalade and walk into the manor beside Andrey.

"I know you're tired, but we have to make sure the baby is okay."

With one hand on the small of my back, he steers me upstairs to a gorgeous guest bedroom on the second floor. We pass no one and I'm grateful for that. The thought of seeing even Mila or Katya feels overwhelming.

"Dr. Abdulov will be up soon," Andrey informs me. "He's just seeing to Misha first."

That gets my attention. "Misha," I whisper, drenched with new shame.

I rushed past him when I ran. I remember his shocked, ashen face. The way his body teetered to the side as though he no longer had any control of it.

"He must hate me, too."

"He wants to know that you're safe. Just like I do."

My chest constricts so tightly I have to fight to breathe. Luckily, I'm spared from having to respond when the door opens and the doctor walks in.

"How is Misha?" I butt in before Andrey can ask.

If Dr. Abdulov is surprised to see me, he shows no indication. "Doing well. The shoulder will heal in time and the concussion will fade in a few days."

"Concussion?" I repeat anxiously. "But—"

"Thank you, Doctor," Andrey interrupts. "Let's just stick to a quick examination, shall we? As you can see, Natalia is very tired." The *shut-up-and-don't-give-her-any-more-information* in his tone is very much implied.

Abdulov takes the subtle reprimand in stride. "Of course, sir."

I turn my attention to Andrey. "I want to see him."

"You'll be able to see him in the morning when you're rested."

"No deal."

He glowers at me and I glower right back as Dr. Abdulov begins his examination.

"Ms. Boone," he remarks after a few tense, silent minutes, "it seems everything is okay. Your blood pressure is a little higher than I would like—" He looks between us as though the answer to why is obvious. "—but we'll monitor it closely and see if we can bring it down over the next few days." His smile falters even as he tries to brighten his tone. "As for the babies, they are perfectly healthy."

Andrey is still staring at me with daggers in his eyes when suddenly, his mouth falls open. He turns to the doctor. "What did you say?"

I squeeze my eyes closed, and I *am* tired. I could go to sleep right now. Maybe I should.

"The babies are healthy," Dr. Abdulov repeats warily.

The silence stretches. I wait for Andrey to turn his anger on me. Clearly, I knew about the twins and didn't tell him. How many mistakes can I make in one day before I become unforgivable?

"Thank you, Doctor," Andrey finally says. "That will be all."

I crack my eyes open as an immensely relieved Dr. Abdulov gathers up his equipment and retreats.

The moment the door clicks shut, Andrey turns his smoldering gaze on me. "You knew."

"I found out during my check-up this morning." Technically, it was yesterday morning. But since I haven't slept, it feels like we're still living the same impossibly long day.

"Twins," he breathes as though he's trying the word on for size. "And they're both…?"

"Girls," I confirm. I struggle upright. "Andrey, I know you're angry—"

"Why do you assume I'm angry?" There's a flicker of impatience in his voice. "I'm not."

"You're not?"

"Neither one of us was in the right headspace to have any type of serious conversation." He walks over to the bed and folds back the covers. I'm not going to lie—the gorgeous feather down looks extremely inviting. "And we're still not. It's time for you to get some rest."

I get to my feet. "Not until I see Misha."

"Jesus Christ, Natalia!" he snarls.

I soften my tone and decide to ask rather than demand. "Please?"

With a tired sigh, he gestures towards the door.

There's only one light left on in the infirmary. It illuminates Remi, who's still lying on the examination table. His breathing has evened out since the last time I saw him, though.

I give the loyal dog an affectionate pat before following Andrey to the other end of the room. Misha's sprawled flat on a single bed, his bandaged arm stiff at his side while the other rests across his face. He looks even younger when he sleeps. I can't resist the urge to bend down and press a kiss to his exposed cheek.

I can't see Andrey, but I can sense him at my shoulder. "Thanks for taking care of him for me."

"I didn't do it just for you," he rasps low. "He's just as much my boy as he is yours."

Twisting around, I catch his gaze. Half his face is drenched in shadow. I can see only one silver eye glinting down at me.

"You're right," I acknowledge, placing a hand on my stomach. "He's ours. Just like these babies."

4

ANDREY

"Nat!" Misha protests as she tries to smooth the shaggy bangs out of his eyes.

"You need a haircut," she scolds affectionately. Remi whines as if to agree. The dog woke up a few hours ago and since then, he's remained squarely between Misha and Natalia.

"I like my hair like this."

"It's getting in your eyes."

"That's the point."

She laughs. "Who're you trying to impress, huh?"

As Misha goes on the defensive, I continue down the hallway before either one of them notices I've been observing them. It's good to see both of them smile. Which is one of the reasons I've taken to dropping by every hour or so to check on both of them.

The other reason being that Natalia seems to be doing better

—but for how long? Everything is going to catch up with her eventually, and I want to be close by when it does.

I continue down the hall to my makeshift office, which, up until a few hours ago, was a guest bedroom. Shura is standing in front of the queen-sized bed waiting for me when I walk in.

"What's going on?"

"The Halcones are circling," he says ominously.

I stiffen. "They've made a move?"

"They're trying to infiltrate your clubs to push their own supply."

"You're fucking kidding me."

"I wish. Security from Silver Moon and Maria called this morning. Two different sets of men raised suspicions at each, but they only managed to hold on to one guy. The others got away."

I own a fuckton of property in this city, and the clubs that Shura just named are far from the most glamorous of it. Only one person alive would start a guerilla war against me by sneaking into Maria.

Unfortunately for me, that person is my brother.

"That *mudak*," I growl. I'm already imagining all the ways I'm going to torture Viktor before I end his miserable existence.

Maybe he was informing on me, too. Just like Yelena. Or maybe the defection is recent. A petty act of retribution.

"We need to act, 'Drey," Shura urges.

Squaring my jaw, I nod. "It's time to bring in the reinforcements. If Slavik is successful, then Bujar, Cevdet, and Luca have as much to lose as we do. We need to shore things up before there's any risk of any of them turning on me. Schedule a meeting as soon as possible."

My second nods and leaves. As he slips through the door, I spy Dr. Abdulov hovering in the hallway. I wave him inside.

I stationed the good doctor—rather forcefully—in a guest room on the property. Until I'm sure Misha and Natalia are fine, I want them under near-constant medical care.

The fact Dr. Abdulov is clutching his clipboard against his chest like a security blanket makes me think my instincts were correct.

"What's wrong?"

"The babies are doing well—"

"I know that already," I snap. "I'm not asking about the babies right now. I want to know how she is doing."

He shuffles from one foot to the other, refusing to lower the clipboard. "Natalia was very clear that she didn't want me conveying her personal information to anyone else."

I almost smirk. "You mean to me?"

"She... uh, did mention in passing that... ahem... that you're not her next of kin. Nor are you her husband." The man is sweating and tugging at his collar. "She wanted the details of her condition, unrelated to the babies, to be kept private."

I take a step towards the skittish doctor and he flinches back. "Those babies inside her are mine, Abdulov," I snarl. "She is mine, too—wife or not. I'm not going to let a piece of metal on her finger determine what I can and can't know about her."

He swallows under my unwavering glare. "I suspect that she's experiencing some prenatal depression."

"That's in addition to the PTSD?"

Abdulov consults his clipboard again. "In my professional opinion, I think that perhaps the combination of the two is creating an unstable psychological environment. I spoke to Ms. Boone at length. The pregnancy hormones might be interfering with her existing PTSD. Her fears and panic could be heightened."

Perhaps enough to pick up a gun and pull the trigger.

"So fix it."

The doctor's brow creases. "This is not a condition with a quick and easy solution, sir. Ms. Boone has a history of depression and anxiety." He clears his throat. "Her current mental state speaks to a deeper problem. She should be in therapy. Intensive therapy that will help her work through some of her past traumas so that she can deal with her current responses."

Predictable though his answer is, I don't have time for it. There are enough external threats that I can't spend time on the ones that exist inside Natalia's head.

"What about pills? Antidepressants?"

"There are medications I can prescribe," he admits. "But I'm hesitant to do so considering her advanced stage of pregnancy. Regardless, pills alone won't help. Ideally, therapy and medication should be used hand in hand. No amount of drugs will make her feel safe if she isn't in a calm, nurturing environment."

Nurturing. What a fucking joke. How the hell am I supposed to nurture her when my very presence is a trigger?

"Thank you, Doctor," I say, dismissing him with a wave of my hand.

Abdulov passes Shura once more on the way out of the room.

"Meeting is set," he informs me as he shuts the door. "All three men are in. Ten o'clock tonight at Maria."

"What about the Halcones spy?"

"He'll be waiting for you in a cell beneath the club," Shura says with grim satisfaction. "Along with some toys to encourage him to talk."

5

ANDREY

"Boss?"

I jolt away from the wall as if there's any way I can hide from Leonty that I've been standing outside Natalia's room like a lovesick teenager.

"What is it?"

"Mino has just arrived." When I show no sign of recognizing who the hell that is, Leonty hurries to explain. "He's the physical therapist that you had me hire to help Misha with his shoulder."

"Right." I nod, embarrassingly grateful for the excuse to knock on the door. "I'll let him know."

Natalia, Misha, and Remi have spent the entire day locked away in her room. Even their meals are being brought up to them, Remi's included.

At first, I was just grateful Natalia was content to stay in the main house instead of the pool house. Now, proximity isn't enough. I want to see her.

With an abrupt knock, I let myself in before anyone can reply. Natalia, Misha, and Mila are sprawled across the bed, eating from the same charcuterie board.

"Hey there, big guy," Mila greets in a teasing lilt. "Come to join the party?"

Based on the way Misha doesn't look up and Natalia frowns, I'm not sure I'm invited.

"Misha, Mino is here for your physical therapy appointment."

Remi perks up from where he's napping on the floor when Misha climbs off the bed gingerly. He gives the dog a gentle pat and slinks out of the room without acknowledging me.

Mila hesitates for only a second before she too jumps up, grabbing the tray of food as she goes. "I just remembered I have some… laundry to do."

"Since when?" Natalia hisses.

Mila offers her only a meek wave before disappearing through the door. Remi takes her place, nuzzling his head in Natalia's lap.

She avoids my eyes as I round the bed and sit down at the edge of it, far from her. "How are you feeling today?"

"Misha's acting like everything is fine, but I know it's not."

"Why do you say that?"

"Intuition."

"He had a big shock yesterday," I say, reminding myself once again that I need to give her a calm and nurturing environment. "Just give it time."

She shakes her head. "He's angry at me. He's just not admitting it."

"Leave the kid alone, Natalia—"

"He's in pain, Andrey!" she snaps. "Maybe you can ignore it, but I can't."

I grimace. *We're off to a great fucking start.*

"Maybe I should speak to him."

She eyes me suspiciously. "No offense, but you're not exactly great with emotions. Or other humans."

I fall back, biting down every snap and retort that's circulating in my head. It's amazing how, even now, she can push all my buttons.

"Where's Katya?"

She picks at the comforter, her lip curling. "Avoiding me, obviously."

"Don't be mad at her. She did the right thing by telling me where you were."

"She should have done what I asked her to do without involving you."

"So you could leave? Again?"

Remi's looking up at her with those bright, brown eyes of his. Almost as though he knows what we're discussing.

"Oh, don't look at me like that. You'll break my heart." Sighing, she drags her eyes back up to mine. Any trace of affection she had for Remi is gone when she looks at me. "It was the only way, Andrey. The only way."

"To do what, exactly?"

She throws a hand up. "To protect myself and my children. And yes, I understand why Misha would be upset by that—but I didn't leave him behind because I wanted to. I *had* to."

"And what about me?"

She stops short. "Huh?"

"You were leaving me behind, too. Did you ever stop to think about that?" It's hard to keep the note of bitterness from my voice.

She presses her lips together. "I won't apologize for trying to give our babies a better life. A safer life."

"I'm not asking you to. I can see why you thought you had to leave. It's not like I made you feel very safe in the end, did I?"

Her mouth opens and closes, uncertain of whether I'm being sincere or leading her into a trap. Even that uncertainty proves how badly I've failed her.

I rise to my feet. "I have to step out for a bit. If you need anything, let Leonty know. He'll be stationed outside your door at all times."

Her eyes go wide. "That's not necessary—"

"It's not negotiable, either."

"Andrey—"

The argument freezes on her tongue when I bend down and kiss her forehead. "If you need me, call me. I *will* answer."

"So, the old *pakhan* is really back?" Luca asks, sliding a hand over the lapels of his double-breasted suit.

"With a vengeance," I confirm.

The club we're in, Maria, is teeming with trendy young people, their skin dappled with sweat, smoke rising up in curls from the tips of their thin French cigarettes. Electronic music pulses dully through the walls, like the place itself has a heartbeat. The frantic energy infects all of us, myself included.

Luca is nodding along with the bass while Cevdet watches me with an excited glint in his eyes. Bujar alone looks apprehensive.

I have a feeling I know why. He's the most vulnerable link in our chain. He doesn't have the manpower to protect his business interests the way the rest of us do.

"Don't worry," I assure them. "I plan on taking out the threat soon enough."

"I hope so," Luca warns. "The longer this takes, the more money we'll lose."

Cevdet rolls his eyes. "Really, Luca, talking about money at a time like this? It's so crass. This is an offense against our young *pakhan* and it cannot stand."

"Two things can be equally true and equally important at the same time," Luca quips with a wave of his hand.

It's one of the things I appreciate most about Luca: the man is straightforward.

"We need to close ranks," Cevdet booms, reaching for another cigar. "Strangle those pesky birds before they take flight."

"Who exactly is this new enemy we're facing?" Luca asks.

"No one you've heard of. Just a small-time cartel that started to gain some traction around the time I took over as *pakhan*," I answer. "They call themselves The Halcones."

Luca wrinkles his nose. "And they're dangerous?"

"They cost me dearly once."

All three men are watching me carefully, waiting for me to volunteer more. But I'm not here to dredge up past losses.

"My father is more capable than I imagined," I say. "He can be very persuasive when he wants to be."

"Are you unsure of your Bratva's loyalty?" Bujar asks.

My jaw clenches. "Of my inner circle—not at all. But there are a lot of men under my command, and many of them swore their allegiance to my father first."

The mood of our meeting wavers beneath the pulse of the strobe lights. Cevdet leans forward. "If we're to win, we need to act fast."

"As we speak, there's a man being held in the basement of this club," I inform them. "Shura hasn't managed to get much information out of him. But I'm going to see if I'll have better luck."

Bujar keeps his eyes fastened on me. "You think he could be useful?"

"He's our only lead," I say, rising to my feet. "I intend to make him useful. Whether he likes it or not."

Cevdet's lips curl into a sinister smile. "Let us know how it goes."

"You three just sit back. Enjoy my booze and my cigars. I'll return soon enough."

They raise their glasses as I walk out of the VIP room through a hidden panel door recessed into the wall. The moment I step into the narrow corridor, motion sensor lights flicker to life, lighting the spiral path down towards the basement of Maria.

The temperature drops as I descend. My shoes echo off the rough-hewn concrete floors.

Shura is leaning against a wall to the side, a toothpick dangling between his teeth. The man across from him is suspended from the ceiling by his arms. Blood coats his bare chest and sweat sticks his gray briefs to his legs. If the bruising on his torso is anything to go by, his insides are as ugly and beaten as the rest of him.

"Who do we have here?"

"This is Diego," Shura explains.

The man, balancing precariously on his tiptoes, flops as hard as he can. It's pitiful. "P-please. Let me go." Blood trickles from a split in his lower lip. Now that his head is raised, I can see his black eyes and the blood crusted along his chin.

"You haven't told us anything interesting, Diego," I tut. "What makes you think you deserve to be let go?"

"Please!" he begs. "I'm innocent."

"You snuck into my club, assaulted one of my waitresses, and tried to push an inferior product on my premises." I unleash a calm, eerie smile on him. "That doesn't sound like 'innocence' to me."

"Please," he tries again. "I'll do anything."

I cock my neck to the side. "'Anything'?"

"Yes, just… let me go."

"I might let you go, Diego—*if* you give me something useful. If your intel proves accurate, then you will earn back your freedom."

"I don't know anything!" Diego wails. "They sent us here to push the product. Those were the orders, so that's what I did."

Shura looks incredulous but he doesn't question me. Instead, he walks to my side and whispers, "Don't you think I tried this already? He's a puppet. No better than Misha was to Nikolai. He doesn't know shit."

Determined, I walk over to Diego. Fresh sweat carves a path through the dried blood smeared over his mouth. "Give me something, Diego. Your life depends on it."

His face crumples. "I was just… following orders. P-please…"

"Whose orders?"

"The man I was with—Edgar Vargas—he was the one telling me what to do."

"Who is he?"

His eyes flicker to Shura. Then back to me. "He's a cousin of one of the Halcones. That's all I know. I was told to follow his orders."

Judging by the way he's trembling, Diego is ready to sing like a canary if it means he gets to live. Problem is, he doesn't know the song I need to hear. I guess I'll have to make do with a few measly notes.

"If tonight had been successful, where would you have gone?" I press. "There must have been a meeting point."

He squints, blinking furiously as a bead of sweat drips right into his eye. "We were staying at a motel in the middle of the city. Last Resort Inn."

Slapping my hand against his bloody face, I nod in approval. "You just earned yourself a few extra hours, Diego. Spend them wisely."

6

ANDREY

Luca glares at the peeling walls of The Last Resort Inn, his nose wrinkled in disgust. "This establishment is beneath us."

Bujar rolls his eyes. "We're not here for a slumber party, Luca. Or are you and your alligator skin loafers too good to even set foot in a place like this?"

"We should have sent our men to handle this, is what I'm saying."

"Where's the fun in that?" Cevdet asks.

I glare at all three men until they fall silent. Then I step in front of them, my shadow falling across the dark parking lot, distorted into something monstrous by the low-angled light at my back.

"We agreed on our purpose tonight, gentlemen," I growl. "We're here to make a statement and show a united front. The Halcones don't know what they're up against yet. Maybe if they do, they'll be more wary about starting a war they can't possibly win."

"Hear, hear." Cevdet applauds, his soft clapping the only sound in the eerily quiet night.

He's not used to doing the grunt work anymore. This is probably the first mission he's been on in well over a decade, so I understand his excitement. He practically foams at the mouth every time he looks up at the corner unit where Edgar Vargas is supposedly sheltering for the night.

Luca pulls out a sleek knife, the blade glinting in the moonlight. "Well, then we might as well get this over with."

The four of us trudge up the steps of the motel, having already secured a second key card from the receptionist's desk. Shura has his gun aimed at the poor schmuck manning the front desk so he can't alert Vargas about our impending visit.

"Who's going in first?" Luca asks.

"I think our fearless leader ought to do the honors," Cevdet suggests.

That subtle thread of sarcasm running through everything he does and says irks me, but I set the irritation aside. Now is not the time for me to lecture him on his tone. Instead, taking the key card from Bujar, I hold it against the access point until the light flashes green. I push my way inside, only to hear the fevered rhythm of grunting and heavy breathing.

The woman underneath Vargas is staring listlessly at the ceiling, chewing on her bottom lip as though she's staring at a clock, waiting for the bell to ring.

Vargas is too busy with his pale, scrawny ass in the air, pumping into his less-than-enthusiastic "date" for the night, to be aware of the audience standing in his room.

It's the woman who realizes they're not alone. She frowns at the new shadows thrown across the ceiling and then her gaze flickers to the door.

She takes one look at me and screams right in Vargas's ear, causing him to roar like a bullfrog. "The *fuck*, woman?!"

He slaps her across the face, still determined to fuck her even as she fights to get out from under him. Only when she refuses to lie back down does he follow her gaze to the door.

"*¡Mierda!*" He jolts, nearly rolling off the bed.

The woman hurls herself to the filthy carpeted floor and scrambles backward to a seat on the far wall, naked and trembling. Vargas attempts to lunge for his gun on the end table, but Bujar beats him to it.

Suddenly, Vargas finds himself staring down the end of his own gun—stark naked and completely unprepared.

"Who the fuck are you?" he croaks.

Cevdet looks offended by the question. "Who are we? Only your worst nightmare."

I resist the urge to roll my eyes at the cliché machismo as I stride further into the room where the hooker is pressed against the wall, her mascara running in black streams down her hollow cheeks.

I kneel in front of her. "What's your name?"

Her teeth are chattering so badly she barely manages to get the words out. "I-I-Ivy."

"Known this useless fuck for long, Ivy?"

"N-no. He picked me up on the street corner… Said he wanted me for an hour."

"Has he paid you?"

Her eyes widen nervously. "No."

I pluck out a couple of hundreds from my wallet and hand them over. "A little friendly advice: always take payment up front. Now, go."

She stares at me incredulously for only a second. Then she grabs the money I'm offering, pulls on her clothes at the speed of light, and gets the hell out of this godforsaken shithole.

Part of me wishes I could do the same.

"We're off to an exciting start," Cevdet chuckles, taking one of the two patchwork chairs beside the bed with a relieved groan.

Vargas looks past Bujar and the gun he has pointed at his head to meet my eyes. "You're him, aren't you?"

He's trying to sound confident and nonchalant, but I don't buy his bluster for a fucking second. The man is unarmed and unclothed, surrounded by enemies, and sporting a shriveled pair of blue balls.

It's not exactly his lucky night.

"My reputation precedes me."

He glowers. "Your reputation has been exaggerated. What's the matter, Kuznetsov? Too weak to kill me on your own?"

Cevdet scoffs. "We're all here to protect our own investments, not because Andrey needs our help. "

Vargas looks from me to each one of my allies. He's a fool for not doing his homework prior to kicking this hornet's nest. It's about to cost him his life.

"You didn't think I was expanding on my own, did you?" I ask as I saunter closer. "Unlike my father, I learned to play well with others. This way, we all get what we want. And right now, you and your little gang are threatening that."

"You don't know what you're up against," he snarls.

I pull out my gun and wave it carelessly in the air. "Then, tell me. I'm dying to know."

His eyes track my gun. "You don't want to kill me. My cousin is a lieutenant... He's high up in the Halcones. Killing me will only piss him off."

"You assume I care whether I piss him off or not."

Vargas's hands are shaking now. He balls them into fists, but he can't hide his fear.

"You're also assuming that you're important to your cousin," I continue. "But let's face it, Vargas: he sent you on a suicide mission when he aimed you at one of my clubs. You're not nearly as important as you think you are."

Cevdet giggles under his breath, but I keep my face still and grim.

"You're gonna kill a defenseless, unarmed man?" he asks.

"What makes you think I'm going to kill you at all, Vargas? Maybe I just want to have a little chat."

"You won't get anything out of me, so you might as well just get it over with and fucking kill me! I won't talk."

"Then you'll die," Cevdet interjects cheerfully.

I give Cevdet a warning look. I need answers before this *mudak* realizes he'll be far worse off if I let him go back to his masters than if I execute him myself.

"You don't really want me to kill you, do you, Vargas? It'll be much easier if you do what I ask and agree to take back a little message from me."

Sensing an opportunity, Vargas's eyes go wide. "A message?"

"To your bosses."

He pales. "W-what's the message?"

"Stop."

His gaze darts to Bujar, then Luca, then Cevdet, hoping for a reprieve or a punchline or maybe just a goddamn miracle.

He gets none of it.

When no one says a word, he swallows, a bead of sweat sliding down the side of his face. "I can't tell them that."

"Why not?" Luca barks.

"Because they'll kill him," I guess.

"Then the man is useless," Cevdet decides. "Just kill him now and be done with it."

"No!" Vargas cries, twisting in my direction. "No, don't kill me. I'll do it. I'll take the message back to the head Halcones."

But I sense the lie hidden behind those confident words. He's got "runner" smeared across his face in big, bold letters. He's exactly what Cevdet called him: useless.

Sighing, I raise my gun and shoot.

Vargas drops to the floor, his eyes glazed over in disbelief.

Luca steps forward and looks distastefully at the body. "I thought we were keeping him alive?"

"I was sick of hearing him blather," I reply. "And besides: his body will carry the message just as well as his lips would have. Maybe better."

7

NATALIA

"Don't look at me like that. I'm fine."

Remi cocks his head to the side and gives me a little bark that I roughly translate to mean, *I'm on to you, woman.*

Ignoring him, I peel back the covers and drag my sorry ass to the bathroom. He pads in after me, observing me with a cool gaze that feels entirely too human to belong to a dog.

I brush my teeth, wash my face, and twist around to find him still in the same position, staring at me with a skeptical expression. *You need some serious help.*

"They were just dreams, okay?" I insist to him. "Everyone has them."

Although not everyone soaks the bed with sweat because of them. Not everyone wakes up shaking and screaming because of them. Not everyone has to clutch their support animal for dear life just to steal a couple more hours of disturbed sleep.

I drop down to my knees and press my forehead against Remi's nose. "I know I was crazy last night, but… it'll pass."

Mhmm. Convincing.

"Stop," I scold him. "I don't need therapy."

He licks at my fingers and I head back into the bedroom, my restlessness reaching an all-time high.

It's not just my botched escape plan that's bothering me. It's all the relationships I managed to sever by leaving the way I did. They flap around me like cut threads, useless and dead.

Katya and I still haven't spoken. Misha and I seem okay on the surface, but I know he's not as unaffected as he pretends to be. Even the dog thinks I'm full of shit.

After I've changed into stretchy pants and a light sweater, I open my bedroom door to find Leonty sitting in the hallway on an uncomfortable-looking chair, his phone in hand.

He's got dark circles under his eyes and crease marks down the side of his face. "Morning," he yawns.

"Did you actually stay here all night?"

He shrugs. "Orders."

No prizes for guessing whose orders they were. "Where's Andrey?"

"Not here."

"Then I'll just have to find another time to yell at him," I mutter. "Let me know the moment he's back."

Judging by the look on Leonty's face, he's not going to tell me shit. But I'm too tired from last night to insist. Instead, I make my way downstairs towards Misha's room.

"You're following me now?" I ask, when I realize that Leonty is shadowing me.

"Just going in the same direction," he replies innocently.

I exchange a glance with Remi. "He thinks I was born yesterday."

Leonty suppresses a smile. "How did you sleep?" He asks the question with a deceptively innocuous inflection that makes me twist around and jab a finger into his chest. "Ouch," he complains.

"Don't you dare tell Andrey anything about last night."

"Nat, you're struggling—"

"You're the one who's gonna be struggling if you tell Andrey anything. They were just dreams, Leonty."

He looks even less convinced than Remi. "Maybe it would help to talk about them…?"

"I'd rather not relive them, thanks." I step towards Misha's door, ready to end this conversation. "Now, if you'll excuse me, I have to check on Misha."

I step inside and shut the door on his open mouth, cutting off whatever else he was going to say to me.

When I turn around, Misha is sitting on the divan in front of his bed, a textbook splayed open across his lap. He tucks it away when he sees me, clearing space for Remi to jump up next to him.

"How're you doing?" I chirp, my voice full of fake cheer.

"Fine."

Misha is smiling down at Remi, so I don't immediately notice the dark circles under his eyes that are even worse than Leonty's. Or the puffiness around them.

Has he been crying...?

My whole body stiffens with unease. But I can't exactly fault him for keeping his feelings close to his chest when I'm guilty of the same thing.

I decide to try a different approach. "What do you say we go out today? Take a car and grab lunch somewhere?"

Misha looks less than enthusiastic. "I have physical therapy in a couple of hours. And the concussion makes me tired."

"That's okay. We can just talk here."

He looks alarmed like I've just sprung a pop quiz on him. "Talk about what?"

"About the fact that you're upset with me but you're trying to hide it."

"I'm not mad at you," he protests. But he looks at Remi when he says it.

I inch close enough to place my hand on his knee. "Misha, you have every right to be mad at me. I know I hurt you when I tried to leave."

"Which time?"

I raise my eyebrows.

His mouth turns down with guilt. "I'm sorry—"

"You have nothing to be sorry for, Misha. I'm the one who should be apologizing." I squeeze his knee. "I didn't leave because I wanted to. It just felt like the only way to protect the babies."

"Bab*ies*?" Misha gasps.

"Twin girls." I nod, giving him a bracing smile. But just as quickly, it fades. "Leaving everyone was harder than I could have imagined. Especially because it meant leaving you as well."

He shifts in place, color rising on his cheeks. "You don't have to say that."

"I'm saying it because it's true. I wasn't lying earlier when I said I thought of you as mine, Misha. It's just… You're on your way to becoming a man, and I didn't think you'd want to sign up for the kind of life I planned on living."

His eyes crinkle at the edges as he frowns.

"I figured you'd be better off with Andrey. I was hoping you and Remi would take care of each other."

Remi perks up a little when he hears his name. Misha strokes his head thoughtfully. "Do you still think leaving is a good idea?"

I had hoped to avoid this line of conversation, but now that he's asked…

"Sometimes."

He lifts his gaze to mine. "So you're still thinking of going?"

I would love to tell him what he wants to hear. But I also don't want to lie. "I haven't made up my mind yet… but I'm leaning that way," I admit.

He sighs, his chin drooping back down to his chest. "I was afraid of that."

I force his gaze to mine again. "But Misha, this time, I can give you the choice. You're under no obligation to, but if you really want… you can come with me."

A ripple of pleasure flits across his face. But almost immediately, it dulls. "Do I have to decide right now?"

"No, not right now."

He nods, clearly relieved. Then, as if he can't help himself, he adds, "I'll miss you."

I lean in and wrap my arms around him. "You have no idea how much *I'll* miss *you*."

Remi whines for some of the attention to be directed his way. We break apart, both comforting the dog. It's easier than comforting each other.

8

NATALIA

"Katya's here."

"Is she?" I shrug like I could care less. "You should let Shura know."

Mila sighs. "She's here to see you, Nat."

My instinct is to go all snotty bitch on her ass. But the emotional upheaval of the last few days tempers my less-than-gracious nature. "Oh, fine," I concede. "Let her in."

Katya slips into my room a few minutes later with a nervous smile. "I'm so glad you're alright, Nat."

No thanks to you. But at this stage, I'm not even sure that's true.

What kind of life would I be living now if Katya had listened to me? Sure, I'd have some money and a ticket out of this city. But where would I have gone? Who could I have relied on? I'm seven months pregnant with twins, and as much as I wish I could deny it, it feels more and more like Katya was the sensible one between us.

I'd like to say I'm evolved enough to let her off the hook immediately. But I don't. Let's blame it on pregnancy hormones.

"Define 'alright.'"

She sighs, exchanging a glance with Mila that clearly says, *She's behaving exactly how we thought she would.*

Needless to say, their telepathic shit-talking doesn't improve my mood.

"I know you're pissed."

"Why is it that every time you meet a man, your loyalties shift?"

Katya's jaw drops. There's pin-drop silence in the room before she regroups. When she does, she looks as pissed as I feel. "This has nothing to do with Shura. My loyalties have been and always will be towards you!"

"Yeah? You sure have a funny way of showing it."

Mila drifts between us as though she's worried someone's going to throw a punch. I happen to know that Katya has a mean right hook. Courtesy of years of practice dating assholes.

Me, on the other hand… well, there's a first time for everything, right?

"You freaked me out when you called, Nat!" Katya cries, brushing past Mila with fire in her eyes. "You sounded bad on the phone. It reminded me of… of…" She sucks in a deep breath before charging through the end of her sentence. "…the time you first told me what happened to your parents."

That shuts me right up.

"I figured you were in shock, and, sue me, but I didn't think it was a good idea for you to be wandering around New York City, pregnant and alone. Particularly not when you'd just *shot the man you love!*"

My heart is hammering against my chest and my arms are alight with goosebumps.

"So yeah," she continues, "I called Andrey. Not because of loyalty to Shura or Andrey or anyone else, but because my best friend was having a mental fucking breakdown and she needed help."

I still don't know what to say. How to breathe. What to do with my hands.

"If you're looking for an apology, don't hold your breath," Katya says, still standing tall on that soapbox of hers. "Because I don't regret calling Andrey. I'd do it again if I had to."

Mila reaches gingerly for her. "Kat—"

"No!" She swats away Mila's hand. "I get that she's fragile right now, but she doesn't get to blame me just so that she has an outlet for her anger. I'm her best friend, not a punching bag."

The truth hits me like I'm its punching bag.

"You're right," I croak.

It does feel good to channel my helplessness into anger. It does feel good to blame someone else, even if that person doesn't deserve it. Maybe even especially when that person doesn't deserve it.

"I am?" Kat coughs and tries again. "Uh, I mean… Yes, I know I am."

I swallow my pride. "You don't owe me an apology, Kat. I'm the one who's sorry."

"OhthankfuckingGod." She lunges at me, wrapping her arms around my shoulders and squeezing like a python. "You're forgiven."

I can't help but laugh. "You didn't make me sweat long."

Katya releases me with a teary laugh. "I'll save the sweating for when you've delivered those babies safely."

"That's generous of you."

She winks. "I'm nothing if not generous."

Just like that, the tension breaks. Not the guilt, though. That stuff has a way of lingering.

Katya claps her hands decisively. "Okay, now that you no longer want to kick my ass, what shall we do today?"

"I'd really like to get out of the manor for a bit. Even if it's just to your place."

Mila opens her mouth like she's going to argue, but Katya plants her hands on her hips. "I'll make it happen. Leave it to me."

She prances out of my room and then shimmies right back in a few minutes later with a huge smile on her face.

"All set. We're heading to my apartment to spend the day. How does that sound?"

"Perfect."

Misha will be busy with physical therapy for the next few hours and Remi's with him, so I peek in to say goodbye.

And mostly, to reassure Misha that I'm not going anywhere. Not yet, anyway.

Then Mila, Kat and I crowd into the back of a blue Escalade driven by Leonty and we head out of the nice part of Manhattan en route to Hell's Kitchen, which is… well, slightly less nice.

The closer we get to Kat's place, I'm reminded of the days when it was just the two of us, sitting on the floor of her living room, knocking back boxed wine and cheap candy. Just us. No distractions. No fears.

It'll be like that again, if only for a few hours.

Or a few seconds, since the moment I walk into Kat's living room, I come face to face with Shura. Kat greets him with a quick peck on the cheek, refusing to look at me.

"Hello, ladies," Shura says nonchalantly. "I'll just retreat to the bedroom and give you some privacy."

I stare between the two of them. "Are the two of you living together?"

Katya blushes and shakes her head. "No, no, of course not. It's way too soon for that."

That's when it hits me. "You're here on Andrey's orders, aren't you?"

Katya swats Shura's arm. "You were supposed to stay out of sight!"

"It's a small apartment," he says with an unapologetic shrug. "My only orders were to stay inside with you."

"My orders are more important than Andrey's," Kat argues.

"Leonty's parked out front in the Escalade," I say. "What could possibly happen?"

"Nothing," Shura announces. "Your two shadows will make sure of that."

Kat cringes, shoving Shura in the chest. "Jesus, Shura. You couldn't have phrased it a little better than that?"

"She might as well get used to it. Andrey isn't going to let her out of his sight until—" His voice trails off as I storm into Katya's bedroom and pull out my phone.

Snapping the door shut, I settle on her bed and concentrate on dialing Andrey's number. "Hello, *lastochka*. What can I do for you?" His voice is deep and silky smooth.

My heart does this weird, trembly little quake that makes me want to smack myself in the head. "You can tell me why your freakish little goons are following every single step I take."

"Shura will keep to himself. You can still have your girls' day."

"Not the point."

"The point, Natalia, has always been to keep you safe. Now more than ever."

"I'm safe," I retort. "Now, tell Shura to leave."

"I'm not going to do that. If that's all—"

"No, that most certainly is *not* all! We need to talk about this. There has to be some sort of compromise."

Despite my anger, his deep, dark chuckle sends a wave of excitement and longing shooting through my core.

"I'm not the compromising type, *lastochka*. You should know that by now."

9

NATALIA

I plop into my seat after visiting the copier, my desk swirling in my vision. I have to grip the arms of my chair to try to right the world before I faint and/or yak my lunch up everywhere.

It's been happening more and more lately, ever since I moved out of the manor—unofficially speaking—and into Katya's tiny, cramped one-bedroom apartment.

I could sit and wonder why it's happening, but it would be a waste of time. I mean, take your pick: I'm pregnant, I haven't been sleeping, my entire life is balanced on a razor's edge and I don't know which way it's going to fall. There are no wrong answers.

It's a recipe for another imminent breakdown.

The most confusing part?

The main reason for my problems might also be my antidote. In other words: the tall drink of water with a killer, if elusive, smile.

I haven't heard from Andrey since I decided three days ago that I wasn't going back to the manor. I decided to take a stand for myself.

And he decided to punish me with indifference.

Also, added security.

Mindy appears at my desk with a stack of files. "These need to be taken to Mr. Ewes. Can you handle it or should I?"

I've been getting a lot of those questions recently. *Can you handle this? Are you okay? You look dizzy—do you need to sit down?* A result of the accessory putting all of my maternity clothes to the ultimate test. "All good, Mindy. I'll take them to him now."

But even as I rise to my feet, my head spins and my knees threaten to buckle.

I just pulled a muscle during prenatal yoga this morning. That's all.

Kat and I cleared out her living room so that we could get in a yoga sesh before work every morning. It's about the only thing that relaxes me these days. And considering the number of worries percolating in my head—Misha, Remi, Andrey, this, that, and the other—I need all the help I can get.

One step in front of the next, Nat. Just keep walking.

I manage to get all the way to Richard's office before the dizziness wins out over my resolve. I teeter to the side, gripping his desk and sending half the files careening to the floor.

"Oh, God," I gasp, mortified. "I'm so sorry."

Richard bends himself in two trying to help me pick up the scattered papers. He's been inordinately nice to me ever since Byron's "resignation" and my "promotion." Every time he looks at me, there's this crease that appears just between his eyebrows. A crease that might as well say, **Andrey Kuznetsov Was Here.**

"Why don't you sit down, Natalia?"

The plan was to apologize my way out of the office and retreat back to my desk to collapse, but another dizzy spell hits me, and I find myself sinking into a chair as Richard brings me a glass of water.

"You don't look so good," he remarks.

"Just what every pregnant woman wants to hear."

He actually pales. "I didn't mean to offend—"

"You didn't offend me," I assure him. "I was just joking. Thanks for the water."

He breathes out a sigh of relief. Almost like he's scared I'm gonna report back to Andrey and he's gonna have a giant shit-storm on his hands. Oh, who am I kidding? That's exactly what he's scared of.

He leans against the desk. "Are you doing okay?"

Well, let's see: I'm having a crime lord's babies, I'm basically his hostage for all intents and purposes, and I may or may not have shot him accidentally-on-purpose…

Oh, and there's that other small, unimportant detail…

I might just be head over heels in love with the guy.

"There's a lot going on in my life right now," I admit. "I'm just… coming to terms with it all."

He nods and clears his throat. "I think it might be a good idea if you were to take some time off. It might give you the chance to get your head on straight."

It's a nice suggestion. So why does the thought of taking a sabbatical fill me with such dread?

Because then you'll be all alone with your thoughts. Duh.

"No," I insist. "I need to work."

He doesn't push, but the crease is back between his eyebrows. "Why don't you finish that glass of water and go home early then? Get some rest."

This time, it's not a suggestion.

With a reluctant nod of thanks, I head back to my desk, dreading the idea of going back to Kat's apartment. I know I'm the one who chose to live there, but that doesn't ease the loneliness clawing at my chest.

The loneliness only one person can ease.

My phone pings with an incoming message, and if his name flashing on my lockscreen is a sign from the universe, I choose to ignore it.

ANDREY: *Come over for dinner tonight. We can talk.*

Only Andrey can turn what should be a romantic question into a command. What's even more annoying? It's actually a turn-on.

Things are simple when I let him make decisions. He's fearless. He doesn't question or second-guess. He just *does*.

What a way to live that must be.

But if I want to be in charge of my own life, my child's life, I can't succumb to that easy temptation of letting Andrey control me. I have to stand up for myself. For *both* of us.

Even if a part of me *wants* to be ordered around.

NATALIA: *I don't think that's a good idea right now. But I will come over to get Remi.*

ANDREY: *Dinner will be on the table either way. It'll give you a chance to spend some time with Misha. Or should I tell him you're busy?*

Apparently, I won't let him order me around. But I will let him manipulate me.

Damn him.

NATALIA: *No, I'll make the time.*

ANDREY: *I'll let him know.*

The "checkmate" is very much implied.

Okay, I'll admit it: since Andrey was the one who issued the dinner invitation and suggested we "talk," I kind of expected him to actually *show up* for dinner.

Instead, it's Misha and me side-by-side at one corner of the sprawling dinner table, suffering in the thickest of silences.

It was clear the moment I arrived that Misha wasn't in the best mood. He's claimed it has to do with a lot of different things—his concussion, physical therapy, tutoring lessons—but stops just short of saying, *"Actually, this is all your fault, Natalia."*

He doesn't need to say it. I already know.

"I can leave Remi, you know?" I offer for the third time since I got here.

He shakes his head. "No. Remi's yours. Not mine."

"It's not forever," I tell him gently, patting his wrist. "I just need some space from this place. And from Andrey."

"Or what? You'll shoot him again?" I raise my eyebrows and he flushes with instant regret. "Sorry."

"Low blow, but I deserve it."

"No… no, you don't. I'm sorry, I shouldn't have said that." He picks at the orzo on his plate, pushing it around with his fork. "I just hate being cooped up here all the time."

"It's just until the concussion clears."

He grimaces, his fork clattering against his plate. "I'm sick of being useless."

"Misha! You're not useless."

He avoids my eyes and turns to Remi, who's got his head resting on Misha's thigh. "Don't forget to take his bone toy. It's his favorite."

"Kat's place is just so small. Otherwise, I could have arranged for you to—"

He pushes up from the table, sending his chair skittering back with an angry screech. "I'm going to bed. I'm tired."

I have no choice but to watch him shuffle from the dining room, his shoulders slumped.

Remi whines, but he doesn't follow Misha. It's like he understands that he's coming home with me today.

"Okay, buddy," I sigh, scratching Remi behind the ears. "Let's get your stuff and go, huh?"

Except his stuff seems to have disappeared in the three days I've been away. There's nothing in the pool house or in the garden shed.

Even more suspicious: neither Mila nor Leonty seem to be around.

In fact, no one is.

With no other recourse, I resignedly make the long trek into Andrey's office. I don't really expect him to be inside. I mean, if he was, why wouldn't he join us for dinner? But when I open the door, Andrey is sprawled across the sofa, his long legs dangling over the side.

Some pitiful part of me jumps at the sight of him, desperate to get close.

There's no surprise on his face when I walk in, so I do my best to hide mine.

"Where are Remi's things?"

Remi sniffs at the coffee table between us, eyeing the whiskey glass sitting on a coaster as though he'd like to take a lick.

"Good evening, Natalia. Nice to see you as well."

Scowling, I cross my arms over my chest. "You purposely hid his things so I'd have to come in here and speak to you."

He doesn't deny it as he pushes up and gestures to the chair behind me. "Why don't you sit down?"

"I'd rather stand, thanks. Remi's things?"

"Here. Which is where they'll stay."

My frown deepens just as my heartbeat picks up speed. "Listen, I'll bring him back for his training regularly, but I do need his stuff."

"You don't need anything," he says, rising to his feet. "Because Remi's staying right here. As are you."

I search his face for some sign of a punchline. There's none to be found. "What do you mean? I'm staying with Katya."

"Not anymore. A situation's come up and it's better that you stay at the manor from now on."

I gape at him like an idiot. "What kind of situation?"

"A few men were spotted outside Kat's place this morning," he supplies. "Another group of men were seen just outside Sunshield as well. All on Nikolai's payroll."

I can't pretend that news doesn't affect me. But a part of me does question it. It sounds like something someone who wanted me to move back under his watchful gaze would say.

"Does it matter? You have a whole army shadowing my every move."

"I'm afraid that's not going to cut it. Until the threat has passed, *this* is your home."

"But I left because I needed— I want—" I blow out a harsh breath. "I need space."

Space I can't get when Andrey demands so much of my attention. Being in such close proximity to him feels more dangerous than ever.

"I know, *lastochka*," he says. "Unfortunately, you're going to have to find space under this roof."

To which I say: "Fuck. That."

I get as far as the foyer before I'm stopped. Leif towers over me, his broad shoulders blocking the front door working in direct contrast to the apologetic grimace on his face. "Sorry, Nat, but I can't let you leave. *Pakhan's* orders."

There are a trillion different comebacks burning on the tip of my tongue—maybe even a right and left hook—but Leif doesn't deserve them. He's only following orders, same as the rest of us.

So I swallow down my unkind thoughts, whip around, and make straight for the son of a bitch who *does* deserve to hear them.

When I burst back into his office, Andrey doesn't bother to look up from his papers. "Back so soon? What happened to needing space?"

"You're already holding me hostage here. There's no need to belittle me on top of that."

His impassive expression doesn't change, but he rounds the table and walks over to me. "I'm not belittling you, little bird. I'm trying to keep you safe."

Those silver eyes hold me captive as he brushes his knuckles against my cheek. Heat courses through me, and I somehow find the willpower to step away from him.

"Come," he says, taking my hand. "Let me show you to your room."

There's something so comforting in letting my fingers lace through his. In letting him lead me. He could be guiding me straight to hell, and I'd just be following along blindly, happy to be holding his hand.

Getting a hold of myself, I pull my hand from his. "I know the way to the pool house."

"I'm not taking you to the pool house."

That's when I realize we're not heading outside, but up the stairs.

Pure curiosity is the only thing that drives me to follow.

That and the perfect view I have of his ass. He's fighting dirty, it seems.

He leads me back to the gargantuan guest bedroom where I spent the first few days post-escape, except... it's different.

There are new shelves on the walls and pictures I remember decorating the pool house with. The baby grand piano is tucked into the window nook.

"What's this?" I demand as Remi makes a run for the window seat and nestles himself between the cushions.

"It's your room."

My glare turns suspicious. "The pool house suits me just fine."

"I said you'd have to stay under my roof for the time being. *My* roof, specifically." He sweeps a hand around to encompass the room. "All your things have been brought here from the pool house. Including the stuff you left at Kat's. You'll find everything you need."

He actually has the audacity to move towards the door, as though the conversation is over.

"Everything I need *except* peace of mind," I blurt.

He pauses. Lingers. "I'm working towards that."

An inexplicable tremor travels down my spine. It's not what he says or how he says it—Andrey Kuznetsov is far too practiced at holding his emotions in to give anything away that cheaply. But if I look close, if I squint and tilt my head… I could swear I see genuine fear in his eyes. Just a glimpse of it. But enough.

"How serious is this situation?" I croak.

Andrey lets the silence sit for a moment. "I'm not going to let anything hurt you, *lastochka*," he says at last, a fire in his eyes that feels like it could burn me if I get too close. "I failed Maria. I will not fail you."

The lines of his face could be carved from stone. But as beautiful as he is, he also feels untouchable. He feels far away, removed from me by the weight of some unspoken responsibility he's taken upon himself.

The chasm between us ripples and bends. There are moments when it feels insurmountable and moments when it feels like it's shrinking and I could jump across, if only I was brave enough.

Right now, I'm caught in between, straddling a fine line between what I want and what I need.

"You really loved her, didn't you?"

I don't know why I ask. A part of me knows that hearing him confirm it will make me bitterly jealous. Another part of me is hopeful—if he's loved one woman before, then maybe, just maybe, he could love another.

You shouldn't want his love. His love is dangerous.

"She was mine to protect," is all he says.

He takes a hesitant step towards me so that we're practically nose to nose. Or chest to nose, as the case may be. One hand strokes my belly and the other curls around my chin, tilting my face up to meet his.

His whiskey breath warms my face. I could bask under the silver glow of his eyes forever. It helps clear out the white noise, the terrifying images in my head.

"I know you want to keep me safe," I whisper. "I just don't know that you can."

His head dips down. For a moment, I think he's going to kiss me. What will I do if he tries? Slap him? Pull back? Give in?

"My enemies don't know what I'm capable of, *lastochka*. And neither do you."

Then, just like that, he's gone.

10

NATALIA

If hiring a new housekeeper-slash-chef was meant to make us all forget Yelena, Andrey should try again.

Pilav is the exact antithesis of Yelena—young, efficient, and professional to a fault. Still, it's impossible not to see Yelena between the cracks.

Sure, his cooking is a heck of a lot better, but somehow, mouth-watering pierogies don't quite make up for his sour face every time Misha or I walk into the kitchen to sneak something from the fridge.

In my defense, I'm pregnant. In Misha's defense, he's a growing boy with nothing to do all day.

At least Remi seems not to mind him. And for the moment, that's good enough for me.

Misha and I are sitting in the garden with a fully-laden tray between us. It's sunny and the glare off the water is particularly brutal, but it beats the heat we have to endure in the kitchen under Pilav's sullen gaze.

"I can't wait to start training," Misha sighs, squinting towards the pool. "I'm so sick of lying in bed all the time."

"You just got over a concussion," I remind him. "Take it easy."

"Andrey says I'm as good as in the Bratva. I want to earn my mark for real, though."

I can tell he's been wanting to share this with me for a while. His chest puffs out proudly as he turns to me, waiting for some form of congratulations.

But my tongue feels like it's turned to sand. "Don't you think you should wait a little longer?"

"No, I'm ready."

"Misha—"

"Don't even start." Indignation flashes across his face. "You think I'm just this stupid little kid who can't take care of himself."

"That's not what I'm saying—"

"I've been through a lot that you don't know about," he huffs over my protests. "I'm the one who protected my mother against men five times my size. I'm the one who cleaned the girls' wounds when a client beat them stupid. I'm the one that looked after the kids when they came to the compound, terrified and panicking."

The moment he finishes speaking, his complexion pales. As though he's just realized that he said too much.

Or maybe it has more to do with the open-mouthed, dumbfounded look on my face. This is the first time he's really talked about his life in Nikolai's clutches.

"It sounds terrible," I acknowledge softly.

He shrugs and looks out into the distance, where Remi is busy tunneling his way through the bushes.

"There were moments when it was quiet," he admits. "But when things happened, they really *happened*."

I have no idea what that means. I'm not sure I want to. But as horrible as this might be for me to hear, he actually went through it. The least I can do is listen.

Provided he's willing to open up to me, that is.

I decide to go with the least incriminating question. "What was your mother like?"

He swallows. "We weren't very close. She was around, but… not really. She was very beautiful, though. The men used to say she was 'popular.'" He flinches as the full meaning of that word hits him, maybe for the first time. "She looked like me. Or maybe I look like her, I guess. But she used to tell me that I had my daddy's nose and a birthmark on my shoulder in the same shape and position that he had."

He pushes down the neckline of his t-shirt and displays a sickle-shaped birthmark right under his collarbone.

"You never met your father?"

"No. But… I don't know." Misha shrugs awkwardly. "I don't think he was all that bad. She said he would bring her sweets. Reese's Cups, because they were her favorite."

Whoever Misha's father was, he might not have been all bad, but he can't have been all that good, either. At the best, he paid to have sex with Misha's mother. At worst, he was responsible for owning and selling her.

"And this compound you lived in… Was it nice?"

He wrings his hands together. "It was just this long stretch of houses that looked like barnyard sheds. But instead of grass, we had sand. And there was a well where we collected our drinking and bathing water. We had to be careful because each shed was only allowed one bucket a day. We were allowed two because Mom was a mare."

I almost choke on a bite. "A *what?*"

He cringes with embarrassment. "It's just how they differentiated between us. The stallions were the men over eighteen. The mares were the women over eighteen. The fillies were the girls. And me... I was a colt."

I put down the sandwich I'm holding. I've suddenly lost my appetite.

He squirms in place. "I was the oldest kid, so I guess I was put in charge of the others."

"Do you know where they came from? The others, I mean?"

"Most of their mothers were mares. I would look after them while the women went to work at night."

"Were there a lot of kids?"

His eyes grow distant. "Usually, only three to four at the most. But for a while, Olivia helped me with the smaller kids."

"Olivia?"

His knuckles are white. He bites his lip as though he's regretting mentioning the name. "She was my... my friend," he admits at last. "She was a year younger. Her mother was a mare, too. She also had a sister who had just become a filly..."

He trails off and I don't have to ask to know what became of Olivia. If her mother and sister were already conscripted into Nikolai's reprehensible skin trade, then she didn't stand a chance.

"We used to talk about running away sometimes," Misha confesses in a hushed voice. "Olivia used to come up with plans to escape."

"Did you ever try?"

Misha shakes his head. "We were too scared. We'd seen too many fillies try to escape. They were always caught and punished. Our escape plans were just dreams."

At a loss for words, I reach out and take his hand. He winces, but I just grip his hand a little tighter. "I'm glad you had someone."

He shrugs, shaking me off as though physical touch is more than he can deal with right now. "For a little while. Then Olivia disappeared, too."

Even though I'm expecting it, my heart sinks like a stone.

"It happens." There's a bitterness in his voice I wish I could override. Years of pain and heartbreak I wish I could take away. "Everyone comes and goes. Even the children. Olivia and I were the only kids who'd been around for over a year. Maybe that's why I didn't expect it to happen. But… you just have to move on."

"But you didn't, did you?"

I know the answer already. It's laughable that anyone thought Misha could be a spy. He's loyal through and through. Of course he looked for Olivia.

His chin sags down to his chest. "I asked her mom and sister, but neither one knew what happened to her. They said she was probably bought."

"I'm so sorry, Misha."

"I'm used to it. People always disappear." His eyes snap to mine when he says it and guilt scourges through me.

I told him he was as good as my kid.

And then I tried to leave.

"I'm sorry, Misha. I'm so damn sorry."

He doesn't say anything and I don't explain myself. I don't really need to.

We both know what I'm apologizing for.

11

ANDREY

"The Black Brigade?" I nearly choke on my own disbelief. "You've gotta be kidding me."

"If I was gonna joke, I'd tell a better one than this."

Shura is not wrong. Nothing about this is funny.

"The Black Brigade hasn't been active since the 1960s," I say. "And even then, they didn't cause trouble."

"Maybe Slavik made them an offer they couldn't refuse."

"*Fuck!*" I pound my fist against my desk and rise to my feet. "It's bad enough that the Halcones were brought in. Now, the fucking Black Brigade, too? What's next?"

"Godzilla destroying downtown, probably." I side-eye him, and he shrugs. "Maybe jokes aren't for me. Should I inform the allies or…?"

"One band of mercenaries trying to horn in on my territory is one thing. But two?" I drop down on the edge of my desk, arms folded. "It's going to look like incompetence if we don't contain this situation fast."

Shura's on the verge of saying something when Efrem bursts into my office without knocking. Never a good sign.

His wild eyes land on me. "We have a situation."

"Of course we do. Who's moving against me now?" I hold up a hand. "And if you say Godzilla, you're fired."

He glances in confusion at Shura, who waves him on.

"Bogdan and Artyom..." he grits as though the words are poison on his tongue. "They've defected."

Shura's spine snaps straight.

My hands curl into fists. "Let me get this right: Bogdan Dimitriev and Artyom Balakin, two men who wear my mark and swore their allegiance to me over a decade ago, *defected?*"

Efrem looks at his feet. "Yes, *pakhan*."

Running a hand through my hair, I turn to the window as the weight of this latest blow sinks in. "They've been loyal members of the Kuznetsov Bratva for as long as anyone can remember."

"I think that's the point," Shura suggests quietly. "They were your father's men before they were yours. They clearly think his return has changed something."

"Then they were fucking mistaken, weren't they?"

Both men take a step back, and I lash down the wild rage in my chest. There's no point alienating the men who are genuinely loyal to me.

"I want this knowledge contained," I order once I'm under control. "Only our inner circle can know about the defection."

"But—"

"Do it," I rasp, cutting both men off without so much as raising my voice. "Go. Now."

Efrem backs out of the room while Shura fixes me with a wary gaze. "He's moving faster than we expected."

Once again, my second is more right than I'd care to admit. I'd hoped to avoid this kind of messiness, but Slavik isn't afraid to play dirty, which means an internal war is almost a guarantee. And more betrayal is imminent. My alliance with the expansion partners remains strong—but not for one second do I believe their loyalty is absolute. It extends only as far as I can ensure our joint venture is safe. As soon as another, more lucrative offer appears, they'll ally themselves with the same men trying to destroy me from the inside out.

My gaze flits to the bottom right drawer of my desk. There's a pack of cigarettes stashed away there. For the first time in years, I'm dangerously close to cracking it open.

"I've got it under control," I tell him.

Shura stops at the edge of my desk, his hand over the drawer like he's holding it closed. "You forget who you're talking to, 'Drey. I can tell you're worried."

"The only thing I'm worried about right now is Natalia."

Shura frowns. "Natalia is fine. She's safe."

"Physically, maybe," I accept. "But mentally, emotionally, I'm not so sure."

When I woke up in the middle of the night, I could've taken the back stairs down to the kitchen, but I wandered through the halls until I passed Natalia's room. Leonty was on duty, standing by the door in full sentry mode… as Natalia screamed inside.

"What in the hell are you waiting for?" I growled.

Just before I could plow through the door, Leonty shifted in front of me. "It's a nightmare. She's okay. She's dreaming."

Natalia's scream tapered off into a whimper before… silence.

I fell back against the wall, my heart racing. "She's been having nightmares?"

Leonty couldn't meet my eyes. "She didn't want you to know."

"What is the fucking point of you?" I shoved him away from the door just as another scream tore through the silence.

Everything in me wanted to tear into that room, to hold her. To save her from the monsters in her own head.

The problem was, I might've been one of the monsters.

Instead, I dragged Leonty further down the hall and grilled him on the secrets he'd apparently seen fit to keep. There was a lot to tell.

Natalia had been having nightmares every night. She'd wake up screaming, and only Remi seemed to be able to calm her back to sleep. On the nights when even that didn't work, she'd turn all the lights on and sit in her room for hours until she crashed out around dawn.

How the fuck am I supposed to handle attacks on my house when I don't even know what's happening inside the walls?

"Let Mila and Katya worry about Natalia," Shura says in answer to the question I didn't ask. "Misha is here for her, too."

"I'm her husband. *I* should be there for her."

Shura cocks an eyebrow. "I get that you're concerned, but we've got bigger problems."

"Nothing is more important than she is. Do you understand?" We're so close now that our noses are practically touching.

His eyes spark violently, but in the end, hierarchy wins out. Shura steps back. "I understand."

"Speaking of which: did you get into contact with—?"

"Done," he assures me. "She doesn't usually make house calls, but she'll make an exception for you."

I nod, reasonably satisfied. I won't be completely satisfied until Natalia simply accepts that I know what's best for her.

"When are you going to tell her?" Shura asks, eyeing me skeptically.

Apparently, I'm not the only one who predicts Natalia won't make this easy. "Tonight," I decided on the spur of the moment. "But first, I'll need to get her in a good mood."

"I'd suggest you make yourself scarce then," he mutters.

Flipping him off, I sit down behind my desk. "Invite Mila and Katya over for dinner. And arrange for Aunt Annie to surprise her. We're going to have a dinner party."

Shura looks like I've just told him I'm running away to join the circus. "A dinner party? *Now?*"

I tell myself that this makes sense. An apple rots from the inside out. If I want to get a handle on things, I need to start with Natalia.

I nod. "She's happiest and most compliant when she's surrounded by her friends and family."

Shura sighs. "Ah, the subtle art of manipulation."

Blunt honesty and directness haven't worked for me so far.

Might as well give this a shot.

12

ANDREY

The night has unfolded perfectly. Natalia wasn't sure about a dinner party, but Mila and Katya were so excited that she couldn't refuse. They're the ones who coaxed Natalia into the gold wrap dress I haven't been able to take my eyes off of all night.

Her dark hair is draped over her shoulder, and the neckline dips low across her chest, flashing a teasing amount of cleavage.

I could've attempted to look unaffected, but I played my hand the second Natalia walked into the room, so I didn't even bother. She's caught my eyes on her time and time again throughout the dinner, but she seems pleased by the attention, smiling quietly to herself from across the table.

Good.

She saved the full wattage of her smile for the evening's biggest surprise: the arrival of Aunt Annie. The woman practically blew the front door down with her walking stick, sashaying into my house in the dress I sent for her to wear.

I thought Natalia was going to collapse in shock. But as the surprise faded, a wide smile I was beginning to worry I wouldn't see again spread across Natalia's face, and it hasn't left since.

Not while she and Annie caught up in the living room.

Not while Annie figuratively and literally twisted Natalia's arm to get her to play something for us on the piano.

Of all the songs she could've chosen, Natalia went with "Celebration" by Kool & The Gang. The fact that both she and Annie were teary-eyed by the end of it was mystifying to me, but I filed that away as a question for later.

As I'm kicking back after a successful dinner—Pilav did exactly as I requested, cooking all of Natalia's favorites in a bizarre lineup that ranged from lobster to Caesar salad to spaghetti and meatballs—I decide that Natalia might just be pliable enough to enact the final part of my plan.

Cherry pie with homemade vanilla bean ice cream is brought out from the kitchen, and I open my mouth to speak—but Aunt Annie beats me to the punch.

"Sweetheart," her tender voice carries from across the table, "how have you been? I mean, *really*?"

A shadow flickers across Natalia's face, followed quickly by a forced grin. "I'm doing better."

It's a passable lie. Some people might even buy it.

But those people didn't hear Natalia screaming in her sleep.

"Are you?" Aunt Annie presses. "Because, as gorgeous as you look right now, you also look tired."

There are dark circles under her eyes. I was distracted by my own ruse—the dress and the nice dinner—but I see them now, too.

"I don't think she's been sleeping very well," Mila butts in.

Natalia can't seem to decide if she's mad at Mila or Leonty for blabbing. Pillow talk was definitely the source for that little snippet of inside information. "That's not true. I sleep fine."

Mila shovels in a bite of pie before she says anything else incriminating, but Aunt Annie isn't so easily swayed. She frowns at Natalia. "You need to take care of yourself, honey. You have to think about your babies."

"I am thinking about the babies," she insists, stealing a quick glance at Misha. "Dr. Abdulov suggested some medications, but they make me feel fuzzy. If I'm going to be here, I want to *be* here."

Without even realizing it, my fists have clenched under the table.

"What about therapy?" Mila suggests brightly. She says it like it's a fun day at the park—an obvious ploy to talk Natalia into it, though not necessarily a bad one.

But Natalia doesn't bite. "I don't need therapy."

"Yes, you do."

The table goes quiet. Only then do I realize that I've voiced the emphatic thought in my head. It feels so damn good to finally say it out loud that I can't even mourn the demise of my perfectly executed night.

"Excuse me?" Natalia's cheeks are scarlet.

"You're struggling, Natalia. You need help." I can feel Shura's eyes on me, cautioning me, but I charge ahead anyway. "Which is why I've scheduled an appointment for you next week with a therapist. She comes highly recommended, and I think she can help you."

I know I need to hold my tongue, display some level of sensitivity. But the woman's stubbornness grates on my nerves like nails on a chalkboard. Why won't she take care of herself, goddammit? Why won't she let me do it for her?

My announcement is followed by a few seconds of drawn-out silence. Everyone looks between Natalia and me, waiting for one of us to break the tension.

Natalia does the honors. "I should have known. I should have known this dinner came with a catch." She looks around the table as though she holds everyone around it equally responsible for the ambush. "Who else voted for this plan? You, Kat?"

Kat rises out of her chair, shaking her head. "No, Nat. I had no idea—"

"But you agree with him, don't you?"

Katya hesitates. "Nat—"

"You're supposed to be *my* friend!"

"I am!" Katya wails. "We all are. We love you, Nat, and we can all see that you're struggling. Right, Mila?"

Mila shrinks down in her seat like she might be able to escape notice, but she sighs when everyone turns to look at her. "Kat's right: we do love you. We just want you to get to a place where you can face your demons head-on."

"I don't have demons." Her fury sputters, drowned out by a barely-concealed sob. "What I have is a bunch of friends who don't have my back."

"Natalia." Annie's voice is quiet and calm, but Natalia's eyes snap to her as if she'd yelled. "That's not fair."

"What would any of you know about it?" she demands, a single tear sliding down her cheek. "None of you understand what I've been through!"

"Because you won't talk about it!" Katya interjects, a little more forcefully than the last time. "Which is why therapy might help."

Natalia ignores Katya and turns her accusing gaze on me. "I don't know how you managed to hoodwink all of them, but it won't work on me. You've interfered in my life enough. I'm not about to let you do any more damage."

There it is. *Damage.* The crux of all our problems.

"I'm only trying to help repair the damage I've caused, *lastochka*," I try again.

She shakes her head as Remi bounds towards her and licks her hand in consolation. "Just stay away from me, okay?" Her gaze sweeps over the whole room. "All of you."

Then she runs out into the dark garden with Remi at her heels.

13

ANDREY

I can just about make out their silhouettes from my office window.

Aunt Annie braved the wet grass with her walking stick to follow Natalia out to the backyard, and I think guilt alone forced Natalia to stay put and listen to her.

At least, I hope she's listening. She won't stay within earshot of any of the rest of us, and the devil only knows what she intends to do next.

Remi is sitting between them, barking occasionally at the bats taking flight overhead.

I feel helpless. Useless. Marooned at a distance, unable to wade into Natalia's thoughts and beat the fucking brakes off the demons haunting her.

Something has to puncture through that thick skull of hers. But my usual brute force isn't getting anywhere close.

"Knock, knock." Mila sticks her head through my door. "Can I come in?"

"Only if you have something important to say."

She raises her eyebrows. "Everything I say is important, Andrey. Otherwise, I wouldn't say it."

Suppressing a sigh, I gesture her inside. "What is it, Mila?"

"I know it's frustrating, but you have to be patient with her," Mila advises. "She's not thinking straight at the moment."

"Is she ever?" I ask bitterly.

Mila ignores my grouchiness and glances out the window. "Ah, you've been spying."

"It's just a nice night, that's all. I'm inspecting how the new grass is coming in." I shove my hands in my pockets. "How did it go when you tried to talk to her? Did she hear you out or did she shoot you down?"

"Head shot, immediate kill. I retreated before I got a word in."

"Coward."

She scowls. "She called me your spy. And considering where I am right now, I don't really have a leg to stand on."

"You're not here for me, Mila. You're here for her."

"That's not how she sees it."

"Because she's not in her right mind," I growl. "Which is why she needs the damn therapist."

"Hey, I'm already convinced," Mila says, holding up her hands. "We just need to hope that Annie can do what all of us failed to do."

She joins me at the window and the two of us watch the

distant silhouettes shamelessly. "I could just force her into the room. Tie her to the damn leather couch."

"And how do you expect to pry open her mind? Is there some martial art that can tear down the walls people have built around their hearts?" Mila purses up her lips. "She has to want to help herself before it has any shot of working."

I'm distracted from arguing with her good point by Natalia rising to her feet. She offers Annie a hand and the two of them meander back to the manor together.

I don't notice her leave, but when I look over, Mila is gone.

I'm still stewing in tonight's failure when the door is thrust open again. This time, it's Annie hobbling unsteadily on the special teak cane I had custom-made for her. She doesn't say anything until she's sitting in front of me, her stick leaning against the arm of the chair.

"I love my Nic-Nat. But there are some days I just want to shake the girl."

The bark of laughter that escapes me is stained with disappointment. "I take it you couldn't get through to her, either."

"I couldn't tell what she was thinking, if I'm being honest," Annie admits. "She was very quiet, and I doubt she was even listening. She just couldn't tell me to 'fuck off' like the others."

"I told you that cane would come with benefits."

She grimaces at the thing. "Sympathy or not, I still hate it."

Smirking, I pour the two of us some whiskey from my private collection. "I can see where Natalia gets her stubbornness from."

Annie accepts the glass with a smile. "Next time you invite me to dinner, warn me there's going to be an ambush."

I tense. "You think I handled it wrong?"

"I think you've handled a lot of things wrong where Natalia is concerned."

She is, for all intents and purposes, Natalia's mother. I should have expected this conversation sooner or later. Personally, I had hoped for "later." It seems none of us are getting what we want tonight.

"I know I'm probably the last thing you wanted for her."

She cocks her head to the side and grips the hook of her cane. I wonder if she might try to beat me with it.

Then she takes a hearty sip of her whiskey and smacks her lips. "Hm, reminds me of an old boyfriend. Terrible in bed, but he knew his spirits." She's got a twinkle in her eye when she looks at me again. "Natalia needs a strong man, Andrey. Someone who can match her spirit and her stubbornness."

"Matching stubbornness hasn't done me a damn bit of good so far," I mutter.

She sets her glass down and leans forward, her elbows on her knees. "Stubbornness isn't just about being bullheaded and getting your way. It's refusing to stop trying to connect with someone. It's loving someone even when they make it hard. You need to have the stubbornness to listen to what she's really saying, not just the sounds her lips make when they move. Keep pushing your way and she'll push you right back. Or worse: retreat into herself and close all the doors."

I grimace. "I'm as worried about that as you are."

"Then trust me and take my advice. Natalia's biggest fear is losing the people she loves. She has a hard time opening up to anyone. It's easier for her to shut down than to face her feelings."

"How am I supposed to help her there?"

"By being stubborn enough to stay even when she screams at you to go."

I roll my neck, trying and failing to ease the tension in my shoulders. "I'm the last person she wants to be around right now."

"She's just terrified of being hurt again, Andrey. At the moment, she feels like nothing more than a broodmare for your legacy."

"That's not what she is to me."

Annie smiles. "Do you think I'd be here at all if I thought she was right?"

"So why can't Natalia see it, too?" I growl.

"Because, when it comes to you, she can't see clearly."

Rising out of my seat, I start pacing. "What if I build Natalia the perfect nursery?" I suggest. "She made a vision board a while back. I could use that to bring her vision to life. To show her how I feel, what she means to me, what our family—"

Annie looks disappointed as she taps a finger against the head of her walking stick. "Don't you understand, Andrey? She doesn't need your money. She needs your time. Your attention."

"I—"

"Find a way to reach her how *she* needs, Andrey," Annie interrupts, climbing back to her feet and regripping her cane. "Or you'll end up losing her altogether."

14

NATALIA

Misha kneels down in front of Remi, the two of them sharing an overly cinematic goodbye, as if they won't be connected at the hip eight short hours from now.

I tousle Misha's hair while he presses his nose to Remi's. "How about we play some chess when I get back home after work?"

"Only if you're prepared to lose again."

"You little stinker!" I swat at him, and he skitters off, laughing.

His limbs look long and lanky. I swear he's visibly grown in just the last couple weeks.

Suddenly, I'm the one in need of an overwrought goodbye. He might grow another inch in the eight hours I'm gone at work. By the time I get home, he'll have a goatee and a credit score.

I walk into the foyer, not even sparing a passing glance for the tall figure leaning against the front door. I've resigned myself to the overbearing presence of my bodyguards.

"Are you ready?" I ask, expecting Leif, Leonty, or Olaf to open the door for me—if I have to be under lock and key, at least they're gentlemen about it.

But the man who turns his broody, silver eyes on me is no gentleman.

"Good morning, *lastochka*."

I successfully avoided Andrey all weekend. To his credit, he made it easy. He gave me a wide berth. Even still, this huge manor felt too small for the both of us. It's why I need to get out now.

"I don't have time for this. I'm going to work."

He bands an arm across the doorway, silhouetted by the sunrise. "I think it's better if you stay home today."

"You'll have to schedule your next bullshit intervention outside of work hours if you want to trick me into attending."

Andrey doesn't move. He just lowers his chin, his silver eyes piercing into my soul.

"You've already given me a full-scale security team," I argue, even though Andrey isn't arguing back. "Not to mention a personal guard dog. What is the point of any of them if I can't go out and live my life?"

His brow furrows. He seems to be searching my face for something, but I have no idea what that is.

I screech in frustration. "You've hijacked every aspect of my life and I'm freaking sick of it. If you—"

"Okay."

I fall silent. "What?"

He drops his arm and steps back, waving me through the door. "If it means that much to you, go to work."

He says it like he's doing me a favor. Like I should be grateful he's letting me leave the house. But I'm not so pissed that I'm going to kick a gift horse in the mouth… no matter how satisfying that would be.

"Right. I'll, uh… I'll just… be going then." I shimmy sideways, staying carefully out of reach as I skirt past him to the driveway.

Andrey stands watch in the doorway as I climb into the car and start down the drive.

For a second, I feel a slight modicum of shame. After all, he *is* just trying to protect me and the babies.

But the feeling lasts only until he disappears from view.

"Have you heard?"

"I know, it's just awful!"

I turtle deeper into the collar of my shirt, trying to pretend I can't hear the whispers floating around the office and, most importantly, that I'm not regretting coming into the office today.

Andrey cannot be right about this, too. I refuse to let that happen.

The crown of Abby's head passes by my cubicle before her nails click against the laminate paneling of the cubicle across the hall. It's her calling card—the same way Freddy Krueger laughs as he slices through teenagers' abdomens, Abby Whitshaw raps her fingernails on the walls right before she comes to annoy the hell out of me.

"I did wonder when he never responded to my texts," Abby whispers. "It's not like him…"

How often was she texting Byron? Was he trying to sleep with her, too? Not that he'd really have to try.

"What do you think happened? Do you think it had something to do with *her*?"

I stare fixedly at my laptop screen, but I can feel the heat of their gazes burning through my cubicle. They're not making any secret about who the "her" is in this scenario. How the hell did I manage to become the punchline and the suspect all in one year?

Bitterness flares through me as I connect the chaotic last months with the only thing that has changed in my life recently: Andrey.

I rise from my desk slowly, calmly… like someone in need of a stale coffee from the break room and not someone who may or may not have murdered her boss.

Unfortunately, my attempt to draw zero attention to myself is shattered when my Schwarzenegger-sized shadow follows me into the breakroom.

"Are you okay?" Leonty asks, closing the door behind him.

"Keep it open," I order. "Otherwise, they'll think we're fooling around in here."

Leonty actually blushes. "That's ridiculous."

"What? I'm not your type?"

His blush only deepens. "You know that's not—"

I wave a hand in his face. "I'm only teasing." I grab a juice pack and slump down into one of the plastic chairs. "I'm guessing you've heard the rumors, too?"

"I don't pay attention." He places a finger against his temple. "It's just elevator music in here most of the time."

I snort. "You're my bodyguard. Your job—and, knowing Andrey, your life—depend on you paying attention. Tell me what you've heard."

Leonty helps himself to a juice, too. "The rumors don't concern you, Nat. Don't let it bother you."

"Byron is missing!" My voice comes out even shriller than usual. "Everyone thinks I have something to do with it. And honestly, that may be true."

"It's not."

"Please. You expect me to pretend like this doesn't have 'Andrey Kuznetsov' written all over it? Byron just quit his job and disappeared without a trace right after they had a chest-banging, dick-swinging, testosterone-fueled showdown."

"People go missing all the time."

I groan, dropping my face into my hands. "Like I don't have enough to worry about."

"Exactly. Don't put this on your plate along with the rest of it. Let those bitches talk all they want. No one can accuse you of hurting another human being."

I frown through my fingers at him. "This from the man who literally saw me shoot a human being at point blank range."

"Oh, shit." He chuckles through a wince. "Forgot about that."

"Lucky you. I haven't."

Leonty gives me a sympathetic smile. "Let's cut out early today. That way, you won't have to deal with the rumor mill."

"You're just suggesting that because you wanna get home to Mila."

"She did text me this picture earlier—"

"Urgh, no, that's enough. Stop right there," I say with a shudder. "I don't need details. You've convinced me. Let's go."

The only thing worse than approaching the manor mid-afternoon and knowing Andrey is waiting for me inside is realizing that he was right about me skipping work today.

I expect for him to meet me at the door with a therapist in one hand and the kind of sign you'd see at airport arrivals that says, "*I told you so.*"

But the entryway is empty and I don't see anyone as I make my way through the house and up to my room.

I click the door closed and kick off my shoes. I'll take a nice, long shower and then go off to find Misha and tell him I'm letting him win every board game we play, but we'll both know it's a lie. He's absurdly good at every game we play, and I don't stand a chance even if I am trying my hardest.

But just as I'm about to undress, I notice a folded white card sitting on my duvet.

Heart hammering in my chest—though I'm not sure if it's frightened hammering or excited hammering—I open it.

Go next door.

I flash the card to Remi. "You know anything about this, Mr. Guard Dog?"

His tongue lolls out of his mouth. I take that as a "no."

Letting my curiosity win out, I drop the note and head into the hallway. The door next to mine is cracked open, and Remi pushes through it like he can't wait any longer.

I follow him in and my jaw drops.

It's a nursery.

Not just any nursery, either—it's the dream nursery from my vision boards. Everything is exactly accurate, from the snowy, sheepskin wool rug to the Egg Dodo baby basket I pinned to my board more as a joke than anything else.

I slip deeper into the room, running my hands over everything to make sure I'm not in a weirdly realistic dream. Part of me wants to throw off all my clothes and roll around in that sheepskin rug just to be really positive.

But Remi steals my thunder and divebombs the rug, rubbing himself all over it. He looks so happy that I don't have the heart to stop him.

"Nat?"

I recognize Mila's voice instantly and turn towards the door. "In here!"

She pops into the room, takes one look at it, and her jaw drops, too. "Oh, no. He didn't."

I twist around and find my expression mirrored on her face. "Andrey did this?"

"Who else?" she asks. "You've got to hand it to the man: he sure has taste."

I don't bother telling her that I'm the one who picked out half the stuff in this nursery. That may be true, but he's the one who has elevated it in ways I couldn't have even imagined. There's art on the walls and books on the shelves. Someone must have picked all of that out, and I have a feeling Andrey is too much of a control freak to hand that responsibility off to anyone else.

"Hey, there's a note." Mila holds up a folded piece of paper just like the one that led me here.

I take it gingerly from Mila's extended hand and flip it open.

Dear Natalia,

I wanted to make your dream a reality. I've taken some liberties in filling in the blanks, but you can change anything you don't like. Consider it my gift to you. The only thing I ask in return is for you to reconsider therapy.

Yours, Andrey

I read the note again and again.

"Nat? Everything okay?"

"'Consider it my gift to you,'" I grit. "'The only thing I ask in return is for you to reconsider therapy.'"

Mila is chewing on the inside of her cheek when I make eye contact again. "Annie warned him that this wasn't a good idea."

I throw the note on the floor. "Of course she did. And of course he didn't listen. Because Andrey Kuznetsov doesn't listen to anyone but himself."

I give the room another once-over. I no longer see a sweet and heartfelt gesture—I see a bribe. Another way for him to control me with his money.

Mila winces. "What are you going to do?"

"I'm gonna donate everything to charity," I decide, content with my decision the moment the words leave my lips.

Not even Mila's horrified face can deter me. "Donate it to— Nat! This stuff is expensive as hell. And it's all so beautiful. I know you're angry, but this room is perfect. You can't just get rid of everything."

I meet her eyes, steady and determined. "Watch me."

15

ANDREY

She's sitting on the window seat, regarding me with eyes made lighter by the sun pouring through the glass. She breathes evenly. Says nothing. Waits for my reaction.

Until, finally, she concedes that she'll have to speak first if she wants to talk about what the fuck just happened in here.

"Why so quiet? Not a fan of what I've done with the place?"

The careful planning—not to mention the tens of thousands of dollars I spent—seems to have faded into nothing.

Quite literally.

I'm standing in an empty fucking room.

"Where is everything?"

"Gone." She shrugs like she's all easy, breezy sunshine, but I see the fire behind her eyes. The *fury*. "I donated it all to charity."

"You were the one who dreamed of this place. You designed it. Why would you give it all away?"

"Because I'm not going to be bribed, Andrey." She leans forward, and I notice the cherry pendant that usually hangs around her neck is gone.

For some reason, that pisses me off more than anything else.

I run a hand through my hair, avoiding her eyes so I don't explode. "I can't keep having the same goddamn fight with you over and over again, Natalia."

"And yet, when I tell you I want more freedom, more autonomy—when I tell you I want to freaking leave—you increase my security, shadow my every move, and force me to live under your roof." She rises and glides forward until her feet touch the bare floor. "If you want to stop fighting, you have a weird way of showing it."

"Maybe I wouldn't have enacted all those precautions if they weren't necessary."

"So I'm supposed to just trust you? Here's some news for you, Andrey: I haven't trusted you since the day we fucking met."

She spits the words at me, her breathing coming in harsh bursts, her eyes narrowed. But her anger falters for just a second when I step closer. She pulls back like she thinks I might hurt her, and fuck, maybe she's serious. Maybe she really doesn't trust me.

"I know exactly what's at stake here, *lastochka*. Considering you were so recently Nikolai's prisoner, you should, too."

I wait for my point to seep into her pretty little head and make some difference—for her to realize how much I don't want her to end up like Maria—but it's like there's an invisible wall between us. No matter what I say, nothing makes any difference.

She lifts her chin. "You're just trying to trap me here."

"Jesus Christ, woman, I was prepared to let you go!"

The furious words explode out of me, but when Natalia responds, she's not meeting fire with fire. It's disdain she gives me instead. Venomous, desert-dry disdain.

"You really expect me to believe that?"

"Do you really think I didn't know about your 'plan' to escape?" I hiss, moving closer still.

Her breath catches in her throat. Her eyes go wide.

I hold her gaze for a second before I continue. "Mila and Katya didn't have to say a word because Shura was standing just outside the door. I knew from the start that you wanted to leave. And if you don't believe anything else I've said to you, believe this: I was prepared to let you go."

Her breath squeaks out in a single word. "Why?"

A cruel bite of laughter escapes my lips. "Because I failed to protect you. I let you down and you felt that leaving me was the only way to give our children any kind of future. I understood that."

"You would have just let me go?" she breathes, her brows knitting together. "Just like that?"

"No. Not 'just like that.'" I trail my fingers through a loose strand of hair that hands carelessly down her shoulder. "How could I live with myself without making goddamn certain you would be alright?"

"You were going to watch me." It's not a question, but a revelation. Hoarse and trembling, it sounds like it's an effort for her to talk at all. "That's not letting me go, Andrey."

I shake my head. "You would never have known we were watching. You could have lived the quiet suburban life you wanted… but from the shadows, I'd make sure you were always, always safe."

She searches my face, hunting for the lie, but I stare back at her, waiting for the truth to sink in.

"I was fully prepared to let you go, little bird. But Yelena—" She flinches at the name. If I were a weaker, less trained man, I'd probably do the same. "Yelena forced me to realize something: just because I was prepared to let you go doesn't mean everyone else would. Nikolai, Viktor, Slavik—they're all out for blood. And the best way to draw my blood is to go after yours."

My fingers curl around her infuriatingly bare throat, and I pull her into me until we're flush. Until her soft curves meld with my hard lines. She's trembling, but she doesn't fight. If anything, she arches into me ever so slightly.

"You're stubborn and desperate for independence, but your life is tied to mine now, *lastochka*. For better or for worse."

She shakes her head. "There has to be another way."

"There is no other way," I warn. "Don't you see?"

"No. As a matter of fact, I don't."

"Like I said: stubborn." Scowling, I draw my thumb over her full lower lip. I'm so hard it aches. "It seems you don't want to believe that I have your best interests at heart."

She swallows. The air between us goes taut.

"So I'll just have to show you."

Her eyes widen with alarm, but before she can get out her rebuttal, I silence her with my lips.

She lifts her arms—though whether to grab a hold of me or push me away, I have no fucking clue—but I pin them back to her sides. Parting her legs with my knee, I grind her against my thigh until she's trembling. I feel her warmth through my pants, and it's been so fucking long that I'm in danger of coming just from the mere thought of being inside of her.

She moans, and I part her lips with my tongue, sweeping in to taste her desperate breathing. Whatever she may say, she's been waiting for this moment as long as I have.

Her teeth bite down on my tongue, but I pin her to the wall and let her take out her anger on me. I don't so much as wince when she leaves her marks all over my body with bites and clawed nails.

I've got two fistfuls of her blouse, ready to rip it to shreds, when Natalia suddenly plants her hands on my chest and gnaws a chunk out of my shoulder.

"What the fuck?" I look down at my shoulder where the bloody imprints of her teeth glisten in the sunlight.

Part of me is stunned.

Another part—one below the belt—fucking loved it.

"I'm no pushover, Andrey." She eyes me like cornered prey. "You can't just kiss me and force me to forget."

"That's not what I'm trying to—"

"You're trying to fuck me into submission. If it's not money, it's sex. That's how you operate, isn't it?"

I'm on her again with a snarl. I shove her pants down around her thighs, and there's not a whisper of space between us now. We're sealed head to toe, my breath mingling with hers as I work a finger between her legs. "As usual, you don't understand the bigger picture. I'm trying to save you—from my enemies. From my sins. From *yourself*."

"Then who is—" She whimpers as I push one finger into her and then a second. She falls against my chest, helpless. "Then who is going to save me from you?"

I withdraw my hand, loving the disappointment that flashes across her face when she looks up at me. "No one, *lastochka*."

Then I free my dick from my pants and drive into her heat.

Whatever protest she had planned, it's gone now. I drive it out of her with slow, deep strokes that feel like coming home. I fuck her into the wall, clawing at her hips and her waist, trying to claim as much of her as I can.

I want to make her feel good.

I want to make sure she has what she needs.

With every thrust, the need to be everything to this woman consumes me.

While she's caught in a moan, I bring my lips to her ear. "I'm not going to let you hurt yourself anymore, Natalia. If you won't take care of yourself, I'll do it for you."

I suck on her earlobe and taste the soft skin of her neck as we come together again and again. Her head falls back against the wall, her mouth opens in a sigh, and I can see my blood on the inside of her lip.

I fuck her harder until her face is burning with desire and her eyes are hazy. Then, I curl my fingers around her throat.

"You're going to talk to someone," I tell her. "You *will* take your meds. You're going to start taking your mental health seriously."

"Andrey…"

"I'm going to teach you how to fight and shoot," I continue, thrusting harder, more urgently, my hands grazing over her breasts. "I'm going to teach you how to defend yourself."

I grab her ass and hoist her up, lacing her legs around my waist as I delve even deeper inside her. "You are not a victim, Natalia. You are a fucking fighter. It's time the world knew."

She gasps. "Andrey…!"

The sound of my name on her lips is what does it. My grip on control slips, and I plow into her until the rest of the world falls away. Nothing matters except the way we fit together—the way she quivers around me.

With a scream, she comes, strangling the orgasm from my cock.

Just when I thought I'd experienced it all.

The high lasts an eternity. When it finally lets us go, her knees are weak. I have to set her down on the window seat. Her clothes are scraps, but she tries to pull them around her chest and her bump.

With every passing second, she's growing more and more distant. I see it happening.

This solved nothing.

"This nursery wasn't meant as a manipulation, Natalia."

She forces her gaze to mine. "No, it was a gift. A gesture. But that's not what I want. It's never what I wanted." A sob bursts from between her swollen lips. "I wanted your time. I wanted *you*."

Should it bother me that she's speaking in the past tense?

Before I can decide, she leaves me with one parting blow. "Maybe I'm not the only one who needs someone to talk to."

16

ANDREY

Considering I just released weeks' worth of pent-up desire, I feel strangely dissatisfied.

Shura tries to hide a cigarette behind his back, but I grab it from between his fingers and take a long draw. "We're a sorry pair," he sighs as I smoke. "How long has it been for you?"

"Almost a year."

"Fuck, you lasted longer than I did."

"What do you have to be stressed about? Your woman isn't determined to drive you insane."

Shura laughs miserably. "I take it the nursery didn't work."

I throw the spent cigarette onto the ground and grind it into the gravel. "Nothing works with that woman. But that's tomorrow's problem."

Shura snaps to attention. "We have new intel from Yorick."

"Can we act on it?"

"The Black Brigade is meeting tonight to discuss the terms of Slavik's alliance." Shura looks longingly at the mangled cigarette. "Yorick will be at the meeting."

My spy, Yorick, has spent weeks worming his way into the Brigade ranks. Access to a key meeting is a minor victory in and of itself. Seeing how rare those have become these days, I'll take it.

"So will we."

Shura's eyes snap to mine. "You're not—We can't—Shit, are you serious?"

"This is no time to play it safe. I need to make a statement."

"News of our double murders will make a grand statement," he drawls sarcastically. "The Black Brigade may have been out of commission for decades, but that doesn't mean they're not dangerous."

"Relax, Shura. I don't plan on underestimating anyone."

He drags a hand over his face as I walk towards the Escalade. The man looks like he could use a smoke, a Xanax, or both. With a grimace and a muttered curse, he follows.

I get in the driver's seat and fly down the road. My plan may only be half-formed, but forward movement is better than standing still. I can think of no better way to channel all my frustration than to strangle it and mash the accelerator to the floor.

The adrenaline gives me a sense of purpose. As long as I'm hurtling forward at a hundred and fifty miles per hour, it's almost possible to block out the image of those bright eyes staring up at me with equal parts longing and disappointment.

It's almost possible to forget her.

Almost.

It's close to midnight when my men gather around me. We're only one street over from the meeting place, waiting on Yorick to secure us a way into the seedy motel where the Brigade lieutenants are gathering.

"Only one man can be in the actual meeting room when it all goes down," I inform my men. "Any more and we'll be noticed."

Shura's jaw twitches, but he doesn't voice his reservations. "What about the rest of us?"

"There will be Brigadiers stationed outside the meeting room. Yorick will let us know the exact number soon. I want you to take them out—*quietly*," I emphasize. "Then wait for my signal before you storm the place."

"And you really think it's a good idea for you, our *pakhan*, to be the one in that room when the meeting goes down?" Shura asks, unable to hold his tongue any longer.

"I don't move forward with bad ideas." He flinches at my tone but falls silent. With a sigh, I toss him a bone. "I don't plan on decimating their ranks tonight, but I do want enough blood spilled to force a change of allegiance."

That's the gist of my gameplan: that, in the absence of loyalty, fear will do the trick.

Right on schedule, my phone pings with an incoming message.

YORICK: *Staff entrance at back of bldg. Take second staircase to fourth floor. Use Bear Door. Meeting in ten.*

YORICK: *Five guards.*

It's clear he's typing fast. As fast as I need to move if I only have ten minutes to get into the room before the Brigadiers arrive.

Quickly, I share the information with my men. "Once I'm in, wait twenty minutes. Use the same entrance. I should be inside by that time and the meeting should be underway."

I turn to Shura, clasping his hand the way we do before every high-risk operation. "You should be able to handle five guards without a problem, no?"

"Leave that to me," he says confidently. "Just make sure you don't get killed before we can get inside."

Smirking, I gather my wits and dart towards the decrepit building.

The minutes fly as I follow Yorick's directions through the building. Ten becomes nine, eight, seven before I reach the Bear Door, which turns out to be exactly what it sounds like —an old wooden door with the face of a roaring bear carved into the surface. Not a single other soul is around as I jimmy the lock and sneak inside.

The second I'm in, voices start to filter up from the staircase on my left.

I press the door closed quietly and turn to the room. Columns and arches ring the perimeter and there's a raised dais in the center. Bedraggled red curtains cover broken, windowless stretches of the wall, leaving me plenty of shadowy alcoves to hide behind. But I find a door that leads to a bathroom and take refuge there just before men start filing into the room.

With the door slightly ajar, I watch the men enter one by one. Amongst the grizzled, scarred men, I spot Yorick.

He's wearing a white button-down, his hair slicked back with an unnecessary amount of gel. I can only imagine he's trying to fit in with the rest of these preening assholes.

By the time the door clicks shut, an incessant chatter fills the room like swarming locusts—until an older man steps onto the dais and the assembled group falls into a pregnant silence.

"My brothers," Dario Krueger booms, his thick, white mustache twitching with every word. "It has been a long time since we've closed ranks in this way. I thank you for being here today."

There was a time when Dario Krueger's name carried weight in this city. But in the last few decades, he's become just another forgotten name on a long list of fallen gangsters.

"We have been content to deal in the shadows, profiting off small deals and meager alliances. But an opportunity has presented itself."

A low rumble emerges from the back of the room—whistles of support, excited murmurs.

Krueger smiles. "Slavik Kuznetsov approached me with a very tempting offer."

There's another rise in volume that Krueger waves away with obvious amusement. He's almost paternal with his men—a father addressing his boisterous, reckless sons.

"He isn't offering us only profit—he's offering us territory. Prestige. We'll have increased drug distribution to expand our market. In addition," he says, "Slavik will give us license to bring back the flesh brothels that brought us to power in the first place."

Flesh brothels? I have to grit my teeth to keep the angry growl at bay.

"It is a generous offer," Krueger states, as though the matter is already decided.

I lean in a little closer, trying to read the atmosphere in the room. At first, there had been an air of excitement and interest. But now?

I can smell the doubt circling in the air. The longer the silence stretches, the quicker it turns to fear.

"What say you, my brothers?" Kruger asks, raising his arms towards the throng of men.

For a moment, no one says a word. Then a man stands. He's younger than Krueger, but still senior enough for a ripple of silence to accompany his rise.

He doesn't bother stepping onto the dais. Instead, he stands where he is, his back to me, stiff and curt. "It's not a good idea to go against the Kuznetsov Bratva. *Pakhan* Andrey will not be pleased."

Finally, a man with some sense.

Krueger's reedy eyes tighten with displeasure, but he maintains his pleasant smile. "You seem to be a little confused, Benioff. Our alliance will be *with* the Kuznetsov Bratva."

"Slavik has not been seen or heard from in over a decade. He is not the true leader of the Kuznetsov clan anymore, no matter what he claims."

Krueger's smile slides off his face. "He is the eldest."

"Seniority means shit-all," Benioff retorts. "It's power that matters, and Andrey Kuznetsov is not a man to be trifled with."

I'm ready to give the man a standing ovation. But, judging from the look on Krueger's face, he's less inclined to agree.

"Andrey Kuznetsov is about to be deposed."

"Says the man trying to depose him!" Benioff pushes back. "What else would Slavik say? Especially since he's trying to win you over. He's succeeded, by the sound of it. You're ready to sign our lives away on a half-baked whim."

Krueger scowls as the men shift awkwardly.

Dissent within the ranks. I can use that.

My plan is forming fast. Krueger is a lost cause. But I have a chance of swaying Benioff in my direction. If I can do that, then—

Before I can formulate the thought, Krueger is talking again. "You're absolutely right, Benioff. We shouldn't form an alliance with Slavik Kuznetsov. Especially when there is disagreement among us."

Without warning, Krueger pulls out a pistol and fires once. The bullet embeds itself in Benioff's forehead and the man crumbles like cheap plaster.

Krueger smiles with satisfaction. The air is rich with the

smell of blood. "Anyone else with an opinion they'd care to share?"

There isn't so much as a murmur. Anyone who was sympathetic to Benioff's position has suddenly switched alliances.

"Wonderful!" Krueger slips his gun back into the holster. "Then we're in agreement. Lieutenants, join me up here while we toast to our fruitful new venture."

Four men join him on the dais. Champagne materializes from some hidden cupboard. Kruger raises his glass with aplomb. "To the destruction of an unworthy *pakhan*. And to the reinstatement of a new dawn for the—"

But I've reached my threshold for bullshit theatrics.

Stepping out of my hiding place, I walk boldly through the throng of men, striding up the center aisle that leads to the dais.

"I'd put the champagne back on ice if I were you, Krueger."

The man freezes, eyes flaring with panic. Apparently, he still harbors a few doubts about who the true *pakhan* of the Kuznetsov Bratva is. Because he looks like he's seen a ghost.

Yorick is only a few feet from me, but he's playing his part, staring daggers at me like all the rest.

"Sorry to crash the party, boys, but I couldn't stand to listen to any more of your fearless leader's drivel."

Krueger's mustache quivers. "How dare—"

He doesn't see the bullet coming any more than Benioff did. One second, he's standing on his platform, raised above all his men. The next, he's falling to the floor, blood spreading across his chest.

My men pour through the doors just as Krueger's head cracks against the stage. With the Bratva at my back, I unleash chaos on the sorry lot of them, already certain of my imminent victory.

This—bloodshed, power games, the skirmishes that live and die in the shadows—has always come easily to me. I know how to act, how to be, what to say, where and when to move.

But my life has expanded. It's stepped *out* of the shadows, whether I like it or not.

And Natalia remains a problem that can't be solved by brute force.

No matter how much I'd love to try.

17

NATALIA

"Nice try, Natalia—you've been spotted."

I was headed back to my room, but then I heard a key in the front door. I thought maybe I could slink back into the kitchen, wait him out, and then run off to hide in my room without being spotted. But those dreams have been well and truly shot to hell.

Which leaves me with no choice but to circle back around the corner and face him.

"Hi."

His gaze drops to the bags of chips, cookies, gummy bears, and chocolate-covered pretzels I'm cradling in my arms. "Hungry?"

"Shut up."

I suppose I can't avoid him forever. Though I tried—successfully—for the last week.

Avoiding his gaze like the plague, I clear my throat. "If you'll excuse me—"

"Have you given any thought to—" I feel my hackles rise in anticipation of the question that's been the very reason I've been avoiding him so thoroughly. Well, that and the whole *we had angry sex we never should've had* debacle. But he saves himself from my wrath by finishing with a totally different question. "—visiting your aunt?"

"Oh."

He raises his eyebrows, probably wondering why I'm gawking at him without replying. In my defense, he looks unbelievable in blue. The stretch of the material across his chest doesn't hurt, either.

Also in my defense, avoiding him has the annoying side effect of making me forget about his ungodly hotness. Which means, every time I find myself face-to-face with him after prolonged Andrey Abstinence, it's like being hit with a blinding light after days in the dark.

"I just thought she might appreciate a visit from you. You haven't seen her since the dinner."

The Dinner. He doesn't need to say anymore. We all know which disaster he's referring to. Kudos to him for mentioning it without so much as a flinch.

But that's the difference between Andrey and myself. *He has no problem being a jerk,* I think bitterly.

"I didn't realize I was allowed out of the house," I remind him with an edge in my voice.

"As long as you're properly accompanied, I have no problem with it."

I have half a mind to tell him to stick his suggestion where the sun don't shine. But I can't pass up the chance to visit Aunt Annie. Much less the opportunity to get out of the manor for a little while.

"Fine. I'll take Misha with me."

A part of me almost wishes Andrey would push back just so that I have an excuse to argue with him. Hell, maybe I just wanna feel like I'm getting my way once in a while.

But as usual, Andrey heads me off at the pass with a shrug. "I can have a car ready for the two of you in half an hour. I'll arrange a second car for your snacks."

My scowl has no effect on him as he disappears around the corner, chuckling softly. Abandoning my snacks—I've lost my munchy mood anyway—I duck upstairs for a quick change before heading back down to rally Remi and Misha.

It doesn't take much rallying. Misha is buzzing at the idea of a day trip, and it makes me realize I'm not the only one who has been cooped up. He hasn't been out much since his concussion.

Remi, on the other hand, isn't fond of the drive and spends the entire ride whining. But the moment we pull up in front of a gorgeous cottage nestled in the middle of a leafy enclave, he's bounding out of the car faster than I can order him to heel.

"Wow!" Misha follows the trail of ivy up the trellises. "This is cool."

We step into the house, which is smaller and cozier than I would have expected for an Andrey Kuznetsov property. But it's still larger than anywhere Aunt Annie has ever lived before.

Her personal housekeeper-slash-caretaker points us in the direction of the parlor, but before I can surprise Aunt Annie, I realize Remi's already beaten us to the punch. He's slobbering all over my aunt, kissing her hands and arms.

When Aunt Annie sees me, she jumps up. "Well, if it isn't my favorite daughter!"

"I wanted to surprise you, but Remi kinda blew it."

Annie scoffs. "Honey, I hate to break it to you, but when the security team showed up fifteen minutes before you did and did a full search of the place, I had an inkling you might be stopping by."

I scowl and drop myself into the cushy armchair next to hers. "Of course. Why did I think he would be subtle about this?"

Aunt Annie just laughs and turns to Misha, who flashes just enough of a sheepish smile to make me wonder if maybe, just maybe, I was the very last person to be informed about today's little field trip.

So much for reclaiming my independence.

The moment Misha's soft snore reaches a crescendo, Aunt Annie gives me a wink and gestures for me to follow her outside.

It's been an hour of snacks and conversation, which has been great for me and Aunt Annie, but the boys couldn't hang. Remi abandoned us for the backyard a while back, and Misha was dozing off and on for fifteen minutes before he finally gave in and curled up on the couch.

Aunt Annie rests her cane against the wall and we settle on the patio sofa where we can watch Remi make sweeping circles of the yard, a fallen tree branch balanced in his jaw.

"He's a good boy, that Misha," Aunt Annie remarks fondly.

"He is, isn't he?" I can't help but smile. "I know it sounds insane, but he genuinely feels like he's mine. Like he was meant for me."

"That doesn't sound insane at all. That's exactly how I felt about you."

My eyes get watery, but I blink it away. "Really? Despite the circumstances?"

Aunt Annie's eyes are awash with tears, too. When was the last time I saw her cry? Probably when I was a little girl—and even then, it wasn't often.

"The circumstances were outside our control, Nat. It happened. But as a consequence, you ended up with me." She takes my hand, clasping it tightly in her own. "I used to think sometimes that you were sent to save me from my own grief."

"I thought the same about you."

"Then I guess we were meant for each other in the same way you and Misha are." She squeezes my hand gently. "Some people really are soulmates."

Andrey's face flashes through my head, despite my best efforts to keep him out. I sigh. "And other people are just lessons."

Aunt Annie watches me, and I get the same feeling I used to get when I was a little girl—like all it takes is one searing look from her to crack all of my thoughts wide open like an egg.

"That's not a bad thing, you know?" she says gently. "We need lessons to help us grow. To evolve."

Biting on my bottom lip, I stare at our linked hands. Aunt Annie's are veined, marked with tiny liver spots that I know she didn't have a few years ago. "I'm sorry, Aunt Annie."

She squints at me. "For what, sweetheart?"

"For everything that's happened. For… the attack on your life, for the fact that you have to live outside your home. You can't even go to work anymore."

"I don't really miss work, if we're being honest," she admits. "It's nice to sit still for a moment, you know?"

"As long as you're happy…"

"I'll be happy when I know you're at peace."

I throw her a sideways glance, taking care not to look her directly in the eye. "I'm… getting there."

She smirks. "I could always tell when you were lying. Nice to know I haven't lost my touch."

I wrap my arms around my body despite how warm the breeze is. "It's… complicated. But I'm fine. Really."

"Andrey tells me that when you're not fighting him, you're avoiding him."

Despite myself, my eyes snap to hers. "When did you talk to him?"

"Last week. And the week before." Her eyes bounce around

as she mentally counts back. "He's been coming every week for quite a while now."

Once a week?!

"He never told me that." Neither did Aunt Annie, but I know I won't get anywhere lecturing her.

"From what I can tell, the two of you don't really talk all that much."

"Because when we talk, we argue," I snap. "And then I make questionable decisions that I wish I could take back later. It's not healthy."

"I would say it's healthier than bottling up your feelings and pretending they don't exist."

I squint at my aunt in disbelief. "I can't believe you're on his side."

She closes her eyes for a moment and guilt prickles at my skin. I shouldn't be giving her a hard time. She may look tough as nails, but she's still in recovery.

"Honey," she says patiently, "don't you get it? There are no sides when it comes to your well-being. There's just you and the people who love you."

"Andrey doesn't love me."

Aunt Annie fixes me with that piercing stare of hers. "Do you really believe that?"

I should've known when Andrey suggested I come visit Aunt Annie that he had her in his back pocket, too. As annoying as it is, I have to admit that the man is good.

"Yes," I double down stubbornly. "He doesn't want me. He doesn't love me."

Aunt Annie pats my knee. "He doesn't know *how* to love you, sweetheart. There's a difference."

Great. We've entered the *let's-justify-Andrey's-bad-behavior* portion of the evening. If I'd known we'd be having this conversation, I might have been open to a little Prozac beforehand.

"Not everyone was taught to show love, honey. Andrey thinks he can buy it the way he does everything else."

"Except that I already told him that it's not what I want. I don't want his gifts or his damn money." I sigh. "It's his way of keeping distance between us. He's just… scared."

Aunt Annie nods in agreement. "So what are you going to do about it?"

I pull in a sharp breath. "What do you mean?"

Her eyes twinkle in the fading sunlight. "Are you going to let his fear win? Or are you going to fight for what you want?" I open my mouth to argue, but she holds up a wiry hand. "And don't bother denying that you want him, because, remember: I can tell when you're lying. You want him, sweetheart. You want him, the family you could have, the future you two could create. I can see it in your eyes."

"I won't deny it," I say at last, my shoulders slumping. "But I also don't know what else to do about it."

Aunt Annie hums as turns her gaze on Remi. "Then maybe it's time to do some inner reflection," she suggests. "Work on yourself so that you're not so confused."

"Now, I know for sure Andrey sent me here with a purpose. I'm not depressed, you know."

"I don't care either way. Depression isn't a dirty word. And your parents saw a couple's therapist."

"Mom and Dad had problems?"

Try as I might, I just can't reconcile the thought of them fighting with the image I have of them in my head—happy, loved-up, kissing over the top of my head as we played piano together.

"They hit a snag about four or five years after they got married. They were both working a lot and they didn't have time for one another. It led to a lot of built-up frustration."

I blink and breathe, because that's all I can manage to do. It's like finding out Santa Claus isn't real.

"I can't imagine them not happy."

"Because you still see them the way you did at seven when life was simple and love made sense. But then you grow up and you learn that things are more complicated. Your parents *were* wonderful parents and they *did* have a great marriage. But it didn't just happen on its own. They worked on their marriage. More importantly, they worked on themselves."

I sit there in silence as Remi barks at squirrels teasing him from the treetops. It's a quiet night, but little by little, Aunt Annie is plucking at the fraying strings of everything I thought I remembered.

"Do you know why they got themselves into therapy?" Annie asks after a few moments of pensive silence.

Another leading question, but I take the bait anyway. "Why?"

"For *you*, sweetheart. They wanted you to have healthy,

happy parents. Parents who were a team, parents who would have each other's backs just as much as yours."

Her gaze slides to my belly and then back towards the house where Misha is still snoring softly in the parlor.

"You need to show your children that it's okay to work on yourself. That there can be an end to trauma. Maybe one day, that will inspire them to do the same with their own demons. Love isn't always what you do for another, Nic-Nat. Sometimes, it's what you do for yourself."

That night, after we're back at the manor and Misha has gone off to his room, I grab Shura's arm before he can slink away to see Katya.

"I need your help with something."

His eyebrows pinch together. "Of course. What do you need?"

"Before I tell you, it comes with one caveat."

His shoulders drop as though he's expecting it. "I can't tell Andrey?"

I smile. "You took the words right out of my mouth."

18

NATALIA

With every passing second that I don't pick up the gun, the *tick, tick, tick* in my head gets louder. I feel like a bomb is about to detonate. It doesn't help that Shura hasn't taken his eyes off of me since I approached the table.

"Stop staring at me!" I snap when I can't take it anymore.

He tosses up his hands. "What do you want me to do?"

"Just... I don't know. Turn around or something."

With a weary sigh, he does as I ask, pivoting to stare towards the pool house. I turn back to the table—and the gun—but I still can't make my hand move.

What was Evangeline thinking?

Evangeline, also known as Dr. Smirnov, also known as my new therapist. I was dumb enough to think she could help me.

Exposure therapy is medieval. What about holding a gun is

going to do anything to help the gnawing panic I feel in my gut every time I even *look* at one?

She told me I could start on a low dose of some medication for my anxiety, but I'm gonna need a tranq dart before I can get within a foot of this gun.

"Come on, Nat," I grit to myself. "It's not even loaded."

Or is it? the anxious voice in the back of my head ponders. Loaded or not, the ugly, metal gun looks far from innocent. I almost think it's taunting me.

Pick me up, Natalia. You know how I work, don't you? You've used me before.

Shuddering, I take a step back. Then I whirl around to Shura. "I'm calling it. This is useless!"

"Don't say that. You're just starting."

"No, it's been half an hour, and I'm further from the gun than when we started." I sag. "I thought I'd at least shoot it before I freaked out."

He turns from the pool house for the first time since I banished him from looking at me. "Stop seeing the gun as a weapon—"

"It *is* a weapon."

"It's a tool," he argues. "What makes all the difference is who's holding it."

All at once, I see my own hands rising in front of me, a gun folded between them… aimed at Andrey's chest.

"Exactly! Look at me—I'm a freaking wreck." I take another step back. "I shouldn't be allowed anywhere near a gun."

Shura looks like he wants to agree. But instead, he walks over and picks up the gun. Without any hesitation, he raises it and aims at a tree in the distance. He mimes pulling the trigger. "You just need to be confident."

"Which automatically disqualifies me."

He lowers the gun, pointing the muzzle at the ground and flicking on the safety before he turns to me. "Confidence can be learned. But if you don't want to do this, Natalia, you don't have to."

I consider going back to my glossy-haired, poreless therapist and telling her I failed my first homework assignment, and my stomach curdles with shame. "No, I want to do this. I'm just... scared."

"Okay. Tell me what you're afraid of."

I glance at the gun in his hand like it's a venomous snake that might strike at any moment. "Everything."

"Care to be more specific?"

"I'm afraid of looking at it, touching it—basically, all of the five senses are off limits," I ramble. "Also, of dying."

Shura looks like he's not sure what to do with me, and I relate to the feeling. I don't know what to do with me, either.

I cover my face with my hands. "I'm sorry, I'm sorry. I know this isn't helping. But every time I see a gun, I see my parents being killed."

Shura puts the gun down and walks closer. "You're thinking about yourself on the wrong end of the gun. Try to imagine holding it. If you were threatened and the only way to save yourself is to pick up this gun and shoot, would you do it?"

Again, I see myself aiming the gun at Andrey, my mind blank as I pulled the trigger.

I shake my head, my chin wobbling. "I don't—I can't—"

"Misha," he says suddenly. "Think about Misha. Would you pick up this gun to save Misha?"

The scene unfurls before my eyes—Misha and I trapped in a room with Nikolai or Slavik. If one of them went to hurt Misha, murder in their eyes, would I be able to pick up a gun with the intention of using it on another human being?

"I would shoot." The words roll off my tongue without a hitch.

Shura nods. "Precisely. Now, pick it up."

I take a few tentative steps forward, my hand reaching for the revolver. *Breathe,* I tell myself. *Just breathe.*

Then my hand clamps, sweaty and slippery, around the handle, and breathing is no longer part of the equation. My lungs are sealed shut, and I rip my hand away so violently that the gun clatters off the table.

Shura catches it before it can hit the ground.

"You touched it," he offers generously. "That's a start."

I'm shaking all over. "Do I have to try again?"

The gun disappears into the holster at his hip. "I think that's enough for today. We'll try again tomorrow. If you're up for it."

That sounds good to me. I'm much more interested in the second homework assignment Evangeline gave me, anyway.

But when I arrive outside Misha's door to get started on "feeding my soul" with things I love, like family time and playing piano, the deep timbre of Andrey's voice is unmistakable. I can't help but lean in and eavesdrop.

"... some real progress here. You should be proud."

"I got five answers wrong," Misha argues.

"And last time, that number was eight. You're improving."

"Barely," Misha mutters.

"Progress is progress, no matter how slow."

I take that little piece of advice and stow it away in my heart. I touched a gun for half a second and almost had a heart attack, but that's still progress.

"I *hate* math."

"You only hate it because it's hard for you to grasp. And now that we know why, we have ways of counteracting it."

I had no idea Andrey was helping Misha with his homework. *Be still, my heart.*

"There's no way to counteract dyslexia," Misha complains. "I just have to deal with being stupid."

I also had no idea Misha had dyslexia. Since when?

I have half a mind to bust through the door and reveal myself as a snoop just so I can tell Misha he is absolutely not stupid. But Andrey beats me to the punch.

"You're not stupid, Misha," he insists calmly. "You just learn differently. And between Mr. Akayev and I, we can help you. I'll bet Natalia could help you, too, if—"

"No!" Misha interrupts, making me flinch. "No, I don't want Natalia to know."

"You don't have a damn thing to be ashamed of, Misha."

In the space of a single, stolen conversation, I've gone from wanting to avoid Andrey to wanting to jump his bones. Maybe it's a simple case of being on the same page for once.

"I'm not ashamed. I just don't want her to know, okay?"

Andrey sighs. "If you insist."

I hear the scraping of chairs before Misha speaks up again. "Is she talking to you yet?"

I'm expecting a generic, evasive answer. The kind of answer you give your kids so they don't worry. *Everything's fine. We're doing good. There's nothing to worry about.*

"She's unhappy with me, and I can't exactly blame her. But… I don't know how to reach her."

"But you want to?"

Is that hope I hear in Misha's voice?

"I do. She's important to me."

My heart leaps the way it did when I saw the gun earlier. Like, somehow, these words are just as dangerous. *Don't fall for it. You'll only end up hurt.*

"Because of the babies?" Misha asks.

"Because…" There's a pause while Andrey thinks, and I'd give everything I own to see the look on his face right now. "Because out of everyone in this world, she matters the most to me."

Bang. The words hit me like a gunshot. I clap a hand over my mouth as tears blur my vision.

Forcing myself away from the door, I stumble to my room. Andrey's never said that to me before, and now, I realize why.

Because it doesn't really change anything.

We each have our issues to sort through, and until we do, we'll just be two people, eavesdropping on each other from opposite sides of a wooden door.

19

ANDREY

"How many routes have we secured?"

"Fourteen." I can practically see the dollar bill signs reflected in Luca's eyes every time he looks down at the route map we've spent the last two weeks perfecting. "I've got men stationed down all fourteen of them, ready to facilitate the drug shipments when they come through. We're as ready as we'll ever be."

I take the map off the table and study it closely. Fourteen thick, red lines wind through the city.

Fourteen ways for drugs to flow in and money to flow out.

Fourteen ways for my Bratva to solidify our future.

Slapping the map back on the sticky tabletop, I point at route number seven. "I need this one taken off."

Luca leans in to hear me over the thumping music of the club. "Route number seven is a strategic meeting point in and out of the Upper West Side."

"So are routes two, five, and eleven. We can do without seven."

Luca eyes me carefully. "May I ask why?"

"Personal reasons. I want it free of interference. That means no drugs and no threat of police activity."

Luca's eyes are bright with curiosity, but he has the sense not to push the issue. "Have you cleared it with Bujar and Cevdet?"

"Considering I'm the one running this operation, not to mention taking on most of the risk, I don't see why any of the partners would have a problem with it."

Luca raises his hands. "No, there's no problem here. Only interest."

"The only thing you should be interested in are the profits we're going to make."

It's a successful carrot dangling in front of him. "Oh, believe me, Andrey, all I've been dreaming of for weeks is profit." He cackles as he helps himself to another cigar. "Leave it to me. I'll have the route cleared for you, no questions asked. We'll talk again soon."

After Luca leaves, Shura joins me for a cigar and a glass of whiskey. "Did he pry?"

"Of course; it's Luca. But I managed to divert him. He'll clear route seven."

I decided early on that we needed a contingency plan on the off chance things went south and an all-out Bratva war breaks out. It's the first time I've ever had to have one.

Then again—save for Maria—this is the first time I've had something to lose.

"Any word from the Brigadiers?"

"Silent as the night," Shura confirms. "Yorick told me that they've severed ties with Slavik. They were a no-show at the last scheduled meeting and his calls have gone unanswered."

I help myself to some more whiskey. News like that deserves a toast.

"Once this expansion is underway, he'll be hard-pressed to find anyone who will be willing to ally with him."

"Let's not forget Nikolai."

I scowl. "Trust me, I haven't forgotten about the bastard. But first things first: I have to deal with Slavik and his takeover bid before I can concentrate on snuffing out the Rostov threat. Speaking of which…"

Shura shakes his head. "No news on that front. The man has retreated into the shadows."

"Which means he's planning something."

Shura's phone rings, and I don't miss the way he tenses before declining the call and placing the phone on the table screen side down.

"Who was that?"

"No one," he answers quickly. I arch a brow and he grimaces. "Katya."

I've known the man long enough now that I know when he's keeping something from me. "Everything alright between the two of you?"

"Sure, sure. She's just been busting my balls lately. Don't wanna deal with it."

He picks up his empty whiskey glass and brings it to his lips. Then he realizes there's nothing in it and reaches for the bottle.

I beat him to it, yanking the bottle out of his reach. "Now that we've got the lies out of the way, you can tell me what's really going on."

Shura swallows. He drops his arm and leans back against his seat. "I've been sworn to secrecy," he admits. "All you need to know is that you don't need to be concerned."

Again, Shura's phone rings, and he flips it over with a groan, Natalia's name clearly visible on the screen.

"Go on," I growl. "Answer it."

Shura eyes me warily, but he answers. "Nat, this isn't a good time."

I can't really make out what she's saying. The club we're in is too noisy and she's speaking fast.

"I don't know about tomorrow," Shura tells her. "Maybe Tuesday." After a beat, he sighs. "Oh, alright. I'll make time tomorrow." He hangs up and glares at me. "You didn't hear any of that."

I cross my heart with a sardonic smile and hand him the bottle. "Not a word."

Shura fills his glass and takes another drink, watching me over the rim.

"I had work for you tomorrow, but I'd hate to double-book you," I say casually. "When will you be busy?"

He downs the rest of his glass and sags back in his chair. "I won't be available at four tomorrow afternoon."

Perfect.

~

I may know what time Shura is busy, but that doesn't stop me from having to wander from room to room to track the two of them down.

I'm on the second floor when I happen to glance out the window and spot them in the far corner of the back lawn.

I tear through the house and stick close to the wall as I make my way towards them, hoping they won't see me. I doubt they're looking for spies, though. They chose the most secluded area of the garden, and it's been so overtaken with plants and trees that it provides the perfect coverage—unless you happen to look out of one particular second-floor window.

"Easy, Nat," Shura cautions. "Remember, if you panic, the gun becomes a liability."

Using the trees as cover, I creep as close as I can to their meeting spot without being seen. There's still about ten feet between us when I settle in to watch the show.

Right now, the show is Natalia with her hands wrapped around a gun, her brow scrunched tight in concentration.

The last time I saw her with a gun, it was aimed at my chest. This time, she's pointing it at a target set up a dozen feet away. One bullet hole is already flapping in the wind.

"Ready?" Shura asks.

"I think so," she squeaks.

"Keep both your eyes open. And remember: breathe, aim, shoot."

Her shoulders rise and fall accordingly. A second later, she squeezes the trigger. The silencer on her gun renders the shot little more than a dull *pop*. The target remains untouched.

"Dammit!" she cries.

"That was good!" Shura claps. "Really good."

"Don't patronize me," Natalia snaps. "You're the only one to actually hit the target today."

"That's because I've had a lifetime of practice, whereas you just got used to holding a gun last week. Give yourself a break."

"Stand back. I wanna try again," she orders, as though she hasn't heard a word Shura's just said.

With a resigned sigh, he steps away and Natalia takes aim once more.

She looks magnificent. Even more so when this bullet grazes the outer edge of the target.

"Yes!" she screeches, jumping up and down. "I did it! I actually did it!"

"Whoa, there," Shura cautions, snatching the gun from her hand and putting the safety on. "This thing's still loaded."

"Did you see that?" she demands, turning to Shura with blazing eyes. "I hit the target."

He laughs. "I did. Well done."

With a squeal of delight, she launches herself at Shura and wraps her arms around him. He stumbles back a few feet before returning the hug.

Something hard twists in my stomach. Before I can decipher what it is, I'm striding out of my hiding place and towards them with only one intention in my head.

Getting Shura's hands off my fucking woman.

As soon as she sees me, the smile wipes itself clean off of Natalia's face. She drops her arms and backs away from Shura, gaping at me like I'm the one holding a gun.

"What are you doing here?" Natalia chokes out.

"I was walking and I heard voices," I lie smoothly. "How long have you been practicing?"

She glances guiltily at Shura. "Um… a few weeks."

I tip my head towards the target. "That's impressive for only a few weeks. I'm proud of you."

She scuffs the toe of her shoe into the dirt, refusing to meet my eyes. "Thanks."

Shura clears his throat. "I'm gonna put the gun away. Excuse me."

He leaves the two of us in the little clearing, and Natalia watches him go like she'd love nothing more than to follow after him.

"How did it feel?"

She turns to me, resigned to a conversation. "Terrifying at first. The first week was kinda sad. I barely even touched the thing. But then…" She can't quite bite back the smile that tips the corners of her mouth. "Then it felt amazing."

"I'm happy you kept trying."

She nods. "It's important to respect my limits while still pushing them." I raise my eyebrows and her cheeks flush with color. "Er... I'm also in therapy. Thus the lingo."

How the fuck have I missed so much?

"And," she adds, "before you think your intervention was some great idea and you're a master of manipulation, you should know that your sneak attack sucked."

"I'm sorry I pressured you," I hear myself say. "I should have approached it differently."

She leans back, eyes wide in surprise for a beat before she can school her face into neutrality. "Well, regardless... It was still a good idea. I shouldn't have rejected your help."

"What changed your mind?"

"It was actually something Aunt Annie said to me." She gives me a tight, accusing smile. "When the two of you orchestrated that little visit for me."

"It wasn't orchestra—"

She waves me off. "Save your lies. I've decided not to be mad about it. Just like I've decided not to be mad about all those clandestine rendezvous the two of you have been having."

I smirk. "What can I say? Your aunt is an intriguing woman."

"I really thought she'd be immune to your charms." She smirks, eyeing me like she's appreciating my *charms* as we speak.

"Actually, I think it was my sincerity that worked with her."

"Well, either way… thank you," she says softly, looking out across the lawn. "For trying so hard to get through to me."

I just nod and say nothing. I don't want to ruin it.

For the first time in a long time, it feels like we're taking a step in the right direction.

20

NATALIA

"He's moving Aunt Annie into the manor with us."

Evangeline's eyes go wide at my bomb drop. "We've been sitting here almost fifteen minutes and you tell me this only now?"

Only because I can still hardly believe it myself. Andrey just told me yesterday, and I haven't wrapped my head around it yet.

I pick at the hem of my dress as Remi burrows his head deeper into my lap. "He said he thinks it would be good for Annie to have some company since she's trapped in the house all day. Misha, too."

"Do *you* think that's the reason he's moving Annie to the manor?"

"Not really." I bite my lip. "I think he's doing it for me."

That's why, when Andrey told me, I couldn't even speak. My throat clogged with emotion, and all I could do was push onto my tiptoes and press a kiss to his cheek.

"How does that make you feel?" Evangeline falls back on her default question.

"Confused, mostly."

"Not touched? Or appreciative? Or happy?"

I purse up my lips. "Way to make me sound like an ungrateful bitch."

"I meant nothing of the sort." Evangeline laughs. "I just want you to articulate why a gesture as thoughtful as that would make you feel confused."

"Because it just complicates everything." As if everything hasn't been complicated from the moment I stepped into that elevator with Andrey. "Sometimes, it's easier to hate him."

Evangeline scribbles in her notes. I've only been in therapy a few weeks and she's almost at the halfway point of her notebook.

"'*Need to up her meds.*'" I pretend I'm writing. "'*The patient is seriously troubled.*'"

She covers her notebook. "You shouldn't spy on other people's journals. I didn't know I was writing that big."

"Hey!"

Evangeline just winks at me with a laugh. "Natalia, it's perfectly normal to be confused about your relationship with Andrey. After all, the two of you have never actually had a conversation about what you both want."

"Sex, mostly." She arches her eyebrows and immediately, I blush. "That was a joke."

"Jokes can be used to deflect serious topics." She adjusts her glasses on the bridge of her nose. "They can also be a very effective coping mechanism—a form of self-preservation."

"And what, in your professional opinion, do you think I'm trying to preserve?"

"Your heart, for one," she suggests.

I cringe. *Well, that's what I get for asking.*

I wait for Evangeline to offer up more professional observations, but she just leans into the silence, letting the room get real weird and awkward.

"I don't really have anything to say," I finally mumble.

She cocks her head to the side. "Nothing at all?"

"I have a few more jokes, but I'm afraid you'll accuse me of using humor to deflect my internal heartbreak again."

More silence.

More weirdness.

"I'm not heartbroken over Andrey, okay? I'm just frustrated."

"And why do you think you're so frustrated with him?"

"Um, hello?" I point at my belly. "He knocked me up, for one. Then he forced me to move into his pool house. Now, I can't even sneeze without four huge bodyguards perking up. I can't breathe! It feels like he's suffocating me."

"*He's* suffocating you?" Evangeline inquires. "Or the *situation* is?"

"Is there even a difference?"

"Maybe, maybe not. You tell me."

I grimace. Honestly, what's the point of a damn shrink if I have to do all the work myself? "I don't know, okay? Maybe I'm too broken to figure it out."

Evangeline snaps her notepad shut and sets it down. "Okay. Let's start with a simple question then. Do you have feelings for Andrey?"

The sad part is, I don't even have to think about my answer. "Yes."

"Are you in love with him?"

Yes. Duh. "I don't know."

Evangeline nods. "Is it possible that you're scared to love him?"

"Can you blame me if I am?" I explode. "The man has no idea who I am or what I want! And that's after I've told him exactly what I want."

"Maybe he's trying."

I can't help but roll my eyes. "Did he pay you to say that? The man has everyone under his thumb, I swear."

"No, you told me when you mentioned that he was moving your aunt into the manor. It sounds like he's trying to me."

She has a point. Clearly, she's doing a much better job of following this conversation than I am.

"Okay," I accept. "Okay, so maybe he is trying in his own way." I unfurl my hands and wipe my sweaty palms against my skirt. "It was a nice gesture. A sweet, thoughtful, touching gesture. But I want *more*."

God, she really knows how to wield these silences.

I sink into the couch. "And I can't help but wonder, what if I want more than he's willing to give me? What if I want more than he's capable of giving me?"

"Putting yourself out there is always going to be a risk, Natalia," Evangeline says. "The question is, do you love him enough to take it?"

I exhale sharply. It's a damn good question. "I'm starting to understand why they pay you the big bucks, Doc."

Evangeline smiles. "You've experienced a lot with Andrey in a short space of time. The two of you have been on a very intense roller coaster since you met. Before you could really get to know each other—or even understand each other—you had other, very serious things to deal with."

Pregnancy. Abduction. PTSD... The list goes on and on.

"Maybe you need to go back to the basics," she suggests. "You're not sure what you want right now or how to get it. So maybe, instead of worrying about trying to make a full-blown relationship work, you need to focus on existing together without the pressures of a romantic entanglement."

"That's a very fancy way of saying we should try being friends."

Evangeline chuckles. "I have to flex my expensive education somehow."

I take a second to chew the idea over. "In your professional opinion, can friends have sex? And before you answer, you should know that the hypothetical sex would be really, *really* good."

There's a lot about Andrey I'm confused about, but that's one point we've never disagreed on.

"If it was mediocre sex, then maybe. But good sex? Definitely not."

Now, who's making jokes?

"Friendship with Andrey." I try the idea on for size. "I don't even know where to start."

"How about with a little honesty?"

I drop my chin, looking up at her from under lowered brows. "No offense, Evangeline, but if I knew how to do that, I wouldn't need you."

21

NATALIA

Evangeline was like the flap of a butterfly's wings somewhere around the world that starts a hurricane. One little suggestion, and it's been days of swirling, spiraling thoughts that have stormed in my head for days on end now. And each and every time the clouds clear, only one way forward remains:

I have to fix things with Andrey.

"If not for myself, then for you guys," I say to my belly.

I want to delay it. Actually, scratch that—I want to run screaming into the hills rather than dive into the thorny mess that is my emotional baggage.

But my babies deserve better.

Which is how I find myself seeking out Andrey for the first time in months. A move that's accompanied by palpitations, severe doubt, and what I'm sure will read as an erratic spike in my blood pressure on my weekly medical report from Dr. Abdulov.

When Shura and I collide as I turn into the kitchen, he grabs my shoulders and holds me at arm's length. "Yikes. You okay, Nat?"

"You should work on your sweet talk," I mumble. Then I gulp. "Actually, I'm looking for Andrey."

His eyebrows disappear in his hairline. "That explains it. He's in his room, I think. We just finished up with a meeting."

I walk upstairs with every intention of stopping outside of Andrey's room, but then I pass it and have to double back. Weirdly enough, I pass it a second time. And a third.

"Stop being a wuss!" I chide myself. "Time to be a big girl."

Finally, on attempt number four, I manage to stop my feet and knock once.

Maybe he's not here. Maybe he's in the shower. Maybe I'll just have to come back and—

"Come in," he calls before I can run down the hall like the scaredy cat I am.

It took so much energy to get here that I have no clue what I'm going to say, but I doubt all the planning in the world will change that, so I draw in a breath and open the door.

Then that breath rushes out of me in a violent burst when I'm faced with the rippling muscles of Andrey's bare back.

He's pulling his shirt over his head with one hand like we're in the middle of a sexed-up fragrance commercial, showcasing his spectacular brawn and the canvas of scars that make my knees weak.

Maybe I should bring that up in therapy.

"Hey," I greet awkwardly.

He twists around at the sound of my voice. "Natalia?"

"Hey," I repeat again. *Cringe.* "Er, sorry to disturb you—"

"You're not disturbing me," he assures. "I was just about to step into the shower."

My face heats up—as does another part of my body that I'm trying to ignore. "I can come back later."

Some time when you have a shirt on and aren't about to be soaking wet would be preferable.

"No need. I'm all yours."

If only that were true.

I squash the internal dialogue in my head. It's really not helping.

"Can I talk to you about something?"

"Of course."

Since he doesn't seem to be in any hurry to cover up all those abs, I keep my gaze north of his neck. "I want to clear the air."

An eyebrow arches with intrigue. "Okay. Clear away."

My heartbeat thunders relentlessly against my chest. Now, I'm regretting my decision to walk in here unprepared. Maybe having a rough idea of what I wanted to say would've been the smarter move. Notecards. A few bullet points in Sharpie on the palm of my hand, maybe.

"You told me that I could trust you, and you let me down."

I walk over to the window and take a seat on one of the two armchairs. Andrey—still shirtless—sinks into the remaining armchair opposite me.

"The thing is, I *asked* for help. I told you what I needed and you didn't hear me. Or maybe you didn't want to. Either way, it felt like… like I was being abandoned."

I curse the tears prickling at the corners of my eyes. I so wanted to do this without crying. But I'd underestimated the intensity of speaking openly and honestly about my feelings.

Especially with the one person who seems to have the most influence over them.

"And therapy has helped me discover that I have abandonment issues. I hate getting close to anyone because I'm terrified that they'll leave me. And you… you left me while you were still around."

His eyes shimmer in the sun through the window. Still, he says nothing.

"You gave me space when what I really needed was for you to lean in. And…" Wringing my hands together, I urge myself on. "And worse, you thought you could solve it all by having sex with me. Like sex was a Band-Aid to make it all better."

I pause, giving him a small window to butt in, say something, apologize, maybe even defend himself.

But he still says nothing.

"And I'm not blaming you entirely. I let it happen. I didn't stop you. I… I wanted it as much as you did." I swallow, ignoring exactly how much my body still wants it right now. "But no matter how good it feels in the moment, that feeling doesn't last long." A straggling sob escapes me. "And it left me feeling used and even more invisible than before."

I open my mouth but then I realize, I don't need to. I've said everything I wanted to. For now, at least.

"Lastochka…"

Despite the coldness in his eyes, despite the hardness in his face, his voice is soft and laced with tenderness. He takes a lock of my hair between his fingers, the same way he did the day he told me he was moving Aunt Annie into the manor. Hesitantly, I meet his eyes.

They're blazing—it's like someone has just set them on fire.

Maybe that someone was me.

"I never meant to make you feel that way."

"I won't let anyone treat me like that again, Andrey. Even if that someone is you." He nods and goosebumps erupt along my skin like wildfire. "If I'm going to be with someone, it's going to have to be a true partnership. If I'm going to have sex with someone, it's going to be with someone who truly loves me."

Shadows flit across his eyes like a veil. As my heart rate increases, I force myself not to lose sight of why I came here in the first place.

"There isn't going to be any more casual sex between us, Andrey. I want a real relationship or nothing. If you come for me, it's going to have to mean something."

Exhaling deeply, he leans back against the armchair. "I hear you."

We sit in the silence for a few minutes longer. I have no idea what he's thinking, and I guess I'm gonna have to make my peace with that.

"Thank you for listening," I blurt, getting up from my seat.

His hand twitches suddenly as though he wants to grab my arm and stop me from leaving. But then the same hand clenches into a fist.

"You're welcome."

I half-turn towards the door before I stop myself and face him again. "There's something else I want to thank you for."

He gets to his feet and steps towards me. I'm close enough that I catch the deep woodsy musk. It's like my own personal version of catnip. Except this cat is going cold turkey.

Whether she likes it or not.

"You saw that I needed help and you wouldn't take no for an answer. No one's ever fought so hard for my mental health before."

"I want you to be happy, Natalia. As much as I want you to be safe."

Dammit—these pesky tears just won't seem to leave me alone. "I'm not the only one who needs to talk to someone, Andrey."

I suppose it's my way of saying, *I want you to be happy, too.*

I'm not sure if it translates though, because he tenses up immediately. "There's a lot I won't be able to say to a therapist."

"Evangeline knows our history," I point out. "And she's discreet. You can trust her."

"That's the problem, *lastochka*: I don't trust anyone."

"You have to try." I inch closer to him without even realizing it. "You don't have to talk to a therapist, necessarily. Find someone you trust and talk to them."

Those silver eyes bore into mine. So intense, so direct… so full of promise. "Can I talk to you?"

The fact my jaw doesn't unhinge and fall to the floor is a small miracle that I'm grateful for as I swallow and nod. "You want to talk—Me? The girl who shot you?"

He actually smiles. "Yes. You, the girl who shot me."

I hide my surprise behind the calmest smile I can manage given the circumstances. "You can always talk to me, Andrey. About anything."

He nods, his lips pulling up at the corners. "I just might take you up on that."

22

ANDREY

The remains of the party are scattered under a huge banner that reads *"Welcome Home, Aunt Annie!"* Half-deflated balloons bob from the banister of the staircase and paper plates and glasses cover every flat surface.

"You missed all the fun."

I turn to find Leonty leaning against the archway, a tipsy smile on his face. "Looks like it was a success."

"It wasn't bad," he admits with a shrug. Six months ago, Leonty would have considered the idea of any party outside a nightclub to be the very definition of pathetic. Times have changed, apparently. "The girls went all out."

I swat at one of the balloons when it creeps close to my head. "I'll bet Annie was thrilled."

"She was. Asked where you were, though."

I loosen the tie around my neck and throw it on the sofa. "I don't get to slack off like the rest of you."

The truth is, I wanted to be at the party. But since Natalia and I had our little chat, I've been keen to avoid her. Not because I didn't mean what I said—but because I want to manage her expectations. I want to give her what she wants.

The question remains whether or not I can.

"Everyone in bed?" I ask.

"Pretty much. Except Annie." He tips his head towards the hallway behind him. "I passed her room just now and her light was still on."

I clap Leonty on the back as I pass him on the way to Annie's room. I knock twice and hear a soft "Come in."

"Well, well, if it isn't my gracious host." She's in a chair by the open window, a chilly breeze filtering in.

"I'm not hosting you. You live here now."

"If you don't start charging me rent, I'm gonna think there's a catch." She shakes her head like she can't quite believe. "Bring me that scarf hanging behind the door, will you? It's cold in here."

Once she's wrapped in a cashmere stole I recognize as one of my early gifts to Natalia, she fixes me with her eagle-eyed gaze. "You better have a good reason for missing my welcome party, or else I might take the offense personally.."

"That candidness of yours is always refreshing." I drop into the chair across from her. "I'm sure you didn't miss me. From the looks of it, it was a great party."

"Are you avoiding my daughter?" she presses.

"Did I say your candidness was refreshing?" I tease. "I meant 'annoying.'"

"I'll take that as a yes."

I run my finger along the arm of the chair. "Has Natalia said anything to you?"

"If you're fishing for information from me, you've come to the wrong pond, young man." She tightens the scarf around her shoulders. "From what I hear, she was vulnerable enough with you. You should know what she thinks. What I want to know is what you think."

"I think Natalia was very brave."

"You're avoiding my question."

"Because I don't have an answer for it yet," I admit. "She wants all or nothing, Annie. I'm not sure I can give her that."

"You're scared."

Despite the truth in her statement, I glower. "It's not fear—"

"Well, something is holding you back. And it's not anything that Natalia has done."

"She did shoot me," I drawl. "Some men might take issue with that."

"And if that had bothered you, you wouldn't have gone chasing after her to bring her home. You wouldn't have her out in your back lawn doing gun training." Her eyes brighten as she leans forward and fixes me with a penetrating stare. "I wasn't born yesterday, Andrey. I know the signs."

"Signs of what?"

"The signs of someone who is too lost in their past to see their future."

I shift my gaze to the window. Just like her niece, this woman sees too damn much. "I wasn't aware I hired you as my therapist."

Annie chuckles. "I have to earn my keep somehow, don't I?"

"I would prefer you just put your feet up and relax. Enjoy your golden years."

"I won't be able to enjoy anything until I know my Nat is happy. That is my only priority. You'll understand in a few months—the moment you set eyes on those baby girls."

I do the mental calculations in my head. She's right: in only a couple months, I'll be a father. The hair on the back of my neck stands on end.

"Did you ever consider that maybe Natalia is better off without me in her life?"

Annie snorts. "Honey, she's carrying your children. That ship has sailed and the two of you are adrift at sea." She does kick her feet up, but the look in her eyes tells me she's nowhere close to relaxing. "I'd consider trying to save her, but it's not what she wants."

My jaw clenches. "What does she want?"

"You." She says it simply, without hesitation. "And you want her, too. If you ask me, it seems like a damn shame to deprive your babies of two happy parents for no good reason. Now, run along. I'm an old lady and it's long past my bedtime."

When I leave Annie's room, I find myself walking the hallway to Natalia's.

Annie made it all sound so simple. So easy. I could knock on her door, lay my shitty hand of cards on the table the way she did, and see if Natalia wants to play.

But as I approach her room, Leonty steps out of the shadows. I almost forgot he's been posted outside here.

"No nightmares tonight," he offers before I even ask. "Actually, she hasn't had any for a few days. Things have been quiet."

Ever since I started keeping my distance.

"Good," I mumble with a nod. Then I keep walking to my room.

Natalia is doing okay without me—better, even. I've given her enough nightmares for one lifetime.

It's overcast as I walk through the cemetery. I can't complain, though—the cold breeze matches my insides. I clutch the large bouquet of flowers I brought with me and brace myself against the pushing wind.

I picked a quiet, shady spot for Maria's final resting place. Not many people make it out this way unless they know who they're looking for. I know exactly who left the wilted purple petunias on her grave.

I sit cross-legged in front of the dark stone, reading the words instinctively, though they're ingrained in my head every bit as permanently as they are in the granite.

Here rests Maria Balakirev, beloved daughter, sister, friend.

There's no sign of me on that headstone.

She wasn't my wife; she didn't get the chance to have my child. More and more these days, our relationship feels like a figment of my imagination. My guilt is the only steady reminder we were anything to each other at all.

At her funeral, her mother sobbed, inconsolable. I tried to comfort her, but this was my fault. I was the reason her daughter was dead. What kind of comfort could I offer?

Maria's older sister, Raisa, pulled me aside later and said what I knew everyone else was thinking: *"This was your fault, Andrey."*

I couldn't even argue. I didn't try.

"I told her to leave you, you know?" Raisa looked towards the closed casket like she could see Maria beneath the glossy wood. *"I begged her to leave you a hundred times. She didn't listen."*

"I wish she'd listened to you."

Raisa's eyes flashed with anger. *"She didn't know any better, but you* did. *You* should *have done the right thing and left her. It would've broken her heart, but at least she'd be alive."*

That was the last time I saw any of them.

I never stopped sending Mrs. Balakirev the money. She gets a monthly check from me and will for as long as I'm alive to make sure it happens. But I stayed away from them, the way Raisa wanted.

Which is why I haven't been to Maria's gravesite since the burial.

I place the bouquet of calla lilies next to the wreath and run my fingers over her name etched into the marble. I blink once and the words start to transform. Instead of Maria's name, I see: **Here rests Natalia Boone...**

I yank my hand back, clench it into a fist.

"Fuck," I growl, dropping my head into my hands.

The wind blows harder. The trees overhead shed their brittle leaves, each rasping against my cheek as they skitter down like fingers rotted to the bone. It's getting colder, but I refuse to move.

I came here for a reason.

Reaching out, I touch my fingers to her name again. The frigid rock. The hard grooves.

"I didn't think I was capable of love before you," I whisper to her gravestone. "Somehow, you showed me what I was capable of. I'm sorry, Maria. I thought I could close myself off again. I thought I could shut down the part of me that you opened up. But I guess it doesn't work that way. Someone else got in through the cracks you left open. And…" I trail off, my chest tightening painfully. *This is why I came here.* "She's important to me, Maria. She might be my redemption. My last chance."

The wind stills. The whole world holds its breath.

"But for that—" I get to my feet. "—I have to let you go."

I stand there a few seconds longer. The clouds overhead break up just enough to let a slice of sun steal through. Warmth washes over me.

I won't be back here again. But it's enough to know that the person who brought those pink and purple petunias will be.

Knowing she won't be alone makes it easier to walk away.

23

NATALIA

When Andrey pushes through the front door, I half-expect it to be raining. For lightning to flash behind him and the power to flicker out.

He looks like a ghost.

His eyes are drawn and haggard, his face paler than I've ever seen it before. His fingers twitch and paw at the empty air by his sides as if he's desperately looking for something to cling onto, but finding nothing.

A second ago, Misha was telling Aunt Annie about the new trick he taught Remi, but now, the table is silent as we all stare towards the door.

It's Aunt Annie who breaks the silence. "Andrey, you're just in time. Pilav made us steak and roast veggies. Join us."

My jaw drops when he nods and takes the seat at the head of the table. Remi wriggles his way between the table legs to give Andrey's hands a quick sniff and a shy lick before he slinks back to lie on Misha's feet.

"How was your day?" Annie asks.

I'd say something, but I'm too busy staring at the dark circles under his eyes. He's death warmed over.

Andrey folds his napkin in his lap. "Fine."

"Do you want some potatoes?" I blurt. It's not my most elegant conversation starter, but Andrey nods, so it must not be all bad.

I load his plate and pass it to him. His lips move as if to say, "Thank you," but no sound comes out.

Aunt Annie catches my eye with a questioning gaze and a raised brow.

I shrug. I don't have any more answers than she does. With a sigh, she drops it and turns her attention to Misha. "How were your lessons today, young man?"

"Ugh, can we talk about something else?"

I haven't forgotten about the snippet of what I overheard him and Andrey discussing, but I won't embarrass him by prodding if he isn't ready for me to know. I want him to *want* to come to me about it.

"I caught the last bit of your lesson," I pipe up. "You did great!"

Misha scowls. "Since when is a C-minus great?"

"Since it's not an F." I toss my napkin at him. "And stop feeding Remi under the table. He's already had his dinner."

Misha grins sheepishly at me. "I didn't think you could see that."

"I see everything." With a nervous laugh, I add, "So there's no point hiding things from me."

If he catches what I'm trying to get at, he shows no sign of it. He just ducks under the table to pet the whining dog.

I look over at Andrey. At some point in the last few minutes, his face softened. He's still pale, still tired, but he looks more alive with every passing second.

He doesn't say much, but he stays with us for dessert. When the dessert plates are cleared away, I'm almost reluctant to stand up. I have no idea what magic brought and kept him at this table, but I'm worried we won't find it again for a long time.

For once, it doesn't feel hard to be near him. I want to hold onto it for as long as I can.

But then Misha yawns. "Okay, time for bed," I announce. "You have an early lesson tomorrow morning."

"Can I skip it?" he groans.

"Only if you want to say goodbye to those C-minuses."

"I hear a C-minus is 'great,'" he sasses. "No one will care if I'm only *good* tomorrow. How do Ds sound?"

"Like I'm too tired to deal with you tonight." I ruffle his hair and push him and Remi towards the stairs. "Goodnight, boys."

I watch Misha slip another potato to Remi before they climb the stairs together. Then Aunt Annie pulls me in for a hug before she makes her way to bed, too.

When I turn around and find Andrey standing in the doorway behind me, I jump.

"Um, well—" Every thought that pops into my head makes *'Do you want some potatoes?'* sound like Shakespeare, so I lift my hand in a wave. "—goodnight."

I climb the stairs, aware of the sound of his footsteps behind me. Then again, his room is just a few doors down from mine. It's not like he's following *me*.

"Natalia."

My breath catches in my throat at the same time I feel Andrey's on my neck. He's standing right behind me—only inches away—wearing that oaky musk like a suit of armor.

I swallow. "It was nice to have you with us for dinner."

"It was a pleasant evening."

'Pleasant' isn't exactly 'sexually-charged' or 'two enthusiastic thumbs up,' but it's better than nothing. And nothing is what I'm used to.

"Where were you? When you came in, you looked…" I let that sentence trail off because insulting him isn't going to turn the evening around.

He hesitates, and no one is as surprised as I am when he actually answers. "I went to visit Maria's grave."

The truth. How strange.

"I haven't been back there since the funeral."

My heart thumps erratically against my chest. I'm torn between wanting to know everything and wanting to forget I asked at all. But he's here, he's talking to me—and I don't want it to end.

"Are you—How did it feel to be back there?"

He's heartbroken, you idiot. He loved her, and now, she's dead, and you're making him talk about it. Way to go.

He reaches out and curls a lock of my hair through his fingers, freezing my lungs. "But... necessary."

Friends can touch each other. That's normal. Just like the flutter in my stomach and the sizzle in the air between us: perfectly normal.

Considering how close we are, it's very hard to avoid his eyes. I can see myself reflected back in them. Forcing my gaze lower doesn't help, either. It puts me at eye level with his lips.

He just visited his dead first love. Give him space. He needs space.

Hell, *I* need space.

I put my hand on his chest and push him gently away. Or maybe it's me pushing myself away—I can't quite decide. "I'm sorry. You've had a long day, so I should—"

"I was saying goodbye. It was time to let her go."

I feel like a tinder box ready to explode. It's hard to think when he's this close. "Are you okay?"

"Should I not be?"

"I don't know what you should or shouldn't be, Andrey. I stopped knowing that a long time ago, if I ever knew it in the first place. I'm just asking as, you know... as your friend."

He smirks. It's sadder than his norm, but it still does what it's always done: scramble my thoughts into incoherent white noise. I can't think when he smirks like that. I can only *be*.

"Are we just friends, *lastochka*?"

My eyes flutter shut and in the space of that tiny, two-second window, his lips brush against mine, softer than a whisper.

I press my hands to his chest, trying to find the strength to push him away. "Of course we are. I—"

But before I can define this newfound friendship of ours, his hand curls around my neck. I'm sucked into his ether, pulled into his embrace. His lips fall against mine and there's nothing soft or whispering about this kiss. It's loud and unyielding.

The kind of kiss that pulls you out of your body.

The kind that makes the thoughts into white noise, and the white noise into nothing at all. Blissful, easy silence.

When he finally releases me, I'm breathless and completely confused.

I selfishly wish the kiss had left Andrey looking as unkempt as I feel. But he just smiles down at me, not so much as a hair out of place.

"Did that feel like a kiss from someone who just wants to be your friend?"

"No," I admit. "But I've been wrong before."

He places his hand against my heart. "I think you can trust this feeling, little bird."

I want to. So badly.

"Were you really going to let me go?" I blurt out as my back hits the wall. "Before, I mean."

"Yes."

"Why?"

"Because you were right: this life, this world... It isn't for someone like you. I couldn't help thinking that, if I had let Maria go earlier, she'd still be out there somewhere, alive."

Tears prick at the backs of my eyes, but I bite them down, determined to see him clearly. "That's why you kept pushing me away."

"You're better off without me."

I stab my finger into his chest. "That's not your choice to make."

He nods grimly. "I realize that. In any case, I'm done trying to push you away. Actually, I'm not letting you go."

I breathe, but my pulse never slows. "Tell me why."

"Because as I sat there, Natalia, I remembered what I am: a selfish fucking bastard. And you're mine," he growls, dipping his hand into the front of his shirt and pulling out the gold pendant that used to belong to my mother.

"You're still wearing it?"

"I haven't taken it off since you gave it to me, *lastochka*." His fingers slide along my jaw. "It's a part of you. And so am I."

A tear traces its way down my cheek. "I told you what I need."

"All or nothing."

"All or nothing," I echo. "Can you give it to me?"

"I will." His jaw clenches. His eyes blaze. "Or I'm going to die trying."

He tips my chin up and our lips crash together. I'm lost in the taste of him, distantly aware that we're moving, that the door is slamming closed and my clothes are falling away piece by piece.

By the time he spreads me out on the bed, I'm wearing nothing but my panties.

He works his way down my body with his hands and his lips until he peels the last scrap of fabric away. His breath fans across my bare skin, warming me at first and then leaving goosebumps behind.

I'm too aroused to worry about my stomach. How could any woman be self-conscious when a man like this looks at her like that?

His eyes burn, simmering with building heat. He pulls off his clothes—slowly, damn near teasing me—and settles in at my side, kissing my ears, my neck, my breasts, my stomach.

I wait for the tide to break. For the beast to rear its head and take me roughly, the way I'm used to.

But Andrey doesn't seem to be in any kind of hurry. As his mouth explores lower—past my belly, the crevice of my hip—a moan rises in my throat. By the time Andrey settles between my thighs, I'm quivering. He tastes me with the same endless patience, licking and kissing until I'm battling dual desires—the urge to push him away against the desperation of drawing him closer.

The wave breaks, and it's hard to know when one orgasm stops and another begins. It feels like it's all variations on the same melody, rising and falling as his fingers and tongue surge and taunt me. I'm wrung dry before we've barely begun.

Andrey's lips are glistening with my desire when he looks up at me again.

"Andrey…" I breathe. "I don't think I can take more…"

"Give yourself to me, Natalia. Just surrender."

He leans over me and the pendant hangs in the air between us. Never has jewelry been so sexy on a man. Wrapping my fist around the chain, I use it to pull him down towards me.

Giving in has never been so easy.

I spread my legs, hugging his hips with my thighs as he slides inside me. We rock together, and I was wrong. I can take more.

And more.

And *more*.

By the time he comes, our bodies are slick with sweat. There are claw marks on his chest. Bruises on my hips.

It's only when we collapse together that the doubts begin to creep in. *What if this time is no different than all the others? What if he changes his mind?*

As if he can hear me thinking, Andrey slips his fingers through mine.

The thoughts become white noise.

The white noise becomes stillness.

And in that stillness, one thought pulses like a heartbeat.

This time is different.

It has to be.

24

ANDREY

"This is the first time in a while I haven't craved a smoke."

She twists onto her side, leaning on one elbow so that she's looking down at me. "You smoke?"

"We all have our vices."

She snorts. "An undercover drug trade isn't enough?" I dig into her side and, giggling, she pushes my hand away. "I've never actually seen you smoke."

"That's because I quit a year ago. But when things get stressful, the craving comes up again."

"And now?"

"No cravings."

Her smile lights up her face. Blushing, she skates a finger up and down my chest. "This is nice."

"All those orgasms and the best you can come up with is 'nice'?"

She smacks my arm. "I was speaking in the general sense. Dinner tonight, having Aunt Annie here—all of it." She keeps tracing circles along my skin. "Thank you for bringing her here to live with us. She really likes you, you know."

"I like her, too. She reminds me of the mother I don't have anymore." Natalia's smile freezes on her face. I press a finger to the corner of her mouth, trying to tip it back into a smile. "Sorry. Bad joke."

"I want to meet her," she whispers.

Why did I have to go there?

"She's in a facility, Natalia. She doesn't even know who I am most days. And her memory is so full of holes. It's impossible to have a conversation with her."

"She's still your mother. And the twins' grandmother." Natalia presses a hand to her stomach. "It matters."

"If you expect her to be happy about that—"

"I don't expect anything, Andrey," Natalia interrupts. "I just want to know where you came from."

"From crime lords and cold bastards, mostly."

Her eyebrows knit together. "Does it help you to be self-disparaging? Or is it just another wall to keep me out?"

She tries to disentangle herself from me, but I grab her and pull her back down against my chest. "Come on, stop—"

"No, you stop," she retorts. "I'm trying to have a real conversation with you."

With a deep breath, I cup her face. "I'm trying, too, okay? You're gonna have to be patient with me."

She sighs into my touch. "I can be patient."

"That requires you to stay in my bed even when I'm pissing you off."

That almost wrings a smile out of her. "You don't have to introduce me to her right away. I don't want to pressure you. I'm just saying I'd like to meet her one day."

I nod. "One day."

"Preferably before the twins go off to college, though."

I plant a kiss on her cheek. "I'll do my best." She opens her mouth and then snaps it shut almost immediately. "What?"

"Nothing."

I roll my eyes. "Come on, *lastochka*. All or nothing, remember?"

"I was just wondering… did you ever introduce Maria to your mother?"

"No."

"How come?"

"Because I had no desire to show Maria my past."

Natalia sits up, straddling me. The little temptress knows exactly what she's doing as she sinks back against me. "Your past is part of who you are."

I grip her hips. "I didn't want to look back. I certainly didn't want Maria looking back with me."

"Why?"

"Are you always this chatty after sex?"

She slaps her palms against my chest. "Answer the question."

"Because my father is Slavik. And because my mother is a mentally fragile woman who was completely destroyed by him. I didn't want to give her a reason to run."

"She wouldn't have," she assures me.

"That's sweet of you. But need I remind you, you didn't know Maria."

"Yes, but I know what it's like to—" She stops short, blushes fiercely, then clears her throat and tries again. "—erm, I know what it's like to care about someone. Deeply."

I sit up, readjusting her on my lap. She flushes, and I know she's feeling the same heat between us as I am.

"I'm Slavik's son, Natalia. Aren't you just a little bit worried that I might be more like him than either one of us knows? I can be as ruthless," I tell her softly. "I can be as demanding, as controlling, as uncompromising as he is."

"But you could never hurt a woman."

Her indignation has me pulling her forward, as close to me as I can get her. For once, I'm actually grateful for her sweet naivete. I push a lock of hair back behind her ear. "I've already hurt you. More times than I can count."

She bites her bottom lip. "That's different."

"At the end of the day, pain is pain. And I don't want to break you."

Her fingers dig into my shoulders. "I know I haven't been myself lately. But you've got to trust me to set my own limits with you, to tell you when to back off or slow down. I haven't done a good job of showing it, but I'm not as fragile as I seem."

"Only if you trust me in return. There will be times I'll push your limits. Will you let me, Natalia?"

"Only if you promise to catch me before things go too far."

She's back to tracing lines up and down my chest. My skin is tingling under her light touch. So is my cock, which is already hard beneath her.

"I promise. Always." Grabbing her tight, I collapse backward onto the pillows. "Though I think we need to seal this promise the old-fashioned way."

Within seconds, the laughter and chatter have given way to low moans and fevered breathing.

There's only her and me and the heat of our bodies as we melt into each other again.

"Andrey, are you asleep?"

No. But up until a second ago, I'd been sure *she* was.

I wouldn't blame her for falling asleep on me—that many orgasms while pregnant can't be easy on her body.

"Sleep, Natalia. We can talk more tomorrow."

She smiles with her eyes closed and sidles a little closer to me. "I was thinking…"

"Stop thinking. It's past midnight. You need to rest."

She burrows her face into my chest. "I will. I just have one more question. It's been on my mind for a while now."

Sighing, I indulge her. "Go ahead then."

"Our girls... Will they be a part of the Bratva?"

Just when I thought I was done being stiff for the day, my body is tense all over again. But I promised her honesty. "As my heirs, they'll have a part to play."

Her eyes flutter open. She squints at me despite the muted light coming from the bedside lamp. "Oh."

I wait for her to add something, but she's silent for a long time. Her eyes stay open.

"What's going on in that pretty little head of yours?" I press.

"Nothing," she whispers. "Goodnight." She turns over, covers pulled to her chin. She doesn't say another word.

With a weary sigh, I extinguish the lamp and try to go to sleep. But sleep doesn't come for a long, long time.

25

NATALIA

As I lounge back under an umbrella Andrey spent twenty minutes getting *juuust* right with Remi yapping at crabs in the sand while Misha chases after him, laughing, I know that squeezing my pregnant body into this swimsuit was worth every grunt, groan, and curse word.

The grunting, groaning, and cursing was from Andrey, obviously, since I can't touch my toes, let alone reach around to tie a bikini into place.

"This is so cool." Misha waves a seashell over his head for me to see. Then he presses it to his ear.

Yep, perfect.

The only thing that would make it better is...

I squint towards the boardwalk, searching for Andrey, but he's nowhere to be seen. His search for hot dogs must've taken him farther down the walk.

It's my fault. I told him I was starving and in desperate need of a snack. That was ten minutes ago, though, and now, a hot dog sounds disgusting. I want a pineapple.

I lie back on my foldable chair, toes curling into the beach blanket as I suck in another big, greedy breath of salty air. "Why don't you get in the water, Misha? It looks amazing."

Misha folds the seashell in both of his hands. "Nah. That's okay."

"Oh, come on! I'd be in there if I were you. But I'm me, and I'd probably float out to sea with this giant flotation device I'm carrying around." I pat my stomach.

Misha kneels down to help Remi dig a hole. A crab disappeared into the sand and then popped up a few feet away, but Remi doesn't know that or else he'd lose his mind barking.

I grab the overstuffed beach bag and pull it towards me. "I'm sure there's a pair of extra trunks in here for you. Andrey thought of everything... Ah-ha!"

I hold up a pair of blue swim trunks, but Misha's smile wilts at the sight of them. "I don't want to get in the water, okay? Leave it alone."

I open my mouth to argue when it hits me. "Misha, do you know how to swim?"

It never crossed my mind until now, but when would he have had the chance to learn? And who would have taught him?

We've been in the pool countless times, but he's never actually swam a lap. I was always the one swimming while he lounged by the side, splashing his feet in.

He drops down onto the sand, his cheeks going scarlet.

"I'm so sorry. I never realized."

"It's easy to pretend around a pool," he sighs. "But the sea is different. It's scary."

"I can teach you."

He clams up. "You're already teaching me enough."

"Oh, Misha, life is all about learning. Do you think it ever stops? I'm pushing thirty and I'm still learning all sorts of things."

"Like how to get along with Andrey?" he prods cheekily.

Using my toes, I whip a little plume of sand at him. "Learning to be a comedian now, are we?"

"Well, it's hard not to notice that you two are… 'getting along.'"

I frown. "Um, why was 'getting along' in air quotes?"

He blushes. "Never mind."

"No, no, go ahead. Tell me what I'm missing."

Misha reaches to pet Remi like the dog might save him, but Remi ducks away. Clearly, he's smart enough to know he doesn't want any part of this. "There's been a lot of… kissing lately."

Now, it's my turn to blush. *And here I thought we were being subtle.* "That's just—We're not—"

"It's okay. It's nice to see you guys getting along for once." He wrestles a seashell from Remi's mouth before the dog can swallow it. "When the two of you fight, it isn't easy on anyone." He grimaces like there's more he'd like to say, but before he can, his gaze shifts over my shoulder. "Andrey's on his way back."

"Please tell me he's got hot dogs with him." All at once, they sound amazing again.

Misha laughs and jogs to help Andrey with all the goodies he's brought back for us.

Like the smart man he is, Andrey bought me a hot dog and then walked another five minutes down the boardwalk to get me a fruit cup, a bucket of caramel corn, and a bag of pickle-flavored beef jerky.

"In case your pregnancy cravings have gone off the deep end and your taste buds are broken," he explains.

Fifteen minutes later, my stomach is larger than ever and my heart is full as Misha sets off towards the shore. Remi's already prancing around in the tide, tail wagging as he splashes. Andrey's sprawled beside me on the beach blanket, arms behind his head, legs crossed at the ankles.

"Thank you for today." I break the peaceful silence. "A surprise beach trip is something I didn't know I needed."

He squints up at me. "I think we all needed it."

Misha is squatting in front of the water, dipping his hand in whenever the waves venture close enough to touch.

"He doesn't know how to swim."

"I know."

I turn to him. "You did? Since when?"

"A few months ago."

"*Months?!*" I gasp. "Why didn't you tell me?"

"I didn't think he'd appreciate me telling you. And I didn't think you'd appreciate me being within earshot of you long enough to tell you. We weren't exactly in a good place at the time."

I hear Misha's voice in my head. *It isn't easy on anyone.* God, it was selfish of me to assume I was the only one suffering back then.

"We can't do that anymore, Andrey. No matter what's happening between us, we have to be able to talk to each other. When it comes to our children, we're on the same team, okay? Always."

He nods. "Always."

The tightness in my chest alleviates. Well, marginally. But I know from experience that making pacts is all well and good—keeping them is the challenge. Especially when you're wading knee-deep in anger and bitterness.

For now, though, the sun is shining and pacts about love and loyalty feel like they'll stand the test of time.

Smiling, I slink my way down onto Andrey's towel—at least, to the extent that a land whale like me can "slink" anywhere these days—and press a kiss to his sun-warmed cheek.

"Always" sounds good to me.

∼

The high of the beach trip carries over to Monday morning.

I pop out of bed with a giddy song in my heart and a pep in my step. It's been hard to get my ass in gear and get to work lately, but I'm excited about it today.

"Who would have thought going to work at an insurance company could put that smile on a girl's face?" Aunt Annie teases from bed when I stop in to check on her in the morning.

I think what Andrey and I did to each other in bed post-beach has a lot more to do with the smile on my face, but that is filed firmly under "Things I'll Never Tell My Aunt."

"I've just got a new lease on life."

"And does that new lease on life have anything to do with the handsome man you've got in your bed every night?"

I almost choke on my tongue as I whirl around. "How do you know we're sleeping—sharing a bed?"

"Your bodyguards talk too much."

"Leif or Leonty?" I demand. "Secrecy is part of their whole thing. I'm gonna make Andrey fire them."

Aunt Annie laughs. "Oh, go easy on the boys. They spend their days following you around, making sure you're safe. The least you can do is provide a little palace intrigue from time to time. Now, off you go. Go remind the world you're a hard-working, independent woman who doesn't need a man."

Laughing, I kiss her forehead and walk onto the porch—and almost collide into Andrey. He grabs me before I can stumble over in my heels.

"You alright there?"

I cling to his bicep. "I'm better now. Where are you off to?"

"Nowhere." Remi nips at my heels and gives Andrey's hand a lick. He's been around the house a lot more the last few days.

Every hour, it feels like we're taking another step in the right direction.

"I wanted to give you this." As I raise my eyebrows, he leans in and kisses my lips. "Have a great day, *lastochka*."

I practically float to the armored jeep. I don't even care that Leonty, Olaf, and Leif are exchanging knowing looks with each other.

I hum under my breath as we meander through the endless Midtown traffic. I'll be a few minutes late, but that kiss was definitely worth it.

As we round the corner to the building, I'm gathering up my bag when the boys start speaking Russian.

That's rarely a good sign.

"What's going on?"

Before they can answer, I catch sight of the police car parked along the curb. Judging from the looks on the men's faces, they don't like this any more than I do.

Leif twists around in the driver's seat. "Don't worry. This most likely has nothing to do with you. Just go about your day as if everything is normal. We'll investigate."

I make it all of two steps into the office before he's proven wrong.

Marge calls out my name. "Natalia," she says as the door swings open. "There are officers here to see you."

I turn around and try to smile—try to take in anything about the men in case it becomes important later—but my eyes keep falling to the shiny guns on their hips.

One is in an NYPD uniform, a gun gleaming in the holster at his side. The second is wearing a sloppy brown suit, a plaid tie, and a curved smile.

"Good morning, Ms. Boone," the one in the brown suit says. "I'm Detective George Harris. We're here to ask you a few questions."

I force my gaze to stay on him instead of looking towards my bodyguards. "I'm sorry—what is this regarding, Detective?"

"The disappearance of your colleague," he says, that smile not moving even the tiniest bit. "Mr. Byron Wells."

26

NATALIA

We're so screwed.

The good-looking detective saunters towards me as my bodyguards close in.

"No need for the display of force here, fellas. I just want to have a little chat with you, Ms. Boone." Detective Harris gives me a friendly, knowing look like there's any chance in hell I'll be on his side. "Can you call off your henchmen?"

"What is this about?" Leif barks.

"That's between Ms. Boone and the city of New York." He points at the badge on his coat. "And this means that I'm not obligated to answer your questions, Cujo. But you are obligated to answer mine."

"Show me a warrant and I'll—"

I step between them before the situation escalates. "It's okay, Leif. I can talk to the detective."

The detective flashes a toothy smile at Leif. "Down, boy. It's all good."

Leif doesn't look at all happy as I place a hand on his chest and force him back a few paces. He doesn't look at me, not even when I mutter in his face, "It's just a couple of questions. I'm sure it's routine. Don't stress."

"I don't like the look of that *mudak*," Leif hisses under his breath.

Leonty draws in closer. "Neither do I."

Remi's on edge, too. He keeps growling at the detective and the cop.

Behind the glass wall that divides the lobby from our office, I can see Abby and the rest of the office popping over their cubicles like meerkats.

"Stop," I order. "I don't want to give them any more reason to be suspicious, okay? Let me talk to them. If I cooperate, I'm sure we can show them nothing shady is going on."

Leif and Leonty exchange a skeptical glance. Ignoring both of them, I force Remi's leash into Leonty's hand.

He tries to reject it. "Take him with you! That's what he's for."

"His job isn't to get Tased for biting detectives. Just keep him calm and keep him with you."

"Fine, but I'm informing Andrey," Leif snarls.

I don't even bother trying to dissuade him from that one. If they're telling Aunt Annie about my sleeping arrangement, there's no way I'm keeping this from Andrey.

I return to Detective Harris and his sour-faced backup

muscle. "Sorry about that. I'm happy to answer whatever questions you have for me."

Harris nods. With one final, skewering glance at Leif and Leonty, we shuffle into a nearby conference room.

The door behind us swings shut with an eerie, disproportionate boom, like a judge's gavel. Inside, it reeks like dust bunnies, mildew, and stale coffee.

Harris directs me into a rickety chair while the officer lurks in the corner. Once I'm seated, the detective leans against the table, his arms folded across his chest tightly enough for the folds of fat on his neck to spill over the collar. He flashes me another megawatt smile. Instinctively, I lean as far back as my seat will allow.

"Ms. Boone, tell me why you travel with a full-on security team."

I cross my legs and shrug. "My partner gets a little paranoid about my safety. He tends to go overboard sometimes." I force a fake laugh. "You know how eccentric these rich businessmen can get."

"And the rich businessman in question is..." He makes a big show of flipping through the small yellow notepad in his hand, as if he doesn't already know exactly what he's about to say. "... Andrey Kuznetsov, is that right?"

I cling to my cherry pendant to keep my hands from fidgeting. I started wearing it after we had our big talk, and I'm grateful for it now.

"That's him."

"I'm curious, Ms. Boone: why would a woman with a man like Andrey Kuznetsov want to work in a place like this?"

I uncross my legs and then cross them in the opposite direction. "Are you here to grill me on my personal life, Detective, or do you plan on getting to Byron Wells any time soon?"

He whistles and looks over at the cop in the corner. "We have a live one, Hernandez."

"You have a *busy* one," I correct acidly. "I have a job to get to."

"Of course. You don't want us wasting your time," he says politely. "Let's get to the point then. When was the last time you heard from Mr. Wells?"

"It would've been the last time we were both in the office together. Months ago by now."

"And what was the nature of your contact?"

Bitter, mostly.

"Professional," I answer instead.

Harris smiles. He lets the silence drag on, long enough to make it clear he's suspicious, at the very least. "Professional, huh?" He rubs his hairy chin. "So there was nothing going on between you and Mr. Wells?"

Gritting my teeth, I shrug as nonchalantly as I can manage given the circumstances. "Mr. Wells had a very one-sided crush on me."

"Hm. And…?"

"And nothing," I snap. "He made an advance in the workplace. I shut it down. End of story."

"Except, it wasn't the end of the story, was it, Ms. Boone?"

I meet his eyes only because it would be really suspicious not to. "I'm not sure what you want me to say, Detective. As far as I'm concerned, there was nothing after that."

"According to several of your coworkers, Mr. Wells had something of an altercation with your 'rich businessman' boyfriend, Mr. Kuznetsov. Do you confirm or deny?"

The bastard is smiling at me as though he's having the time of his life. No wonder he got Remi's hackles up. I'm *this* close to growling at him myself. I'd bite a chunk out of him, too, if I wasn't so sure it would taste like polyester, cigarettes, and gas station aftershave.

"He was hitting on me at work, Detective," I explain tiredly. "He was my superior; I was his subordinate. It was nothing less than sexual harassment, so of course my partner wasn't happy about it. They exchanged words and Byron left me alone after that."

"And by 'left you alone,' you mean that he disappeared."

"By 'left me alone,' I mean that he stopped making inappropriate sexual advances towards me."

"Seems a little convenient, don't you think?"

"That my intimidating boyfriend would tell Byron to back off and then Byron would back off? Sounds like clear cause and effect to me. Even if it wasn't, last I checked, coincidences aren't crimes."

Harris's eyes flare wide for a moment. That menacing smile is back on his face. "That remains to be seen."

"Are you accusing me of something?" I ask. "Because if you are, I'd rather you stop beating around the bush."

There are times I need to learn to shut the hell up.

This is one of those times.

"You're right, Ms. Boone. Let's not beat around the bush any longer. I'm going to need you to come down to the station with me and answer a few more questions."

My body goes cold instantly. That's all the foreboding I need to shake my head. "No."

Detective Harris pops off the desk. "No?"

"I'm not obligated to go anywhere with you. If you want to bring me in for questioning, then show up next time with an arrest warrant. Otherwise—"

I gasp when I feel something cold and hard pressed into my side. I don't have to turn my head very far at all before I come face to face with the silent cop, who's no longer a statue in the corner. He's wearing a look of such cold detachment that I need to double-check to make sure he really is pressing a gun to my body.

"What is this?" I croak.

"This is what happens when people think they're above the law," Harris quips with a pleasant smile that doesn't reach his eyes. "Now, you're going to walk out of here with us right now. Or my colleague here is gonna get real sloppy with his gun."

"Detective," my ass. They're not who they say they are.

I swallow down the sob rising in my throat. "I'm pregnant."

"And if you want to stay that way, I suggest you do exactly as I say." Harris smiles again, sending a shiver down my spine. "Is that clear?"

I can only nod.

"Excellent. Let's go. Arkady, make sure you walk behind her. If she tips off her watch dogs… shoot her."

I wipe my sweaty palms on my trousers before walking out of the conference room behind the fake detective. The police officer stays close behind me.

The fresh air of the lobby is a minor relief. The stench of the conference room was starting to feel like mud in my lungs.

But even fresh air doesn't ease the heaviness in my chest.

"I need to go down to the station for a bit," I say to Leif and Leonty as they crowd toward us.

Both men scowl immediately.

I glance nervously at Harris, who's busy adjusting the collar of his jacket as if nothing is amiss. "Yeah, it's routine apparently. Nothing to be alarmed about. They said they'll release me in an hour or so."

"The hell they will—"

"Leif!" I raise my voice. "It's okay. I've agreed to go down to the station. Just do me a favor: cancel my appointment with Misha Remington, will you? Tell him I can't sign the contract today and send my apologies."

As far as clues go, it's pretty lame, but it's the best I can come up with in the moment. I hope to God they understand.

Leonty is surveilling Harris and Arkady through narrowed eyes while trying to hold fast to Remi's leash. The dog is straining hard, desperate to get to me.

Without waiting for them to protest, I head out of Sunshield, my heart in tatters. I'm ushered into the back of the police car and the moment I'm inside, the doors lock with an ominous click.

"Let's have your phone, baby doll." Harris twists around in the passenger seat and holds out his hand.

Helplessly, I fork over my phone.

I get a glimpse of Leif's ashen face as the fake cop steers the car away from the pavement. The fake detective is busy punching numbers into his own phone.

"Hey, boss," he greets as he puts the phone to his ear. "It's done. We've got her."

27

ANDREY

"How bad is it?"

Vaska sighs and drops into the chair in front of my desk. "It's depressing, is what it is. I'm informing on the men who are supposed to be my brothers—*your* men."

"It's all depressing, but this is where we're at. With Slavik making moves, I need to know where loyalties lie."

Vaska's knee jumps. "Not gonna lie, boss: there are more than a few men who'll defect if it comes down to it."

My fist tightens around the pen in my hand. Slavik abandoned ship over ten years ago and there are still idiots who're willing to abandon my leadership for his? Have I not done enough for them? Have I not led this Bratva out of the fucking Dark Ages? Have I not *provided?*

"The rumors are that Slavik never abandoned the Bratva. They think he merely left you in charge in his absence and his seniority overrides the last decade of your rule." He sighs heavily, hating this every bit as much as I am. "They miss the freedom to do whatever they want."

I snort. "Meaning Slavik let them off their leashes, but I don't let them fuck around like they used to."

"That about sums it up."

"*Blyat'.*" I abandon my chair for the window. "Maybe one good thing will come out of this: I can weed out the weak."

"And if the weak outnumber the rest of us?"

Before I can respond to Vaska's annoying pessimism, my phone rings. It's Leif. "Cops," he grunts in a low voice before I can say a word. "They're here to question Natalia. Something about that shady motherfucker you got rid of."

Fuck.

"Are they with her now?"

"Questioning her. I don't like the look of the detective. They're talking right now, but, boss—"

"I'll be there soon. Keep an eye on them."

Just before I hang up, I hear a strangled whimper. *Was that Remi? Why isn't he with Natalia?*

"Vaska, keep your eyes and ears open. If you hear anything, report it to me or Shura immediately."

"Got it, *pakhan*."

I rush towards my Escalade, determined to get there before the cops are done questioning Natalia. Shura's just turning into the drive when I start the engine.

"What's going on?" he asks, hopping out of his car and running towards my window.

"Natalia." It's all I have to say before Shura jumps into the passenger seat. "The cops turned up to question her about Byron."

"I thought you took care of that."

"I've got a few guys in my pocket, not the whole damn department," I growl. "Leif thinks something is wrong."

"Don't worry: Leif, Leonty, and Olaf are with her—"

"Yeah, but I'm not."

Shura shuts up, and I concentrate on trying not to run over any unsuspecting pedestrians. We're only ten minutes away from the Sunshield building when my phone rings again. Shura grabs it and puts it on speaker for me.

"Leif?"

"The motherfuckers took her down to the precinct for questioning." Cold dread floods through me. "Natalia insisted that she go with them, but she said something strange before she left."

"What did she say?"

"She told me to 'cancel her meeting with Misha Remington.'"

"She was trying to tell you that these guys aren't legit!" I roar. "They work for Slavik. Or Nikolai, or… Fuck. Do you have eyes on them?"

"We're tailing them in the jeep. They're cornering 3rd and 41st, headed north."

I reroute quickly, cutting off half a dozen furious drivers at the same time. "We're close. Stay on the line and don't take your eyes off that fucking vehicle for a second."

"Boss…" Leif's voice is drenched in regret. "She was pale when she came outta that room. I should've stopped her from—"

"Doesn't matter now," I cut him off. "The only thing that matters is getting her back."

"They're turning again. Hold on, hold on…"

He falls silent and my hands tighten on the steering wheel. I'm in danger of breaking it clean off at this point.

"They're slowing down."

"Where?"

"A closed Chinese restaurant at the end of 39th."

"We'll be there in two minutes."

Ninety seconds later, I screech around the corner and park alongside the curb where my men are waiting. Remi bounds over to me the second the door is open, whimpering and growling like even he knows something is wrong.

"It's okay, boy. We're gonna get her back safe and sound." I take in the boarded-up windows and the cracked parking lot before I look at my men. "Let's go."

Shura catches my arm from behind. "We don't know what we're walking into, Andrey."

"We're walking into the building where my wife is being held hostage," I growl. "However many men are in there, we can handle them."

Remi nudges my thigh with his nose, and I whisper to him in Russian, "Stay with me."

The dog's ears perk up and he stays close at heel as though he understands every word.

It takes a single kick to the weathered plywood covering the front window to snap it in half. The woods crashes in on the shattered glass that litters the floor, giving me a perfect place to land.

My men follow after me.

The first few idiots are slaughtered where they stand, dumbfounded and gawking. Remi's teeth are as blood-soaked as the bottoms of my shoes by the time we wade through the carnage. The dog leads me to a rickety door down a back hallway and barks as I join him there.

Another kick, and I send the door careening off its hinges.

The crash almost hides the high-pitched scream that emanates from within. When the debris clears, I find myself staring at Natalia.

She's sitting in a chair, her hands trembling…

As the man standing next to her holds a gun to her head.

He's wearing a sweat-stained suit and a smile that doesn't quite cover the worry lines in his forehead. "Back off right fucking now or I blow her brains out."

I step onto the fallen door, Remi at my heels. He's growling menacingly. The suit isn't sure who the bigger threat is: me or the dog.

"Keep that fuckin' mutt away from me."

As if he knows he's just been mentioned, Remi snarls.

"Get that gun away from my woman." Despite the fact that I barely raise my voice, it carries. "Right fucking now."

The man must realize he's in over his head, because he begins to barter. "Let me go or she dies."

Fucking pathetic.

"If she dies, I'll make you wish you did, too."

His eyes dart frantically around the room until they land on a window in the corner. It's just big enough for a grown man to squeeze through.

"Fine. I won't hurt her," the suit says. "But first, put down your gun."

Natalia's eyes go wide. I try to make eye contact with her, to reassure her with a look. But I'm not in total control of my face right now.

"Done."

Bending down, I switch the safety on and set my gun on the floor. The moment I stand, the suit darts towards the window, intent on making a run for it.

In his rush to make a quick getaway, he's made a grave oversight.

"Remi," I growl. "*Ataka!*"

The dog bolts forward and sinks his teeth into the suit's leg just as he's trying to squeeze himself through the narrow window.

I barely hear the howl as I run to Natalia and pull her into my arms. She sinks into my chest, her hands over her ears to shield from the agonized screaming.

"It's okay," I assure her as I pull her from the room. "I've got you."

Her eyes meet mine. "I knew you'd come."

28

NATALIA

Remi's head is resting on my knee, his nervous eyes scanning up to my face again and again. He's so worried about me that I can almost forget the blood staining his fur and teeth... the sounds he made as he tore into that man...

If I was a little less grateful for the way he saved me back there, I might be more scared of him. As it is, I try to reach out and pet him. But I can't move my arms thanks to my other, less hairy guard dog.

"Andrey?"

His entire body stiffens, his arms tightening around me like he's trying to hold me together. "What do you need?"

"To breathe, for starters." I manage a fractured smile. "You're squeezing me too tight."

He releases me instantly. I want to calm Remi and swear to Andrey that I'm fine, but even with Andrey's arms gone, my chest is still tight. Panic is clawing up my throat, and I really do need to breathe.

I do a round of the calming exercises Evangeline taught me to help manage my anxiety. Nothing changes, so I do a second round. The third time through, I open my eyes and am vaguely aware of movement just outside the tinted windows of the Escalade.

Don't get distracted.

I close them again and breathe until the weight on my chest eases.

When I'm done, I open my eyes to find Remi and Andrey staring at me with almost identical expressions. "Better?" Andrey asks.

"I feel… good. In control." I'm surprised by how true it is given everything I just went through.

He reaches for my arm and gives it a comforting squeeze. "We'll be leaving soon."

I finally let myself look through the car window—only to see men being rounded up and tied down.

Leif drags one man out by his collar and throws him to the ground. When he raises a fist to strike, I turn away. I've seen more than enough violence for today.

Andrey catches my chin. "The babies?"

"They're fine, too. I can feel them kicking."

His jaw flexes. "You sure you're okay?"

I put my hand on his arm. "If I weren't, I would tell you, Andrey. I promise. Right now, I'm doing okay. They didn't hurt me. He didn't even pull out his gun until you kicked the door in."

I hear more grunts and groans of pain outside the SUV. Knuckles meeting flesh. Screams cut off too soon.

"They know too much," Andrey mutters. It sounds like he's talking to himself.

I risk another peek. Bratva soldiers are escorting a line of men with bags over their heads into the back of a waiting van. "What are you going to do with them?"

He doesn't answer or look at me for a while. His throat rises and falls with each breath until, finally, he turns his attention to me. "Nothing, until you're back at home."

Goosebumps erupt on my skin. I'm fresh from yet another kidnapping attempt, but this is the first time all day I've felt true anxiety. "You're going to leave me to go deal with those men?"

"I have to get answers from them, *lastochka*. I still don't know who sent them. You'll be safe at the manor. Leif, Leonty, and Olaf will be with you."

"I don't want *them* to be with me. I want *you*."

His jaw tightens again. Any tighter and it might shatter. "I need to deal with this. I'll be home as soon as—"

"Let me come with you." The words are out of my mouth faster than I can consider just what the hell I'm asking.

"Natalia…" Andrey actually smiles. "You don't want that."

I wait for anxiety and doubt to set in. I wait for good ol' rationality to break through this sudden, burning desire to look those motherfuckers in the face.

Zero. Zilch. Nada.

It never comes. None of it.

"I do. I want to come with you. I want to watch you question them."

He tilts his head to the side as if to see me in a new light. "You don't know what you're asking."

Remi whines like he's agreeing with Andrey. I place a hand on his head and stroke him. "I know what you mean when you say you're going to 'question' them. I'm not stupid, Andrey."

"Then why would you want to be there?"

"Because…" I trail off, fumbling in the dark of my confused thoughts for an answer. "Because this is your world; I need to know if I can stomach it."

"Natalia, you're not thinking straight. It's been a crazy day. You need to—"

"Don't," I interrupt. "Don't tell me how I'm feeling and don't tell me what I want."

Sure, there are goosebumps on my arms and my hands are trembling, but beneath the fear and uncertainty, there's something else. Something new.

Or maybe it's not new. Maybe it's been there for a long time. Waiting.

Gritting his teeth, he leans back in the cushioned seats. "I must be insane to agree to this."

"Is that a yes?"

Before he replies, Leif lurches into the driver's seat and starts the engine. "They're loaded up, boss. I can make a pit stop at the manor before we go to the warehouse."

Andrey's face is indecipherable. I wait with bated breath as the muscles in his jaws thrum and twitch, clenching again and again. Then: "Forget the pit stop, Leif. We're going straight to the warehouse."

I can't stop the triumphant smile from spreading across my face. If Leif has questions about Andrey's decision-making, he keeps them to himself. With an obedient nod, he puts the car into drive and we take off after the van filled with men who thought they could put their hands on me and get away with it.

Time to show them just how wrong they were.

29

NATALIA

The warehouse looks like the set of a slasher movie.

Broken boards covered in mold hang from the ceiling like rotten teeth. Shattered glass is scattered across a floor that could be covered in either rust, dried blood, or both. I contemplate it for all of two seconds before I decide I'd rather not know.

"There's still time to back out." Andrey's lips brush against the shell of my ear.

I square my shoulders and wrench my hand away from his. "I want to be here. I want to see you in action."

He gazes at me thoughtfully. *Is that admiration or disgust?* "You might get more than you bargained for," he warns.

"If I can't take it, I'll walk away," I assure him. "But it'll be my choice. Just let me try."

He opens his mouth to say something, but then thinks better of it. "Then let's go." He takes my hand again and leads me through the warehouse.

I lean into his side. "I know this place is mostly for maiming and murdering, but you could still sweep once or twice."

Andrey smiles wryly. "The worse it looks, the more likely civilians are to stay away from it."

The only light comes from the moonlight slicing through the holes in the roof. It dapples the dusty ground and debris. Further into the space, one shaft acts like a spotlight for a line of men tied up in front of a crumbling brick wall. Their arms are pinned above their heads and their legs are fastened spread-eagle to iron hooks set into the bricks.

I count eleven souls in total. I recognize the one on the end as "Detective" Harris.

Something curls in the pit of my stomach. It's hot and viscous, and I don't have a name for it.

"Natalia?" I flinch at how close Andrey's voice is.

"I'm okay," I assure him. I point one quivering finger at Harris. "I think you should question the 'detective' first."

His tongue sweeps across his bottom lip. "You're sure?"

I circle my hands over my stomach. "He didn't hurt me, but he spent the whole drive telling me about how he was going to hurt my children when they were born. I want to hear him scream."

Andrey watches me for one extra second. I know he's checking to see if I'm okay, but I don't know how to tell him that I'm more than okay. Taking action—even if it's violent and brutish—feels so much better than being a victim.

With one last nod, Andrey turns to Shura, who's manning the prisoners. "Bring me the detective."

Shura unties Harris from the wall and nudges him to the center of the warehouse. A tarnished metal hook designed for raising up cattle to be butchered is dangling from one of the steel beams.

Shura and Leonty loop the rope around Harris's hands to the hook. Someone unseen cranks on a lever and the hook rises just enough to force Harris onto his tiptoes. He groans, his face slick with sweat and blotchy, red patches of panic.

Andrey steps to my side, his breath tickling my ear. "One last chance. If you need to—"

I turn and glare at him. I don't even need to say the words out loud: *I'm not going anywhere.*

Shrugging, he lifts his hand to my face and traces the curve of my jaw. His eyes burn into mine before he turns towards Harris, and I watch him become someone else.

Like a switch has been flipped, Andrey is not Andrey anymore.

He's not a handsome man in a stuck elevator, kissing me back to life.

He's the *pakhan* of the Kuznetsov Bratva.

He's death itself.

"Detective Harris, yes? I don't think we've been formally introduced."

Harris swallows. The blotchiness on his skin fades until he's sheet-white, though he sets his jaw firmly. "You won't get anything out of me."

Andrey lets out a harsh bark of laughter. "What makes you

think I want anything out of you?" He tips his chin towards the line of captives in the far corner. "I have them for that."

"Then kill me and be done with it."

Andrey carefully pulls off his suit jacket, folds it in half, and drapes it over the side of a moldy-looking chair. He's wearing a crisp, open-collared shirt, so white and clean as to look utterly bizarre in this filthy place. A shiver runs down my spine as he paces back and forth, cracking his knuckles one by one.

"'Kill you'?" he echoes. "You abducted my woman and threatened to hurt my children. You won't get the mercy of a quick death."

Harris's eyes flare wide, but he has to blink against the sweat dripping from his forehead.

My chest tightens, but I find that I can't look away.

Andrey unsheathes his gun and toys with it. Harris's eyes follow his every movement. Up until, with a mournful sigh, Andrey sets it down on the same chair where he left his jacket. "My Natalia doesn't like guns. So I'll have to find more creative ways of punishing you."

Andrey snaps his fingers and one of his men wheels what looks like a black, metal toolbox across the floor towards him. It reminds me of one my father kept in the garage.

But the similarities end the second Andrey lifts the lid.

My father had tools for DIY home renovation, but this case is for DIY torture. Pliers, scalpels, and a dozen other gleaming points and razored edges I don't have words for. It's row after row of metal pain.

Harris twists on the hook like a fish. "No! No," he moans. "Please."

"What happened to all that bravado, Harris?" Andrey questions calmly. "Don't let yourself down now."

"Listen, I was f-following o-orders…"

"From whom?"

Harris opens his mouth, except nothing but sweat and spit fly out of it. He's stammering so hard that he's unintelligible.

"Fucking speak, Harris."

"You'll kill me anyway."

"Yes. But you'll earn yourself a quick death. Isn't that worth cooperating?"

Harris's eyes dart from side to side before he finds the audacity to look at me.

"You dare—" Andrey takes a sharp step forward, his voice shaking in a way I've never heard it do before. "You dare to look at her?"

"I-I didn't hurt her!" he cries, meeting my eyes again. "Ask her!"

Andrey storms to the center of the room, stopping close enough that he's snarling in the man's ear. But the harsh sneer of his words carries all the way over to where I stand. "Look at her again and I will cut your fucking eyeballs out and stuff them down your throat. Is that understood?"

He nods in pure, abject fear.

"Good."

Then Andrey punches Harris in the stomach. I wince at the sound of flesh on flesh—at Harris's groan of pain—but it doesn't bring the expected wave of sympathy.

You threatened my children, asshole. You deserve this.

As if he can read my mind, Andrey hits him again and again. His muscles shift and flex as he unleashes a storm of punches onto the tied man, using him like a literal human punching bag.

With every blow, Andrey paints another mark on Harris. A bruise here, a cut there. Blood rises to his skin until it breaks through the surface and drips to the floor. Harris's grunts turn into screams and punctured moans.

He pleads desperately for mercy we all know isn't coming until one blow to the head sends his eyes rolling back into his sockets. His face sags between his shoulders until I'm looking at the top of his head.

"He didn't last long," Andrey snorts.

Shura walks forward with a bucket of water in hand. "Shall I wake the scum up?"

"Not just yet."

Andrey turns in my direction. He walks over and cups my face with his clean hand, the thumb stroking along the edge of my mouth. "Are you okay?"

My mouth drops open when Andrey uses his other hand to unbutton his white shirt. Blood stains the button holes and the cuffs as he pulls it off his shoulders and tosses it over the chair where he left his jacket.

"I'm okay, Andrey," I insist, wrapping my hand around his wrist to hold him closer. "I want to stay."

His eyes brighten as a slow smile spreads across his face. "You're a fucking miracle." He pulls me to him and kisses me hard on the lips.

Then, all too soon, he lets me go. I'm still buzzing from the contact as he stalks back to his prey, muscles rippling under a thin spotlight coming from the moon above.

I can't take my eyes off him. It's true that his life is a dangerous thing. But so is he.

And if I have a prayer of being safe in this world… it's with him.

30

ANDREY

"Please! *Please! STOP!*"

"Would you have stopped?" I snarl as blood pours from his mouth like a faucet. "Would you have stopped if she'd been the one begging?"

"Yes!" he screams.

"You know what liars get?" Keeping my eyes on him, I extend an open palm out. Shura places the scalpel in my hand.

As I advance on him, the stench of urine hits me. It stains his pants on the way down, pooling around his feet.

"Is this the kind of soldier you are?" I ask in disgust. "I shouldn't be surprised. Your boss is a coward. Why would his men be any different?"

Harris raises his swollen, bloodshot eyes to mine. "I am still a Rostov man. I'm no coward."

Jackpot. That's the kind of information I've been trying to literally cut out of him.

"He's going to fucking destroy you," Harris spits, oblivious to the mistake he's making. "He's smarter than you are. Stronger. More ruthless…"

"So smart and so strong that he sent a boy in to do a man's job."

It's a throwaway comment; I'm not expecting a reaction. But Harris's eyes widen, his nostrils flaring. "Did you kill the boy?"

I aim the scalpel at his throat. "Why do you care?"

"I… I don't."

"Maybe you don't. But Nikolai does, doesn't he?"

Through a film of blood, sweat, and tears, Harris goes pale. "The boy is worth something to Nikolai. If he's alive, I'm sure he'd be willing to negotiate. I can take a message to—"

"You're in no fit state to go anywhere, Detective."

"Please!" he pleads. "Give him the boy and you can make a truce. I'm sure—"

"No!"

My men would never contradict or override me, period. Let alone in front of the enemy.

But apparently, my woman didn't get that memo.

Natalia is storming towards us, her eyes blazing. "No one is going to barter with a child. No negotiations. No trades. Nothing."

Harris's eyes narrow. "So he *is* alive?"

Before I can even think to stop her, Natalia swipes a pair of brass knuckles from the toolkit and takes aim at Harris.

The hit isn't square and she falls off balance when she misses his nose and hits his lip instead, but blood pours down his chin, so the damage is done.

"The boy is *mine*!" she shrieks. "And Nikolai's never getting his hands on Misha again!"

Harris stares daggers at her. "You have no idea what you've gotten yourself into, you stupid whore."

Natalia roars as she hits him again. Her aim this time is better, and she opens a nasty gash in the center of his nose. But as she rears back for another hit, I wrap an arm around her waist and drag her back.

"Why?" she spits, kicking and swinging wildly, still cursing at the captive.

I carry her all the way through the warehouse, and she's still fighting when I drop her outside the warehouse doors, well out of sight of Harris and the prisoners.

"Why did you stop me?" she demands, shoving hard against my chest.

"Because that is not who you are, Natalia."

"I'm a mother, and that man threatened my children. That's exactly who I am!"

I drag a hand over my neck. "I shouldn't have agreed to let you come here."

"I'm a grown woman. I can go wherever I want."

"You're also a very pregnant woman. You can't be getting into fist fights."

She looks like she wants to swipe at me with those brass knuckles. Her eyes are brighter than I've ever seen them. I try to cup her face but she swats my hand away. "He was trying to convince you to sell Misha back to Nikolai!"

"And?" I press. "You thought, if he made a good enough deal, I'd bite?"

The fire in her eyes dulls just a little. "Well…" She bites on her bottom lip and sighs as the fight goes whistling out of her. "I… I wasn't really thinking straight. He mentioned Misha and I just got scared. After everything Misha has been through with that beast, I'm not about to let Nikolai come near him ever again."

I frown. "What do you know about what he's been through? Has he talked to you about his time with Nikolai?"

Her gaze flickers from side to side. "Uh…"

"We agreed," I remind her icily. "In fact, I believe you were the one who told me we needed to be on the same page when it came to our children."

"I agree," she sighs. "But he should be the one to tell you."

I pull back, letting her hand drop. "You're right." I flag down my Escalade. Leif drives it over to us.

"What are you doing?"

"Taking you back home. You've had enough excitement for one day."

She pulls the brass knuckles from her hand almost reluctantly. "Are you coming, too?"

"Yes, I am. It's time that we had a chat with our boy."

31

ANDREY

"You're going to be gentle with him, right?"

It's hard to believe this is the same woman who punched a man wearing brass knuckles fifteen minutes ago. The shift from maternal violence to maternal concern is dizzying, but Natalia doesn't seem to mind the altitude change.

Personally, I'm glad we left those brass knuckles behind.

"He deserves respect, Natalia. He's not a child."

"Is that what you were doing back there with Nikolai's man? Respecting him?" she spits. "Misha isn't working for Nikolai!"

"But he was once."

"And you chose not to hold that against him when you agreed to take him in!"

Remi whines, looking between the two of us with a sour face. Natalia is so worked up that she doesn't even notice.

"It may not seem like it," she adds, "but Misha's a sensitive kid."

"That's the problem, Natalia. You insist on seeing him as a kid. But he's not. Not really. He's smart as a fucking whip and he lived on Rostov property his entire life. There's no telling what he's seen and heard."

Her fingers wring together like she's trying to strangle some invisible person beneath her hands. "He was probably kept separate from all of that."

"So why send him to us then?"

"Maybe he was expendable! That's what you said."

"Or maybe Nikolai thought he was the best person for the job."

Her eyes flash. "If you so much as hurt one hair on that boy's—"

I grab the finger she's jabbing at me and twist her hand back. She gasps with shock a second before I ease the pressure and touch my lips to her palm.

"*Lastochka*, I'm not accusing Misha of anything. I don't consider him the enemy, and I don't plan on interrogating him. But he hasn't been totally honest with either one of us."

Her bottom lip trembles. "It's because he's scared, Andrey."

"I'm aware of that." I pull her towards me, cradling her into the nook under my arm. "But I do need us to be on the same page. We need to go in as a united front."

"I don't want him to feel like we're ganging up on him."

"We're not ganging up on him. We're trying to protect him. Especially if Nikolai wants him back."

That seems to get through to her. Her shoulders straighten and she nods. "You're right."

As we approach Misha's room, Remi knows where we're going and runs ahead. By the time we get there, the door is open. Remi is inside, lying on his back while Misha rubs his belly. He looks up to Natalia with a smile, but it falters when he catches sight of me.

Natalia gingerly lowers herself to the floor next to Misha, squeezing the boy's arm.

"Is something going on?" he asks.

I'm about to jump right into it, but Natalia beats me to the punch. "There was a… situation today at my work. There were cops waiting to question me about Byron's disappearance."

"The creepy dude who was hitting on you all the time?" He looks to me, no small amount of accusation in his eyes. "But I thought you took care of him?"

Natalia nods sadly. "They weren't actually cops, Misha. They worked for Nikolai."

Misha goes pale, but doesn't say a word.

"They forced me into their car and took me to a… a bad place. Andrey got to me in time and it all turned out okay," she rushes to assure him. "But, under… questioning, one of the men mentioned something that upset me."

"What did he say?" Misha asks.

Her lip wobbles. Natalia has been so strong for so long, but the day is catching up with her. "Well… h-he—"

"He mentioned you, Misha," I cut in.

Misha's eyes tighten and his lip curls. "What did he say about me?"

"He mentioned that Nikolai might want you back."

"But you don't have to worry, Misha," Natalia insists, grabbing his hand and tucking it in her lap. "We're not going to let him come near you. You're safe with us."

But Misha's not looking at her. His gaze is fixed on me.

"You haven't been honest with us, have you, Misha?"

"Andrey!" Natalia blurts, narrowing her eyes at me. She whirls back to Misha. "It's not that we don't trust you. It's just that—"

"Misha," I interrupt, "I told you that, as far as I was concerned, you're a Kuznetsov man now."

He nods, his eyes fixed on the wall past my shoulder.

"I meant that. I still do."

Natalia sidles a little closer to Misha, as though she might be able to shield him from this entire conversation.

"You are not only a part of my Bratva now; you are a part of my family," I continue. "I wouldn't change that for the world."

Misha's eyes water. He sags under the weight of too much life for someone so young. His chin drops to his chest.

"But I need you to be honest with me."

I flash back to the interrogations right after Misha was captured. He refused to breathe a word no matter how Shura threatened him. He seemed so strong.

But the way he lifts his eyes to mine now and nods is the bravest thing I've ever seen. "I… I'll try to be."

"Then tell me the truth: are you Nikolai Rostov's son?"

32

ANDREY

"Misha…?" Natalia whispers.

He flinches, his eyes trained on the floor. "I'm sorry."

"Don't be sorry. Just—" Natalia grabs his arm, pulling him closer to her. "I don't understand."

"I don't—It's not for sure. I don't have a birth certificate or anything." He's speaking fast, tripping over his own words. "But… I noticed things."

"Like what?" I ask.

"My mother spent a lot of time with him. She was one of his favorites. And he seemed to like us, I guess."

Natalia slowly pushes his sleeve up to reveal his arm covered in old scars. "He did this to you, Misha. He didn't like you. How could he be your—?" She chokes down the word.

"Our shed was nicer than the others," Misha explains. "We got new clothes. I was the only boy with a pair of sneakers."

Natalia is trembling, but with a deep breath, she steadies herself. "Did you ever speak to Nikolai?"

"Sometimes. But only about training, really. He used to supervise some of our training sessions, to see our progress. It was during one of those lessons that..." He trails off, chewing at his lip hard enough to draw blood. "It was during one of those lessons that I saw the birthmark on his collarbone. My mom always said I had one like my daddy. And I have a birthmark on my collarbone. So if his looked like mine, then..." He shrugs.

I clear my throat. "Misha, why didn't you tell us this before now?"

The boy wraps his arms around Remi. "Because the two of you... you're enemies... Nikolai hated you and your father. I know you hate him. I thought, if you knew, then you'd hate me, too."

I lean forward and put my hands on Misha's shoulders. "We can't help who our fathers are. The fact that Nikolai Rostov might be yours means fuck-all to me."

Although I can use this to my advantage, especially if he wants the boy back.

Hot shame follows the casual thought. It's hard to take off the crown and just be what this boy needs right now: a father, not a tyrant. Someone who loves him, not someone looking for any angle to exploit him.

"You're safe with us, Misha."

Those are the magic words. He releases a heavy breath and his entire body relaxes as though I've absolved him of all his sins.

As if I don't have far too many of my own.

"But if you remember anything at all from your days on the compound, if you think it could be helpful—"

"There is something," he whispers.

Natalia looks up at me, a silent warning not to push him too far. I override her with a nod. "Go ahead."

"After I started to suspect that Nikolai might be my father… I guess I was curious. I wanted to know more about him." He winces as though he's ashamed of the fact. "I used to sneak out of our shed after curfew and go down to the warehouse when I saw that the lights were on. Sometimes, I would see Nikolai in there having meetings, or… erm… doing other things."

Natalia is still pale. Her eyes look unnaturally big against her hollow cheeks. She gives Misha's arm a squeeze, encouraging him on.

"There was this one night when a man was dragged in. Nikolai accused him of trespassing. He pulled out his gun and aimed it at the man. Somehow, the man talked Nikolai down."

"How?"

Misha shrugs. "He claimed that he had information that would be useful to Nikolai. He said that it would help him get out on top and… get everything he ever wanted since his parents were put behind bars. That's what he said, word for word."

"And Nikolai listened?"

"Nikolai didn't just listen. They talked for ages, and afterwards, Nikolai shook the man's hand. Then he had one of his lieutenants show the man to an empty shed. And…" He scratches and tugs at a loose thread in the upholstery for a while before continuing. "… my mother was sent to entertain him."

Natalia rubs his shoulder, but we're so fucking close to *something*. I can't let it stop here. "Do you know what kind of agreement they came to?"

"Andrey." Natalia rises to her feet. "It's late and we're all tired. I think that's enough for one night."

The boy looks emotionally wrung out. Exhausted in a way a fourteen-year-old has no right to be.

"You're right," I concede reluctantly. "Let's call it a night."

Natalia hugs Misha tight. "You're the bravest kid I know."

Fighting back tears, Misha nods. Natalia presses a kiss to his forehead and gives Remi a pat on the head. "Stay with Misha tonight, okay, boy?"

Remi gives her an agreeable bark and jumps onto Misha's bed. Only then does Natalia follow me out of the room.

The door clicks shut and we walk towards the patio, each of us lost in our thoughts. The moon is hiding behind dark clouds, so we have to rely on the dull garden lights to illuminate one another.

Natalia breaks the silence first. "He's not a tool to use, Andrey."

Despite myself, I stiffen. "I never said he was."

"No, but you did think about it. Didn't you?"

Her green eyes are shrouded in shadow, but I can still see the worry in them. I consider lying for a moment, if only to preserve her opinion of me. But lying now would be a slippery slope.

"Yes, I did. And I fucking hate myself for it." I reach up and stroke the smooth plane of her cheek. "I won't let Nikolai hurt either one of you, Natalia."

She gazes up at the invisible moon. It's out there, somewhere. Just hidden for now.

Then, with a sigh, her fingers lace through mine. "I know."

33

NATALIA

We sit out on the patio for a while. It's nice to be in the warm, dark silence. It makes my thoughts seem less sharp around the edges. But when my eyelids start to droop, I stand.

Andrey stands with me and takes my hand. We're walking back to our room when I notice that Misha's light is still on.

I pause, staring at the sliver of light coming through the crack at the bottom of the door. Remy's whine is faint but steady.

I glance helplessly at Andrey.

"Go," he says, releasing my hand.

I push myself up on my tiptoes and kiss him on the cheek. Andrey disappears upstairs while I knock gently on Misha's door.

I'm met with a few seconds of silence. Then: "I'm fine, Natalia."

But his shaky voice says otherwise.

"Then open the door."

"No."

"I can break it down," I warn him. "I punched a man in the face with brass knuckles today, so I'm tough now."

A second later, the door swings open. Misha's eyes are red-rimmed and his lower lip has been chewed raw. "You did *what* to *who*?"

I sweep past him before he can stop me and join Remi on the bed. With a sigh, Misha snaps the door shut and leans against his bedpost. "Was it the man who abducted you?"

"Yes, but that's not why I punched him. I punched him because he suggested we leverage you to make a deal with Nikolai."

Misha blinks, his chin quavering for only a second before he catches himself.

"He thought you were his golden ticket to freedom, but I wasn't about to stand by and let him use you like a commodity."

"I'm no commodity." He drops his eyes to the floor. "I'm worthless."

My heart cracks, but I hold the pieces together and offer him my hand. "Come sit by me."

"I shouldn't be here. I don't deserve—" He looks around the room as though this level of comfort is too good for him. "—any of this."

"Did you hear what I said about the brass knuckles? I can knock some sense into you if I need to."

Finally, a smile pokes through the anxiety. "Did you really do that?"

"Sure did. It felt great, too. I felt powerful—and you know what? I would never have been able to do it if it weren't for you."

He frowns.

"I'm serious, Misha. I would do anything for you. It's the nature of being a mother."

His bottom lip trembles. "My mother didn't always jump to defend me," he admits, sitting down on the very corner of the bed.

"Because she knew that getting involved would only make things worse for you," I suggest with more conviction than I have any right to feel. I don't know the woman from Adam, but I feel confident in my assumptions. "But she did protect you, in her own way. She made sure to be on Nikolai's good side. You were the only boy on the compound with sneakers, remember?" I clutch his forearm. "Your mother was a brave woman, Misha. She did what she could to protect you with the tools at her disposal."

A tear slips down Misha's cheek. Then another, and another, until he's full-on crying and I can't hold myself back anymore.

I pull him into my arms. His head crashes on my lap and he sobs as Remi licks his hand. "It's okay, sweetheart. Let it out. Let it all out."

With every sob, my heart forms a new crack. But I just hold him tighter, whispering words of comfort into his ear, hoping that my arms will keep him together the same way Andrey's did for me.

When Misha's crying finally subsides, his eyes are red and puffy and his cheeks are stained with tears. "I'm sorry."

I cup his face. "You have nothing to be sorry for."

He bites his lip, though the poor thing is already shredded to ribbons. "Is… is Andrey mad?"

"Of course not!"

He flinches. "But I'm his enemy's son."

"You didn't ask to be."

"But… I've done things, Natalia," he insists. "I've done things I shouldn't have done because of Nikolai—"

"It doesn't matter. You were trying to survive. We all do things we're not proud of when it comes to life or death. You didn't have a choice, Misha. Neither did your mother. Andrey knows that."

He keeps scratching at his own bleeding lip.

"Misha," I say, drawing his eyes to mine, "what is it?"

"My own father couldn't care about me," Misha whispers. "Why would Andrey?"

I have to bite down on my tongue to keep myself from sobbing like a baby. *Be strong for him, Natalia. Be strong.*

"Because Andrey is a different man. It's the family you choose that matters, Misha. And you are the family we choose."

He blinks and two fat tears drip down his cheeks.

"Now, you're going to lie down and I'm going to stay with you until you fall asleep, okay?"

I expect some pushback, but Misha just nods and lies down obediently. It takes only a few strokes of his hair before his eyes get heavy. Soon after that, his breathing is a soft, even snore.

By the time I get upstairs, I'm exhausted to my bones, but my mind is whirring.

Andrey is sitting up in bed, waiting for me. "How is he?"

I pull off my clothes and climb under the covers. "Broken."

Andrey touches my chin until I have to look him in the eye. "How are you?"

I dab away the tears still glistening on my cheeks. "Drained. And pissed. What kind of man—what kind of *monster*—would use his own son like that?"

Andrey's silver eyes smolder, and I know he feels the same way I do. "The kind of monster that needs to be stopped," he grits.

"You have to kill him, Andrey."

Andrey smiles, though it's tinged with sadness. "My little bird has talons. Who knew?"

I'm in no mood to make light of things, though. "You need to talk to Misha again tomorrow. He's convinced that a part of you will hate him now that you know who he really is."

"Of course I don't hate him. My only instinct is to protect him. As much as those babies in your belly."

I throw my arms around him, and he falls back against the bed under my weight. "You're amazing."

He snorts. "You're only saying that because I saved your life."

"I'm not." Hiking myself up on one elbow, I look down at him, tracing the lines of his face. "Watching you work today… that was amazing, too."

He chuckles. "Now, I know you're tired."

"I'm being serious. It was actually—" I sink my teeth into my bottom lip. "—kind of a turn-on."

He stops short, his eyebrow arching. "A turn-on, you say?"

"Don't get me wrong; I'm still not into violence. But I don't know—something about the… brutality." I slap my hands over my eyes. "That didn't come out the way I meant it to."

Pushing me down, Andrey slides his body over mine. "Then try again," he whispers into my ear.

My skin tingles as he pulls at my earlobe with his teeth. "Now, it's hard to think straight." Especially with the way his erection is pressing against my thigh.

"Should I get off you?"

I grab his shoulders. "Don't you dare."

Smiling, he presses his lips to my neck. "Then I suggest you give it another try."

I wrinkle my nose in concentration. "Well, it's just something about seeing you take charge like that. Watching you be the *pakhan*—you never faltered, never backed down. You were confident and determined and… *hot*."

"I knew it. I'm just a piece of meat to you."

Half-heartedly, I try to push him off me, but he's circling his lips over my nipple, wetting the thin material of my shirt.

"You're much more than just a piece of meat to me," I say softly. "So much more."

His face rises up to hover over mine. I can see myself reflected in the bright silver of his eyes. "You like when I defend you?"

My eyes flutter. "I… love it."

"Do you know why I do it?"

I bite my lip. "Tell me."

"Because you're mine." The words send a shiver down my spine like I knew they would. "And anyone who tries to hurt you will suffer for it."

He works his hand between my legs and a finger into my wetness. I devolve into a writhing mess beneath him. Everything from there is a blur of sensation and heat, pressure and breath—and the underlying bedrock of it all is Andrey.

So solid.

So real.

So *there*.

34

ANDREY

There are three names on the piece of paper Shura hands me.

Anatoly.

Vasily.

"Efrem?" I try to hand the paper back to him. There must be a mistake. "What the fuck, Shura?"

He crosses his arms tightly. "You told me to keep my eyes and ears open and vet the men. Those are the names. I stand by them."

"Efrem is part of the inner circle."

"His father was on the plane with Slavik when he flew out of here," Shura reminds me. "Or have you forgotten?"

I rise to my feet. "I forget nothing."

My hands flex, the paper crumbling in my palm. I'm so fucking close to upending my own damn desk. It's one thing to lose lesser *vory* to Slavik—it's a whole different ball game losing my most trusted men to his cause.

"Are they all on the grounds?" I grit out.

"All of them."

"Send them in."

"Together?"

I make a split-second decision. "Together."

Shura slips out of my office as I turn to the windows. The night is dark and quiet except for the rustling of trees. Leonty is outside Natalia's door on duty. She was sleeping when I left a few hours ago. It took all my willpower to disentangle myself from her arms.

Only to leave and deal with *this* shit.

When Shura returns a few minutes later, accompanied by the three traitors, only Efrem seems bothered by being summoned. His eyes are puffy with sleep and he doesn't even try to hide the scowl on his face.

"Who's making trouble now, boss?" Efrem asks. "Slavik or the Rostov fucker?"

My heart clenches as I search their faces for signs of what they've done. "Sit down, all of you."

Shura alone remains standing behind the three men. Only I spy the gun in his holster.

"Efrem is already aware of this," I start, addressing Vasily and Anatoly first, "but Slavik is back."

Vasily nods. "We've heard rumors, boss. Is he here for good?"

"Not only is he here for good, he's here to take back the Bratva."

Vasily and Anatoly make a good show of looking shocked, but I won't be so easily swayed.

"Can he do that?" Vasily demands.

"He thinks he can… with enough support."

"Does that mean Vladimir is back, too?" Vasily tries not to look at Efrem, but he loses that fight. We all watch for his reaction.

Efrem clears his throat. "He tried to contact me a few times."

I stand, planting my fists on my desk. "You never mentioned that to me, Efrem."

"He's my father, okay? I had to pick up. That doesn't mean I do everything he says."

"He called for a reason."

"Yeah, he called for a reason: he wanted me to defect," Efrem admits. Anatoly and Vasily lean away from the man as though he's contagious. He scowls at both of them. "I'm still fucking here, aren't I?"

"Yes, you are," I agree. "The question is: why don't you seem happy about it?"

Efrem pales. "It's not a question of being *happy*. I just… I don't fucking get it," he snaps.

"Get what?"

"This *who's-the-pakhan* business. Why the fuck does it matter?" He throws up his hands. "It's the same damn family. Even if Slavik were to step back in, you'd get the title eventually."

Shura's hand strays towards his weapon. I caution him against it with the subtlest flick of my eyebrows.

We need answers right now, not bloodshed. Not yet, at least.

"Slavik fled and left us here to drown in his mess, Efrem. He took a personal jet, filled it with his men, his whore, and most of the Kuznetsov money, and he fucking ran." I grip the edges of my desk to keep my hands from curling around Efrem's throat. "Do you think this Bratva would have survived long without me? Slavik drained the coffers before he left. It took my leadership to salvage this Bratva."

"Yeah, well, Slavik says otherwise," he mutters.

"You would know, wouldn't you?"

Efrem clears his throat again. The color still hasn't returned to his cheeks. "I just listened to what my father said. I didn't agree, and I didn't defect."

"But you don't think defecting would be that big a deal."

The *mudak* has the balls to look me in the eye. "His men would be yours eventually."

"They already are. Most of them, at least."

Efrem swallows. "What are you saying?"

"I'm saying that you have a choice to make, Efrem. If you choose to accept my leadership, it means rejecting Slavik. It means that, one day, you might come face to face with your own father on opposite sides of the war."

Panic blooms across his neck and under the color of his shirt like burning red scabs. "I know where my loyalties lie."

"Problem is, brother, *I* don't."

Efrem leaps out of his chair as though it's just electrocuted him. "You're accusing me."

"Prove yourself. What did Vladimir tell you?"

"Nothing," he answers without hesitation. "Only that the true *pakhan* was back."

"And how did you respond?"

His chest rises and falls indignantly. "I hung up on him."

I sigh. "I think you're telling me what you know I want to hear."

Sweat has beaded across Efrem's forehead and is dripping down his neck. Fear in liquid form. His eyes dart from Vasily to Anatoly like he's looking for someone to throw on the sword instead.

"I'm not lying!" he shrieks, his hand jerking towards the waistband of his pants.

I act without hesitation. I pull my gun out and send a bullet straight at Efrem's head. He's dead before he even hits the ground.

"Fuck." Shura has his gun out, too, and is staring down at the body spilling blood across the Persian rug at his feet. "That's gonna stain."

Anatoly is slack-jawed as he watches the life drain from Efrem. "Boss, are you sure he was—?"

"It's time everyone got the message," I bark. "Fuck with my family and you die."

Vasily stuffs his hands into his pockets. "I'm no defector. Call me what you want, but I'm no traitor."

Anatoly nods his agreement. "The same goes for me. I have no loyalty to Slavik. As far as I'm concerned, there's only one Kuznetsov *pakhan*."

I look both men in the eye. Their faces are resolute. "If that turns out not to be the case—"

"Expect a bullet to the forehead." Vasily spits at Efrem's corpse. "We got the memo."

"Now, you can make sure the message carries. If there are defectors in our ranks, I want them to know exactly what they're in for. Slavik is nothing compared to the hell I will unleash on them." I step over Efrem. "Take care of this bastard before he starts to stink."

Only Shura follows me out of the office. I chase the need for a cigarette all the way to the patio that looks over the pool.

"You think you got your message across?" he asks once we're alone.

"I thought Slavik leaving would've been enough." I sigh and stroke my chin. "If Efrem could be swayed, what hope do I have that the others won't be?"

"Don't underestimate your hold on the men."

I turn to him, eyes flashing. "Don't assume everyone has your standards of loyalty."

"Are you feeling sorry for yourself, 'Drey?" he asks with a cheeky smirk. "That's not like you."

"It's not myself I feel sorry for. It's the people I've involved in this mess."

He knows precisely which "people" I'm talking about. "Natalia's a grown woman. And she chose you."

Yeah. But how much longer until she regrets that decision?

35

ANDREY

I look around at the men surrounding my desk and tell myself I can trust them—even as a voice in the back of my head warns me not to trust anyone.

Shura steps forward. "Nikolai's attempt on Natalia can't go unanswered."

"I'd agree, except…" As I pause, Shura's eyes widen in surprise. He's not the only one. "I think it's what Slavik is counting on. Nikolai and Slavik hate each other. So why haven't they made a move on each other?"

"Maybe Nikolai doesn't believe Slavik is really back?" It's the first suggestion Leif has made the entire meeting.

It's his first day standing in Efrem's place in the circle. No one has mentioned the absence yet, but it looms between all of us like a black hole sucking the life out of the room.

"*Nyet*," I say. "Slavik hasn't exactly been subtle about his return. They're both playing the long game here."

"They're relying on each other to take you out first," Shura realizes. "You're the biggest threat to both of them right now."

Leif perks up like an overeager pup. "What if we try to take them out together?"

"Because," I explain patiently, "I can't be sure of my own men. If I plan that kind of attack and I'm betrayed from the inside, it won't just be a defeat—it'll be a fucking massacre."

Jaw clenched and fists tight, I drift away from the circle. "We need to weed out all the men who might move against me and we need to do it quietly. I don't need rumors of disloyal *vory* circulating. Not to Nikolai or Slavik and certainly not to our allies."

"We could use their help, though," Yuri says.

"If they sense even the smallest hint of weakness, those fickle *mudaki* are more likely to jump ship than risk dying on it. We need to be discreet."

A murmur rumbles through my men, but no one seems to have a clue what to do. They're all looking at me for answers.

"Who's been keeping tabs on my useless brother?" I ask.

Yuri raises his hand. "It's a waste of time. All the man does is get drunk, get high, and get laid."

I'd hoped that keeping eyes on Viktor would pay off eventually, but so far, no dice. I run a hand through my hair. "This meeting is over. Get out."

They file out of the room, but Shura is the only one who dares to linger.

"I'm not interested in company right now, Shura."

From the stubborn set of his jaw, though, I know he's not going anywhere. "We need someone on the inside, 'Drey. Someone who can get close enough to extract valuable information."

"Don't you think I know that? But there's no way we can plant anyone trustworthy at this stage."

Shura arches a brow, waiting for me to follow his train of thought.

It doesn't take long.

"No. *No.*"

"Think about it," Shura persists. "The boy knows Nikolai. He's lived in the compound. He can convince him that he managed to escape from our hold and now has inside information on you."

"Do you think I haven't thought of that already?"

"Then what's the problem?"

"For one, Natalia. She'd have my fucking balls if I sent the kid in there. And for another..." I drop wearily into the closest seat. "I'd never forgive myself for sending him back to that hellhole."

"Since when do you have a conscience?"

I laugh hollowly. Fuck if I know, but it's a beast to carry around. "The boy is off-limits. I promised to protect him."

"Maybe you should let him decide."

"He's fourteen years old and desperate to prove himself. Of course he's going to want to jump into the fray. That doesn't mean we should let him."

"'Drey—"

"It's not going to happen, Shura."

Shura falls silent, the vein in his forehead throbbing. The tension feels at the point of spilling over when someone clears their throat from the doorway.

And then, of all people, Katya steps into the space between us. "Before someone walks out of here with a black eye, might I make a suggestion?"

"You're not supposed to be here," Shura grits.

"Well, I am, and I heard everything. Andrey's right, Shura: sending Misha would be a huge mistake. And I'm not just saying that because Natalia would burn this house to the ground in a rage."

Shura scowls. "This doesn't concern you, Kat. These are Bratva matters."

She meets his scowl with one of her own. "Since it concerns the safety of my best friend, I'm making it my concern." She pushes past Shura to face me. "Send me instead."

I wait for the punchline.

It doesn't come.

"Have you lost your fucking mind?!" Shura roars.

Katya doesn't so much as glance in his direction. "I'm smart and resourceful. I'd make a good spy."

"*Prygat!*" Shura grabs her arm and steers her towards the door.

She shakes him off. "Touch me again, buddy, and I'll kick you in the nuts."

Shura's hand drops along with his face. His anger drains away, and his voice wobbles in a way I've never heard before. "Kat, baby... you can't."

"I can. I'd do anything for Natalia. Do you think that's changed just because you and Andrey entered our lives? We've had each other's backs long before you two showed up."

Shura reaches for her, but stops himself when she levels him with a glare. "If you think I'm going to let you get anywhere near Nikolai Rostov—"

"I'm not planning on getting anywhere near Nikolai Rostov," she interrupts. "I'm planning on getting close to Viktor."

Oh, for fuck's sake. She might be right.

As much as I understand Shura's fury, Katya is onto something.

"Viktor knows you're Natalia's friend," I remind her. "Why would he trust you?"

"Because as far as he knows, Natalia cut me off after we crashed his wedding to Mila. I'll let him think we're on the outs, and I'm looking to get even." She gives me a dark, melancholy smile. "I'll make him believe what I need him to believe, Andrey. I've always been good at that."

"This isn't fucking happening." Shura throws his hands in the air. "Andrey, you can't seriously be considering this."

Reluctantly, I force my eyes to my second's. "She makes a good case, brother."

"She is my woman!"

Katya stamps her foot on the ground. "I'm my own damn woman, Shura. Just because we sleep together doesn't mean you own me."

He steps towards her, getting right in her face. "Doesn't it?"

I shift between them if only because the heat in their gaze has me worried about my office. "Shura, you're my right-hand man and the closest thing I have to a true brother. If you're against this, I won't insist. But I do think Katya's plan has a chance of working."

Katya is crackling with outrage. "Who cares if he's against this? Back me up, Andrey!"

"If it was Natalia wanting to do something like this, I'd feel the same way." She opens her mouth to argue, but I hold up a hand. "Convince him to get on board with your plan, and I'll agree to it. But if Shura says no, it's dead in the water. That's my final offer."

She turns her ire on Shura, and I slip out of the room. As I shut the door, something shatters.

I don't turn back.

36

ANDREY

I'm on my way upstairs to find Natalia when I spot Misha in the backyard. He's wandering aimlessly, kicking at the grass with every step, so busy staring down at his feet that he doesn't notice me until I'm only a few yards away.

He jolts in surprise. "Andrey! I didn't see you there."

"You looked deep in thought."

"I just… needed a walk." His shoulders straighten and he pulls himself up to his fullest height, but his eyes shift over my shoulder, looking at the house instead. "If you want me to go, I will."

"I told you yesterday how I feel about that."

"Yeah, but that was in front of—"

"I didn't make my decision because of Natalia." I inch closer to him. "I meant what I said. You have a home here as long as you want it."

He holds himself rigidly, but he can't fight the tremors working through his body. Finally, he shoves his fists into his pockets and continues pacing. "What do you want from me?"

"Nothing but your safety. And your happiness, if that's at all possible."

He tilts his head to one side like a confused puppy trying to make sense of things. "You know, Nikolai always said you were a monster who broke up families."

"He must've been looking in a mirror."

Misha doesn't smile, but his face softens. "I'm sorry I didn't tell you before now."

"I understand why you didn't. And we don't need to revisit this conversation again."

He shuffles from one foot to the other. Back and forth, back and forth, like he can't find solid ground. "Is it true that the man you captured said Nikolai wants me back?"

"That's what he said. Whether we can believe him or not is a different issue."

Misha nods and silence falls between us. He's lost in thoughts that I can only imagine.

"Misha, you should know that, when it comes down to it, I am going to kill him—your father."

"He was never a father to me," he spits with more venom than I thought possible. "He's the man responsible for selling my mother. That's all he'll ever be to me."

I'm not sure he even realizes it, but as he talks, his fingers stray toward the birthmark on his collarbone. The one that marks him as a Rostov.

"Andrey..." He clears his throat and tries again. "Do you think it would be possible to track down my mother?"

I've been wondering if we'd have a conversation like this one day. It came even sooner than I anticipated, though. I rest a reassuring hand on his shoulder. "I can't promise you we'll find anything, but I can promise you that we'll search for her. But first, we need to deal with Nikolai and Slavik."

"I want to help."

I've been expecting this, too. Shura's idea would mean Natalia would never speak to me again, but damn if it wasn't a good one. It would be so easy to train him up and send him in. Such a neat solution. Nikolai would have no reason to suspect the boy had turned to my side during captivity. Misha could be perfectly placed to bring about the premature end of the Rostov empire.

Except...

I promised Natalia.

"You can help by telling me whatever it is you remember about Nikolai and his operation."

Misha's forehead scrunches. "You know that's not what I meant. I mean, of course I'll tell you whatever I know. But that's not how I want to help."

"You know I can't let you go back there."

Misha's chin falls to his chest and his breathing quiets to a slow, raspy rhythm. "I don't want to hurt her, either. I don't want to do anything that would cause her pain or stress. But..." He raises his face to look at me again, and as he does, I'm struck by how much of a man he seems to be. Proud and self-assured and resolute. "She needs to accept that I have a choice in this, too."

"We all have choices," I agree. "But this is not yours to make."

"What if we didn't tell her?"

"She's pregnant, not stupid."

"Tell her I ran away."

I laugh. "She'd launch a full-scale manhunt for you. She'd search to the ends of the earth until she got you back."

Misha knows that as well as I do. He crumples to a seat on the grass, head slung low between his knees. "It's not fair. None of this is fair."

No, it's not. It's not fair at all. Between Shura protecting Katya and Natalia protecting Misha, I'm left with nothing except a full-scale Bratva war that will leave me vulnerable on all sides.

Route Seven was supposed to be a contingency plan.

Now, it looks like our only way out.

37

ANDREY

"To our first milestone!" Cevdet toasts his glass of champagne to the sky. "Only one fucking trip and I'm a few million dollars richer. Ha!"

Cevdet isn't usually a sloppy drunk, but his excitement is justified. Our first drug run after the expansion was flawlessly executed.

Luca, however, is always a sloppy drunk. He raises his cigar in a toast and brings his glass to his lips like he's going to take a puff. He and Cevdet roar with laughter at the mistake and clink their glasses.

It's Bujar, as always, who paces himself. "One successful run doesn't guarantee that they'll all go as smoothly," he pipes up over Cevdet's less-than-on-pitch rendition of *"We Are the Champions."* "We need to—"

"Jesus, Bujar, have another drink. It might help pry that stick out of your ass."

Bujar glowers at Cevdet before turning to me for support. "We can't afford to be complacent."

"I agree, but not all of us are in a fit state to talk business." Luca and Cevdet begin an uncoordinated round of the chorus, singing different lyrics and sloshing their glasses together. "There will be time for that later."

"Exactly!" Cevdet roars. "Listen to our fearless leader. The night is ripe with still-untouched pleasures…" His eyes veer towards one of my waitresses in a red mini skirt. "What a wonderful selection you have tonight, Andrey."

I draw Cevdet's attention with a click of my tongue. "The women are not on offer, Cevdet. Not in my clubs. Not on my watch."

Drunk as he is, the man still has the sense to backtrack. "I was talking about your array of poisons." He lifts his empty glass, and it's refilled immediately.

"We should grab our wives and have a formal dinner to cement this new venture." Luca seems to warn Cevdet with his eyes, reminding him he does, in fact, have a wife at home.

Cevdet toasts to the idea even as he watches my waitstaff sashay across the club. "Who will our young leader bring? Is there a woman you'd dare to introduce to us?"

He's teasing, but I have no desire to bring Natalia anywhere near this crew. Still, a meeting of the families is symbolic. It signifies trust.

I give my allies only a polite smile. "I'll set it up."

As Luca and Cevdet launch into the particulars of this dinner, Shura enters the VIP room and looks for me. I rise from my chair. "Excuse me, gentleman."

Slipping out of the VIP room behind Shura, I notice the rest of the club has emptied considerably compared to an hour ago. "What's going on?"

"The cops are here."

I've been getting reports of cops in the area all night, but I didn't really think it would turn into a raid. I press two fingers to my forehead, massaging away the headache forming there. "Where are the supplies?"

"Hidden after the first sighting, but a raid isn't a good look. Especially tonight." We both angle towards the VIP room where Cevdet's voice is rising above the steady thrum of the music.

"It's too late to get them out now," I concede. "Let the cops have their fun. I'll handle the allies."

Shura nods and departs to take care of matters. When I slip back into the VIP room, the mood has stalled. It's clear that all three men are aware that something is up.

"Something the matter, Andrey?" Cevdet asks.

"Just a few kinks that need ironing out, that's all."

Cevdet's smile only gets wider. "This wouldn't have anything to do with the cops that have been sniffing around the area all night, would it?"

I don't so much as blink. "It seems my enemies think practical jokes and minor annoyances are enough to rattle me. If this is the best they can do, destroying them will be easier than I thought."

Cevdet snorts. "They're intimidated, that's what this is."

"Cheap moves to undermine your authority," Luca adds.

Bujar alone stares at the door with his eyebrows drawn together in a worried V. It remains there throughout the entire search, even as Cevdet and Luca return to their drinks.

Minutes later, Shura reappears in the doorway and nods, informing me that the cops have cleared out.

"They found nothing." I make a show of laughing for their benefit. The allies join in, but I'm not sure how much of it is sincere.

After another two rounds of champagne, Cevdet and Luca finally stand to leave. Bujar looks as relieved as I feel as their ruckus departs.

"That lasted forever," Shura grumbles, joining us as Vaska escorts our allies from the room.

"Try sitting through it." I put down my mostly untouched champagne flute and reach for a cigar instead. "Did you find out who called the cops?"

"'Anonymous tip.'" His disgust is obvious.

I roll my eyes. "I expect better from Slavik and Nikolai. Calling the cops is like telling the teacher. It's juvenile."

"Maybe they're desperate."

"Or maybe this has nothing to do with either one of them."

Shura cocks his head to the side. "What do you mean?"

The more I think on it, the more likely it seems. It's too cheap a ploy for men like my father or Rostov. Which leaves only…

"I think it's time to have a little talk with my brother."

The mention of Viktor has Shura baring his teeth like Remi. "There's no point wasting your time with that scum. It's bad enough you have men tailing the useless waste of space. If you confront him face-to-face, he'll just lie through his teeth."

He doesn't mention Katya's plan to confront Viktor, and out of respect for him, I haven't, either. But we're dangerously close to the topic now.

I get to my feet. "He's never been a good liar. Particularly not when he's drunk. And considering the hour, I'd bet he's well on his way to plastered."

I can hear the grind of Shura's teeth. "What if he destroys what we've built? What we have?"

I have a strong feeling he isn't talking about the Bratva.

"Brother, Katya's a smart woman." He flinches, but I keep going. "She can more than hold her own where Viktor is concerned."

Shura's hands ball into fists. "We're not talking about this."

Not yet. But we won't have a choice soon.

"Have Viktor brought to the manor," I sigh. "If you'd rather have Vaska and Yuri handle it, then give them the order."

"I can fucking handle Viktor," he glowers. "I can take that motherfucker with my eyes closed."

I know that much is true.

It's Katya who's more of a struggle.

38

ANDREY

The door flies open and a six-foot-one mess lands on my Persian rug. He smells like shit. Between Efrem's bloodstains and Viktor's filth, I really will have to throw the damn thing out.

Shura fills the doorframe a second later, towering over my brother, who is trying and failing to peel himself up off my floor. Shura, ever the helpful one, "accidentally" kicks him on the way to my desk.

"Delivered as promised."

"*Mudak*," Viktor growls, glaring up at Shura from where he remains plastered on the floor. He half-rises again, trips over the edge of the rug, and falls right back on his ass.

None of us move to help him. It takes a while for the whole circus to spin itself out, so Viktor is practically foaming at the mouth when he finally stands. His clothes are stiff with grime and every miniscule motion sends foul waves of stale smoke and booze wafting toward me.

"Jesus, Viktor." I wrinkle my nose. "You reek."

His bloodshot eyes swirl in their sockets as he focuses on me. "How dare you? If our father knew about this—"

"Running to Daddy to tattle on me, Vicky?"

"My absence will be noticed."

"By the whores who warm your bed at night? I'm guessing they'll be relieved you're not around."

"Fuck you!" He swipes at the spit dribbling down his chin. "Listen, if this is about those cops who raided—"

"How do you know about that?"

Viktor's mouth hangs open. My God—this is going to be even easier than I thought. I'd be pleased if I wasn't so repulsed instead. "What was the point of that stunt, Viktor? Trying to earn Papa's approval?"

"There's nothing to earn. Otets trusts me."

"The old man doesn't trust you for shit," I say. "He doesn't even like you. He tolerates you. For the moment, at least."

"I'm his right-hand man!"

The vile creature wobbling on his feet in front of me is so much more broken than I remember. I can't even bring myself to despise him. Pity is the only emotion left.

"One day," he says, "I'm going to rule the entire fucking Kuznetsov Bratva!"

Shura barks out a harsh laugh. "What self-respecting man would follow you?"

Viktor lists to the side, but manages to clamp a clammy hand around the edge of my desk to right himself before gravity drags him back down where he belongs.

"Who are you to talk?" Viktor crows. "Half your men aren't even loyal! They're coming over to our side in droves. They don't want you as their *pakhan*; they want Slavik. After Slavik, it'll be my time."

"This is your time, brother," I tell him calmly. "As good as you will ever have it. Enjoy the drinking, smoking, and whoring while you can. It's all gonna end soon enough."

Viktor cackles like a madman, sounding lucid for the first time since Shura dragged his carcass in here. "You don't know what you're in for. Otets will win. He's got a big ally on his side. He doesn't need any of the others—the Brigade, the Halcones—none of them matter compared to—" His eyes bulge mid-sentence. Then he twists to the side and throws up.

"*Blyat!*" Shura recoils in disgust.

Viktor is still dry heaving like a cat hacking up a hairball when I grab him by the scruff and shove him towards the door. "Get him out of my sight."

Shura takes over, hauling a slurring, screaming Viktor all the way to the front door.

But traces of him remain. My brother's vomit seeps into the carpet fibers, and I decide that merely throwing it away won't be enough. I'll have to burn it to get the stench out.

Half an hour later, Shura finds me next to the pool. He drops into the chair next to mine with a weary huff. "I dumped him in a ditch outside the brothel I found him in."

I nod, but the silence lasts no more than a second before Shura is back on his feet, pacing.

"He mentioned a strong ally. Do you believe him?"

I've done my own pacing for the night, and my answer is ready. "Yes."

"Do you think it's—"

"I don't know."

Shura lapses into silence. His eyes are far away as he stares up at the cloudless night sky. Finally, he shakes his head. "He was a fucking mess, man. Even by Viktor's standards, that was low."

"I don't know what made him think he was better off with Slavik. He always saw Viktor as weak." I run a hand over my sore neck. "When I look at him, I'm disgusted by what he's become. The problem is, I also see the little five-year-old who used to follow me around and demand that everyone call him 'Andrey Junior.'"

Shura's eyebrows arch. "He did that?"

"He wasn't always a broken mess. Somewhere along the way..." I exhale loudly. "Sometimes, I think I failed him."

"You did everything you could for Viktor. Including making excuses for him when he didn't deserve any. He was nothing more than your dead weight. Now, he's Slavik's dead weight. Until the old man cuts him loose, at least."

I look at him sidelong, trying to gauge how easily he could shove me into the pool if he doesn't like what I have to say.

"He would be easy to crack, Shura."

"*Yebat'!* Don't you think I know that?" He runs a hand through his thinning hair and swears again. "But it doesn't matter how easy the job would be. It would be *her*—Katya—doing shit that I ought to be protecting her from."

"She's a grown woman."

"So she keeps reminding me." He turns to me with fire in his eyes. "She won't talk to me because she says I treat her like property. Are you gonna stop talking to me, too?"

I keep my voice calm. "We both know I would react the exact same way if I was in your place."

"I sense a 'but' coming."

I raise my hands. "Just a piece of advice: accepting who Natalia is has worked a lot better for me than trying to mold her into something she's not."

Shura curses once more under his breath, but he stops pacing.

"Natalia was never and is never going to be a traditional Bratva woman, Shura. She's got a mind of her own. Goals. It's the whole reason I could never convince her to quit her stupid day job. And, need I remind you, she started training with guns long before I knew about your lessons."

Shura cringes. "Are you holding that against me?"

"Not at all. It was the right thing to do. All I'm saying is, there was no point denying her the right to train. She found a way to do it anyway. I had to learn to let go a little. And, as much as it wasn't always easy, it's only made our relationship stronger."

Shura clicks his tongue in irritation. "I can't believe I'm taking relationship advice from you."

"I can't believe I'm giving it."

He plummets back into his chair with a groan. "What if Katya can't convince Viktor that she's on the outs with Natalia? What if he suspects that she's working for you?"

"We're not going to send Katya in blind, Shura. If she goes in, she'll have backup. We'll keep tabs on her constantly."

"Things can still go wrong."

"Katya's smart and resourceful. She can handle this."

"Fuck me," Shura moans. "I can't believe I'm actually considering it."

"It might be the only way to get Katya to talk to you again. She holds grudges, that one."

He folds his arms over his chest and scowls. "If it's the choice between never talking to her again and keeping her alive, I choose the silent treatment."

I turn to face him. "Nothing's going to happen to her. I give you my vow."

I can see the conflict in his eyes and I understand it completely. It goes against our very natures to put our women in the path of danger. He and I, we were born to protect. Born to bear the scars and the nightmares and the burdens so that others don't have to.

"Like I said, if you decide against it, I'll support that."

"I know. But… fuck me, you were right: I might not have a choice." He looks back up at the sky as if it's holding answers for him. "I need to go talk to her."

Shura rises from his chair and trudges to the house like a man making his way to the executioner's block. I don't envy what waits for him inside. I, for once, don't have to worry.

When I finally slip into my bedroom, Natalia is sitting by the window wrapped in one of my shirts.

"It's late, *lastochka*. You should be asleep."

She turns to me with a soft, sleepy smile. "I could say the same to you."

"*Pakhans* don't get to sleep."

She screws her face up with disapproval. "Then we're going to have to change that. Because I like going to bed *with* you."

She makes room for me on the window seat, and I slide in next to her. My arms wrap around her waist and she nuzzles into me with a happy sigh.

"Was that Shura I saw out there with you?"

"You were spying on us?"

"As a matter of fact, I was. I even cracked the window to try to hear you, but your voices didn't carry." She folds her hands over mine, twining our fingers together. "It looked like a serious discussion."

"Nowadays, they're all serious discussions."

"Anything I should be worried about?"

I genuinely consider telling her, but I'm tired of talking about it. I press a kiss to her forehead instead. "Nothing I can't handle, little bird."

She twists in my arms and cups my face with her palm. "You don't have to carry the burden alone, you know? You can talk to me, Andrey. You can tell me anything. We're partners now."

"You know what I really need right now?"

"Tell me."

"You," I whisper. "Just sitting here in the quiet with you."

She smiles and scoots closer. "I can handle that."

39

NATALIA

"Where's Katya?"

Mila checks her phone from the couch where she dropped it after the fourth time I asked the same question. "She just texted. She's on her way."

I appreciate Mila being here, I do. But Kat is my hype girl. She knows what to say to get my ass in gear. Sure, sometimes, she talks me into crashing a wedding and I end up pregnant with twins, but a lot of the time, she says just enough to get me out the door and having a good time.

I've never needed that so badly.

I eye the midnight-blue dress hanging on the wall with skepticism. "What if it doesn't fit?"

Mila groans. "Your makeup looks great, the shoes won't break your toes, and the dress is going to fit like a dream. We've been over this."

"The dress fit last week, but I think I put on ten pounds in the last two days."

"That's literally, scientifically impossible."

"Five pounds then. I swear."

"Natalia," Mila sighs, "you need to—" I'm positive she's about to tell me I need to get a grip, which wouldn't be completely unjustified. But then the door bursts open and Katya rushes in.

"Sorry!" she cries. "I couldn't get a taxi and it was raining downtown and… It doesn't matter. Natalia, you look amazing."

"Don't lie to me."

She turns to Mila with a grimace. "Things aren't going well, then?"

I drop my face into my hands. "What are the chances I can get away with pretending to be sick?"

"None at all," Katya declares, snatching the dress from the hanger and walking it over to me. "I'm not gonna let you back out of this."

"Why not?"

"Because this is a big freaking deal, Nat. And you need to make an impression tonight."

"I know. Hence why I want to back out. I look like a planet."

"Helloo, Earth to Natalia?" Mila waves a hand in my face. "Do you think Andrey would take you anywhere if he wasn't desperate to show you off?"

Katya wraps an arm around me. "Look at how far you two have come, Nat. There was a time when Andrey was all frowny and sullen and wouldn't share your bed. He's still two of those things, but at least he's sleeping with you again."

I swat her arm, but she just laughs.

"Now, here you are, eight months pregnant with his babies, ready to step into his world. Isn't this what you wanted?"

I give her a silent, reproachful nod.

"Verbal answers only, please." She curls a hand around her ear. "I need to hear you tell me how right I am."

"Yes," I mumble. "Yes, that's what I've always wanted."

She claps her hands together like that settles it. "Beautiful. Because I'm failing to see this as anything but a good day."

I lift my eyes to my two best friends. "This is a big step. Meeting the partners and their wives."

"It is a big step," Katya agrees. "For a man like Andrey, introducing you to his allies is like a proposal."

That's not as comforting as she thinks it is, but before I can point that out, she reaches to tuck a strand of hair behind my ear.

I snatch her wrist out of the air. "What the hell is that?"

Katya rips her hand away and tucks it out of sight. "It's nothing."

"It's not nothing." I bring her arm closer to inspect it. "That's a bruise. Are those *fingerprints*?"

Mila runs a gentle finger over the welts. "You should ice that, Kat."

"It's really not a big deal," she insists. But her voice is far too high-pitched for me to believe her.

I cross my arms. "If Shura did that to you—"

She gasps. "Of course Shura didn't—!"

"Someone grabbed you, Kat. Who was it?"

She's pale and fiddling with the ends of her hair, which is a classic caught-in-the-act Kat move. "I was at a club with… colleagues. People were drinking. A guy got obnoxious. It was no big deal. Someone pushed him off of me, and I'm fine."

"Who was the guy?"

"Who the hell knows?" Katya shrugs. "Some nobody who thought I was interested. I let him know that I wasn't. End of story."

I squint down at the ugly, purple bruise. "Are you sure that's the whole story?"

"Would you stop making a big deal about this? I don't need Shura to—" She breaks off mid-sentence. "Just don't mention this to Shura, okay? He'll overreact, as usual."

"I won't need to tell him. If I noticed the bruise, he definitely will."

"Not if I avoid him until it's gone."

"Kat!"

She grins cheekily at me. "Knew I could count on you. Okay, enough about me. We've got to get Cinderella ready for the ball."

"We're not done talking about this," I warn with a point of my chin toward her wrist.

"Yes, yes, to be continued. Now, up you go. Time to get dressed."

Between Mila and Kat, they help me into the dress. After I'm zipped up, they steer me in the direction of the mirror and step aside with "tadas" and jazz hands aplenty.

The dress really is gorgeous. It has an empire waist that flows over my bump. The sheer sleeves sit off-shoulder and make me feel like a grown-up fairy princess. I look quite nice, actually.

"Are you a knockout or what?" Katya chides, nudging me on the shoulder. "This dress is gorgeous."

With his trademark flawless timing, the door opens and Andrey walks in. "It's not the dress," he remarks the moment he lays eyes on me. "It's the woman wearing it."

Katya meets my eyes in the mirror. *Swoon*, she mouths.

She's not wrong.

"But there is one thing that's missing," Andrey adds, revealing a stack of three velvet boxes from behind his back.

"Ooh" Kat cries, clapping her hands together. "I smell jewelry."

Andrey snaps open the latch on the biggest box to reveal a gorgeous necklace dripping in diamonds and green emeralds. "I thought it would complement your eyes."

I can only gawk at it, open-mouthed and breathless. "It's stunning."

He opens the remaining two boxes, containing a bracelet and a matching pair of earrings. Both pieces are made up of the same combination of glittering diamonds and large emeralds.

"Andrey, this is too much."

"You're not obligated to wear any of it. I just wanted to give you the option."

"'Not obligated'?!" Katya shrieks. "Of course she's obligated! I obligate you, Nat. Look at those diamonds. They deserve to be worn. Put them on or I'll put them on for you. Either that or steal them and wear them myself."

Clearly outnumbered, I shrug. "Oh, alright. Put them on me."

Katya plucks the diamond necklace from its perch like just touching it is enough of a treat. "But first, let's take off the cherries—"

"No!" I grab my chain before she can get her hands on it. "The cherry pendant stays on."

Katya gapes at me. "But Nat, it doesn't go with the whole look."

"Don't care. I'm not taking it off."

Katya looks at Andrey for some support, but he just shrugs. "It's up to her."

She rolls her eyes and proceeds to put the rest of my jewelry on over the cherries resting just above my heart.

Andrey leans over my shoulder and presses a kiss to the nape of my neck. "You look perfect."

Feeling confident, I take Andrey's arm and he leads me downstairs, where our chariot awaits in the form of a stretch limo. He opens the door and waves me into the backseat, and for one foolish, wild second, I see a flash of an alternate reality.

In that reality, I'm not wearing a midnight blue dress; I'm wearing a snowy white one. I'm holding a bouquet of white roses and Andrey is in a tux. There are rings on both our fingers and the sky overhead is a fluttering mass of doves.

The vision disappears when I turn back to the house and see Shura standing in the entrance. Apparently, he won't be joining us for dinner, but he will be part of the security detail.

When Katya sees him, she tucks her bruised arm behind her back.

"Ready to go?" Shura asks. He's talking to me, but his eyes are trained on Katya, who seems to be playing hide-and-seek behind Mila.

Every time Shura tries to move closer to her, she moves in the opposite direction. I have to admit, I understand the instinct. The last time a man touched me without my permission, he disappeared. Katya probably doesn't want the same drama.

I maneuver my whale-like body into the back of the stretch limo with Andrey, but just as he closes the door, I see Shura snatch Katya's wrist.

"Oh, shit."

"What's going on?" Andrey is immediately on high alert.

"I don't really know," I admit.

Andrey follows my gaze out the window. Shura and Katya are yelling at each other, their muffled voices making their way into the limo.

Scowling, Andrey hits the top of the limo's ceiling. "Let's go, Vaska."

"Without Shura?"

Andrey glances out the window. "I'd say he's got enough to deal with."

40

ANDREY

She checks the jewels hanging off her ears and neck again and again, as though she's scared she'll lose them. Even when she tucks her fingers under her thighs to control herself, she keeps fidgeting for the rest of the drive. She trips twice on the way up the hotel stairs, even though I've got my arm looped around her waist.

I make no mention of it. Any of it. At least, not until we arrive outside the doors of the private rooms where we'll be having dinner and she comes to an abrupt stop.

"You okay?" I ask.

"I just need a moment."

I stand with her, my security detail spreading around the area, pretending like they don't notice us. Natalia closes her eyes and takes a few deep breaths. When she finally opens them again, she looks ever so slightly more composed.

"You won't leave me, will you?"

"Not until you're comfortable," I assure her.

With that promise secured, she grips my arm tightly and we stride into the lounge.

Cevdet, Luca and Bujar are all present, as are their wives, dripping in jewels and floor-length evening gowns. "Well, well," Cevdet thunders, drawing all eyes to him as usual. "If it isn't the lucky woman who managed to win the heart of our young leader."

Natalia's cheeks burn pink, but she smiles politely. "Pleasure to meet all of you."

The wives eye her from head to toe, and Natalia takes a step back, pressing into me.

"Just be yourself," I whisper in her ear. "It worked on me."

She clears her throat and reluctantly lets my forearm slide out of her hands. With one more mournful sigh, she takes a seat at the ladies' table.

"You'll have to forgive my nerves," she says by way of introduction. "This world is all a little new and confusing for me. So if I use the wrong fork at dinner, please don't, like, burn me at the stake or anything."

There's a momentary pause as if the room is holding its breath. Then, one by one, they all laugh.

Leonora, Cevdet's wife, pats Natalia's arm. "You have nothing to worry about. And if I may say, you look absolutely wonderful. I never looked half as lovely when I was pregnant."

Natalia blushes. "Thank you. I feel like a cow."

Bujar's wife barks out a laugh. "Wait 'til you start breastfeeding. Then you'll really feel like a cow."

"Motherhood," Cevdet mutters in what passes for a whisper from him. "It's the great unifier. They won't stop blabbing for hours now."

As the men make their way to the armchairs in the corner, I catch Natalia's eye. She winks, letting me know I'm free to leave her.

To think I was ever worried about her in the first place.

"She's stunning, Andrey," Cevdet crows once we're out of earshot. "And it seems, very pregnant, too."

"I'm keeping that news quiet for now, gentleman. No need to tempt fate."

"Wise choice, my friend." Luca passes out crystal tumblers filled with whisky and we toast to the future and our new business prospects.

But the revelry lasts only through the first sip.

"I received word of increased surveillance on several of our trading routes yesterday," Bujar informs us, jumping straight into it. "If this continues, we might have to close a few temporarily."

Luca puts down his whiskey. "You think our operation has been compromised so soon?"

"I think we need to tread carefully. We have more people watching us than we might suspect. And not for the reasons we might suspect, either." His gaze falls directly on me. No prizes for guessing what he might be thinking.

"News travels fast, Andrey," Cevdet booms. "Apparently, the Bratva has more to worry about than we originally assumed."

I take an unbothered sip of my whiskey. "If you're referring to my father, I'm dealing with that."

"You don't seem concerned." Luca's eyes bore into my face.

"That's because there's nothing to be concerned about. The old man is out of his depth. I'm simply giving him the respect of a subtle defeat. If he were anyone else, he'd be nothing more than smoldering ash by now."

"Still, we need to consider alternate routes," Bujar says. "And perhaps a little more manpower."

"And if that doesn't cut it?" Luca asks.

Cevdet's gaze sweeps over to me. "Well then, I don't see the point of continuing a business venture that poses more risk than reward, do you?"

I return Cevdet's smile. "Of course not. But there's not going to be much more risk once I've dealt with the complications. You're not going to let a minor setback deter you, are you, Cevdet? I took you for a stronger man than that."

"Depends on what you define as 'minor.'"

"As I said, I've got everything under control." I hold his gaze a second longer than necessary to ensure my point lands.

"Glad to hear it," Luca concludes, raising his glass. "Another toast then. To fruitful new ventures and our enemies coming only close enough to lick our boots."

Once we've clinked our glasses together, the topic falls back to less pressing business prospects. My eyes wander over to where the women are sitting and chatting.

The chandelier dapples Natalia's dress and highlights her

cheekbones. When she tips her head back and laughs, I stand without a firm idea of where I'm going.

"Excuse me, gentleman."

All four ladies look expectantly at me as I approach, but I only have eyes for one. "Natalia, can I borrow you for a moment?"

"Of course." She reaches for the arm of the chair, but I offer my hand instead. She flushes. "Where are you taking me?"

I make eye contact with Olaf as we close in on the ladies' restroom. "We're not to be disturbed, Olaf."

"Understood, boss."

"*I* don't understand," Natalia interjects, looking more and more bewildered. "Andrey! You can't come in here with me. This is the ladies—"

She gasps as I close the door and push her up against it. I slide my hand inside the high slit of her dress, stroking her thighs.

"Andrey! You can't… Wait…"

But her eyes flutter unconvincingly as I pull her panties to the side and bring myself home inside of her.

It's a fast and furious fucking. The door rattles in the frame as I plow Natalia into it, my hand cupped over her mouth to muffle her moans. We come almost in unison, mere minutes after we started. Only then can I breathe again.

"What was that?" she asks while I'm zipping myself back up and helping her do the same.

"I wanted you."

"Cut the shit, Andrey." She grabs my wrists and drags me toward her. "You're worried about something, aren't you?"

I sigh. It'd be easy to lie, to downplay everything. But that's not what I signed up for with Natalia. That's not what we agreed on.

And if I want a future with her, I have to be honest.

"This alliance can't fall apart, Natalia," I grit. "But the longer it takes me to deal with my enemies, the more vulnerable it becomes."

"It's only a matter of time. Soon, Nikolai and Slavik will be a thing of the past. And we can finally focus on our family."

Her arms are tight around my waist. I lean into them. Into her scent, her softness, her sweetness. "You're my secret weapon, you know that, little bird?"

"This little bird is flexing her talons," she winks.

I kiss the curve of her jaw. "My world doesn't know what it's in for."

"Should we go back in?" she asks. "I don't want them to think we snuck off to have sex."

I chuckle. "That's where you and I differ. I sincerely hope they do."

41

ANDREY

"I've got good news and bad news."

Shura is on his feet and inspecting Katya before she can even get close to our table. "If that *mudak* has laid another hand on you—"

Kat silences him with a kiss on the lips. Shura is stiff as she pulls away, but there's a huge grin spread across her face. "Hello to you, too."

I've chosen to have this meeting at a little hole-in-the-wall Italian restaurant I use periodically to launder money. It's always dead in the middle of the day, and right now is no exception. We've got the whole place—all four tables—to ourselves.

"Kat…" Shura warns, fisting her dress and hauling her close.

I understand his overprotectiveness, but we don't have time for it. I gesture for Kat to sit down. "How long do you have?"

"An hour before I need to get back to work. Is that bread? I'm starving!"

I push the basket in the middle of the table towards her, and she tears into a baguette with a dreamy groan. Shura is looking at her the way she's looking at the bread.

"How are things going?"

"Good," she assures me between bites. "I've established some trust. He's started opening up to me."

"How have you established trust?" Shura scowls.

"With a little over-the-pants massage, duh." She's barely even finished the sentence and Shura is turning a violent shade of purple. Kat pats his thigh. "Oh, for God's sake, Shura, I'm kidding."

"Go easy on him, Kat," I warn.

He lets her tow him back into his seat, but he looks as comfortable as if he was sitting on spikes. "You didn't answer my question. How did you establish trust?"

"You really think I would let that asshole touch me?" she spits. "I thought you had more faith in me than that."

Without saying a word, Shura grabs her bruised wrist and holds it up to the light like that's all the proof he needed.

She shakes him off and sighs. "His pride demanded that he punish me for the whole wedding fiasco. He got over it fast."

"Because he wanted to fuck you?"

Katya's confident smile withers and she looks down at her lap. "I had to make him believe I wanted to sleep with him—but I promise you, nothing happened." She risks a peek up at Shura. "You believe me, don't you?"

Shura doesn't move. Doesn't speak. Part of me wants to tell him to grow the fuck up. This is business.

But if Natalia and I were having this conversation, I'm not sure I'd be doing much better.

Kat touches his cheek and turns him to face her. "I got him so drunk that he couldn't tell me apart from Luna."

"Luna?"

A tiny, triumphant smile breaks apart her frown lines. "She's an escort who works at La Belle. About my size, conveniently enough. She comes in once I've got Viktor drunk and in bed, has her way with him, and I get all the credit. We call it the 'master-bait and switch.' Honestly, I'm as proud of the pun as I am of the trick itself."

I bark out a laugh, and Shura glares at me before he grabs Katya's hand. "He really buys that?"

"Like I said, he's drunk off his ass every time." She tucks her hand in his lap. "We should be celebrating. The plan is working. We're getting closer to—"

"I still don't like that the fucker thinks he's having sex with you," Shura snarls.

"*You* don't like it? Think about me. I have to pretend to want to sleep with him." She leans in close, her lips pressed to my second's ear. "He doesn't make it as easy as you do."

Shura might be blushing. I'm not sure because I've never seen it before, but his hand slides into Katya's lap under the table and he settles back without another complaint.

She kisses his cheek. "I'm getting real information out of him. Shit we can *use*! This is good news."

Shura looks like he wants to argue, but time isn't a luxury we can afford. "What do you have for me?" I ask.

"Ah, that's the less-good news." Her gaze flickers around the restaurant, clearly wary of being overheard. "Viktor's put a hit out on Mila."

"On his own wife? The fucking coward." Shura turns to me. "Ivan's gonna blow his lid when he finds out."

Speak of the devil...

Ivan's Bentley pulls along the curb just outside the restaurant. There's no way I can keep this kind of information from the man for long. But that doesn't mean I can't try.

"Leave Ivan to me. Katya, anything else?"

She bites her lip. "Mila's not the only one with a target on her back. Slavik has put a hit out, too. On... your mother."

My mouth drops. Even I never thought my father would stoop that low. "He wants to kill his mentally unstable wife?"

"He wants to hurt you, Andrey," Katya explains gently. "He also wants to undermine your power. By taking out the people you protect, he thinks he can expose you as a weak leader."

"Viktor's apple certainly didn't fall far from that fucking tree." To think the same blood runs in my veins is absolutely repulsive.

Katya checks the time on her watch. "I really gotta get back to work." She turns to Shura and lowers her voice a little. "I'll be thinking of you tonight."

His eyes remain cold as ice, but he kisses her back when she leans in. "Be safe," he commands. "If he tries anything with you—"

"I've been fighting off handsy men my whole life. I can handle Viktor."

With a wave, Katya ducks out just as Ivan walks into the restaurant. He takes her place at the table.

"Gentleman," he says morosely. "I hope you have good news for me."

I don't envy the miserable, balding bastard. He bargained on security and power when he insisted Viktor marry his daughter. Instead, he received an abusive drunk who, if he has his way, will get them all killed.

"I'm afraid good news is in short supply these days, Ivan."

He nods grimly. "How is my daughter?"

"Safe." We're all running off lukewarm promises as of late, but it's the best I can offer for the time being.

Ivan seems to know that. "Then we can move onto business. I assume I was summoned for a reason?"

"You're one of the best smugglers I know, Ivan." I mean it. He wouldn't be here if I didn't. "But this job requires slightly more finesse than usual."

"Why is that?"

"Because what I want smuggled is not drugs." He arches a curious brow, a silent invitation to go on. "We discussed this. Route Seven. One woman. I need it done quickly. Tomorrow at the latest."

Shura spins to me, mouth hanging open. "We haven't lost the war yet, Andrey. We have time."

"Time is the one thing we don't have, my friend," I say

wearily. "My pride is what killed Maria. Say what you want about me, but I learn from my mistakes."

42

NATALIA

"You're not eating."

Katya eyes the plate of olives I just pushed towards her. "I'm not hungry."

"Since when?"

"There's a lot going on at, uh… at the office." She clears her throat. "They've been working me pretty hard. It's enough to make a girl lose her appetite."

Katya once got her head stuck between the bars of a ride at the fair, and in the middle of the fire department sawing her free, she convinced a boy in line to go buy her a soft pretzel. She *always* has an appetite. Between this and the bruise on her wrist, which she is still taking great pains to hide from me, I feel like something is going on.

When she and Mila exchange a look, I know I'm right. "Something is up with you."

"Nothing's going on, Nat. It's just work stress."

"Things are alright with you and Shura?" I press. "Because the two of you have been weird around each other lately. Shura has been an asshole way more than normal."

"He's just feeling neglected because of how busy I've been at work." Kat rolls her eyes. "His big ego can't take being second priority."

Her explanation makes perfect sense. *So why don't I believe her?*

"At least your man lets you get out of the house," Mila complains, jabbing a thumb over her shoulder to where Leonty is sitting near the doorway.

He's on guard duty today. In theory, he's talking with Misha and petting Remi, but his eyes still flit in our direction every few seconds, as if he's worried the earth itself is gonna open up and swallow us whole.

"Leonty's been overbearingly protective the last few days."

"Welcome to my world." I lean back against the patio chair, resting my hands on my belly. "Being pregnant turns Andrey into my shadow, but that at least makes sense. I can't help but wonder what has everyone else all riled up."

Katya chokes on her lemonade and Mila has to slap her on the back. "You okay?"

"Fine," she splutters, going red in the face. "Just went down the wrong pipe." She makes a determined effort to avoid meeting my eyes, though. Just when I'm about to call her out on it, she points towards the house. "Here the boys are now."

Andrey and Shura are walking towards us. Katya winks and blows Shura a kiss, which should be normal, but something is off. She's putting on a show, and I don't know why.

"Ladies." Shura salutes soberly.

Andrey offers us all a grim nod as he sits down next to me and wraps an arm around my shoulders. Same as with Katya—the actions are right, but the motivations feel off.

"What have you girls been up to?" he asks.

Mila wrinkles her nose. "Cooped up indoors, mostly. We were trying to figure out what to do with the rest of our day. Hey! How about a shopping trip to—"

"No!" Leonty barks.

I didn't see him walk over to join our little group, but he's left Misha and Remi on the other side of the yard and is now hovering just over Mila's shoulder.

Kat shrugs. "I'd rather stay in anyway."

"Since when?" I mutter.

"Indoors it is," Mila sighs mournfully. No pushback, no feistiness, nothing but meek compliance.

"Okay, seriously!" I snap. "What the hell is going on?" I turn my gaze on each one of them in turn. "I feel like I'm in high school and the cool kids are keeping me out of the loop. *Something's* going on and everyone's in on it. Everyone except me, it seems."

Andrey kisses my temple. "Nothing's going on, *lastochka*."

I brush his kiss off. "Why am I the only one who is being left in the dark? Everyone—except for me—is being weird. I want to know what it is." I jab a finger at Mila. "You love to shop, and you'd go by yourself before you'd let anyone convince you to stay in."

"I dunno... It's just, everyone's here," she says sheepishly. "It's kinda nice."

"Don't do that. Don't make me feel crazy."

Andrey pulls me back against his chest. "No one thinks you're crazy, Nat. We're just relaxing."

My frown deepens. Am I being gaslit or am I being ridiculous? To their point, it's a sunny day and everyone I love is here. I should take a deep breath and enjoy it.

Too bad I can't.

Anxiety I can't name ripples through me, and I haul myself to my feet. Six pairs of eyes snap to me, and I raise my hands in surrender.

"Stand down. I just need to pee." I scooch between the chairs, my bump brushing the back of Katya's head. "Routine procedure. No emergency response necessary."

I make it all of two steps towards the pool house before the pain strikes.

I double over, and Andrey is instantly at my side. "Natalia?"

"I'm okay," I pant, trying to wave him off even as another round of pain twists my insides. "Ow. *Ow.*"

Mila and Katya are on either side of us now. Kat takes my arm. "Did you pee yourself? Is this a UTI? What's happening?"

I want to laugh. Or cry. Maybe scream.

But there isn't enough air. A fresh wave of agony rips through me, and all I can do is moan.

When it's gone, I look up at three pale, worried faces looking back at me. Behind them, Leonty and Shura are on high alert. Their job is to protect me, but I'm my own threat. What can they do?

I'm about to ask when I hear Aunt Annie's voice in the distance. "Nat? Honey?"

I push Andrey towards her, and he knows what I mean instantly. He helps my aunt over the uneven ground and brings her to my side.

"What's going on?" they ask in unison.

"Um, I'm not exactly sure," I admit. "I just had this really sharp pain in my… stomach? I think?" Misha pokes his head over the crowd, and I reach out to grab his hand. "It's fine, though. Just felt like someone was sticking a cattle prod in my insides, but it's gone now."

"That sounds like a contraction," Aunt Annie remarks.

Now, I do laugh. "No. Not possible."

"You're eight months pregnant with twins, sweetheart. It's almost impossible that you're still pregnant."

"Could it be Braxton Hicks?" Andrey asks, the color leaching out of his face.

"You should get her to a hospital either way. Just in case."

Katya, per usual, takes Aunt Annie's advice as gospel and stirs us all to attention. "Let's mobilize, people. Woman in labor."

"Maybe," I add meekly as Andrey almost picks me up and hauls me towards the house.

Mila runs ahead. "I'll pack a bag for you!"

Shura runs towards the drive. "I'll bring the car around."

Misha falls into step with me and Andrey, still gripping my hand. "Can I come, too?"

I squeeze his hand. "Of course, honey. I wouldn't have it any other way."

Misha and Remi race off behind Leonty and Shura, while I turn to Andrey. Now that we're alone, I feel safe enough to absolutely and completely freak out. "I can't be in labor, Andrey. This isn't happening. What if this is really happening?"

He smiles down at me, all the weirdness from a few minutes ago long forgotten. "Then we're about to meet our girls."

43

ANDREY

I swore to protect Natalia, but there are some things I can't save her from. "Where's the damn epidural?"

The nurse who just brought Natalia more ice chips is gray-haired, stocky, and completely unfazed by my growling. "Labor hasn't progressed far enough for an epidural. Be patient." She leaves the room with a quick nod in Natalia's direction.

"Will you stop harassing the staff?" Natalia gasps between contractions. "They know what they're doing!"

"You're in pain. They need to fix it."

She grabs my hand and squeezes it hard. "Giving birth will fix it. Pain is part of the solution."

"I despise seeing you like this." I dab a wet washcloth across her forehead.

If I can't yell at the nurses, then I can keep her cool and hydrated. It's easier than focusing on my racing heart or the question trying to burrow out of my skull.

Am I ready to be a father?

"I need to walk," Natalia announces, shoving her blankets off the hospital bed. "I need to move. I can't sit here anymore."

I help her up and follow her as we do laps around the small room. When a contraction hits, she doubles over, and I rub soothing circles along her back.

"God, that hurt," she groans.

"Do you need more ice chips? I can have Kat or Mila run down—"

"No." She waddles forward, continuing her looping path. "I just want to walk."

Another nurse walks in with more wet towels. "Where's Dr. Abdulov?" I bark at her.

The woman jolts like I'm holding a gun to her head. "He's doing the rounds. He'll be here soon to check on things."

She flees from the room, and Natalia laughs. "Maybe you should try some deep breaths with me."

"I can breathe just fine. Sit back down." I help her back onto the bed and rearrange the pillows behind her back. "Comfortable?"

"Is that a trick question?"

I slide in behind her on the bed. She leans forward, and I work my thumbs into the knots on her lower back. She moans, and I can't tell if it's in pain or relief.

"You don't have to stay in here with me the whole time, you know," she mutters. "If you need a break, you can send Annie or Kat in for a bit. Mila. Anyone."

"I'm not going anywhere."

"You don't need to watch this. We both don't have to suffer."

"There's nowhere else on Earth I'd rather be, Natalia. Not even you can get me to leave."

"I just meant—" She clenches her teeth and the words die on her lips. I move to the end of the bed and rub her swollen feet. "Forget it. Just… talk to me. Say anything."

Anything. What do you say to the woman who's about to bear your children? What do you say to the light of your world in the midst of a storm that threatens to blot out every last bit of her?

I open my mouth and pray that the right thing emerges. What I hear shocks even myself.

"I'm going to marry you one day."

She squints at me through the pain. "You're just trying to distract me from the pain. To be fair… it's kinda working."

"I am trying to distract you. But I also mean it."

"Seeing my swollen ankles and sweaty back is turning you into the marrying type, huh?"

"Your bravery is changing my mind," I correct. "Your grace and your patience changed my mind. You're it for me, Natalia. You're my future. And I'm never letting you go. Our family is the only thing that matters now."

All at once, she seems to realize how serious I am. "Oh, Andrey…" She smiles dreamily. "I'd be honored to be your wife, Andrey. But—"

The smile freezes on my face.

"—not until after you've dealt with Slavik and Nikolai," she continues. "I don't want to worry about our wedding being hijacked or our loved ones being targeted. I want to put all that ugliness behind us before we start our life together."

I grip her hand tightly. "Baby, our life together has already started."

She nods. "But I want a clean slate. Without the threat of attack hanging over our heads all the time. I want to become your wife knowing that our family is safe."

I hesitate for only a moment. Agreeing feels wrong, but when it comes to negotiations, she's going to win every single one in this state. She cries out with another contraction, and agreeing is the least I can do.

"Okay. We can wait. But as soon as we get back home, I'm putting a ring on your finger."

She laughs. "Only you would propose to me before you've even told me you love me."

"*Lastochka*, how could I not love you?"

Her eyes are watery as she grips my hand. "Yeah?"

"It's you and me against the world. And I will never, ever let us lose."

She reaches for me, and I bridge the distance between us. She kisses me feverishly, her nails digging into my hand as she tries to pull me closer. Then she releases me without warning. "Argh…"

"Too much tongue?"

She snorts. "Don't make me laugh now. It hurts too much."

The door opens and Dr. Abdulov walks in. "How are the parents-to-be doing?"

"She's in pain."

Dr. Abdulov dips between her legs to examine things. "Okay, it looks like it's time for that epidural," he announces, straightening up. "Another few centimeters and you'll be dilated enough to start pushing."

Natalia leans against me as the anesthesiologist comes in to administer the epidural. The massive needle in her spine doesn't seem to faze her when compared to the pain of the contractions, but I can't help wincing in sympathy.

Once it's in and the nurses clear out of the room, Natalia grabs the front of my shirt and pulls me towards her. "Andrey, you have to promise me something."

"Tell me. What do you need?"

"I need to know that our children will be kept separate from the Bratva. I know it's a part of you, but I can't have them involved. Please!"

"Natalia…"

"Please," she gasps again, refusing to let go of my shirt. "I need you to promise me…"

I grab her hand and pry it from my shirt before bringing it to my lips. "I will do my best to keep them safe."

She frowns, her eyes unfocused for a moment. "That's not… that's not…"

But she doesn't get to finish her sentence, because Dr. Abdulov is back in the room. After another quick check, he raises his brows. "It's time."

Natalia tries to sit up. "Right now? No, I'm not ready. I don't feel ready. I doubt it's—"

She screams with another contraction and the entire room becomes a flurry of movement and activity. A nurse drags in two bassinets while another unfolds baby blankets.

"You can do this," I whisper in her ear.

Dr. Abdulov walks her through how and when to push, but it doesn't seem like Natalia needs it. She goes red in the face with every effort, nearly crushing my hand in her grip.

"Okay, Natalia. That's great," the doctor coaches her.

But she looks to me. I kiss her sweaty forehead. "You're doing amazing. Keep going."

With a nod, Natalia grits her teeth and pushes hard, hard, hard. This time, I'm worried she's going to pass out. "Breathe," I tell her, rubbing her back as she prepares to push again.

She takes a deep breath and, with a scream, Natalia delivers our first baby.

"I've got her!" Dr. Abdulov says a moment later, a piercing cry filling the delivery room.

Natalia's head falls back against the soaked pillow. Her face is blotchy, and her eyes flutter closed.

But Dr. Abdulov doesn't give her any time to recover. "I'm sorry, my dear, but no rest, I'm afraid. The second baby is coming. Give me another push."

"I don't think I can push anymore, Andrey," she sobs. "I'm so tired."

"Just give me two more pushes, my *lastochka*. Two more and we'll be done."

She shakes her head, but I grab her face and force her to look at me. "You don't need me to do this for you. You don't need anyone. You're strong, you're fierce, and I know you have two more pushes left inside you."

"Natalia, *now*," Dr. Abdulov orders.

She grips my hand tight and pushes.

"Excellent," Dr Abdulov cries. "Excellent. I see the head. One more push, Natalia."

There's another scream, and then the doctor stands back, another baby in his arms.

Natalia collapses against her pillow, her eyes rolling back with exhaustion.

"Our girls. You did it," I tell her. "You did it."

But Dr. Abdulov is staring down at our second little girl with a slight frown between his brows.

"What's wrong?" I bark.

Natalie's eyes snap open. She just gave birth to twins, but she's almost off the bed trying to get to the doctor. "Nothing is wrong. What do you mean? Are the babies—"

"They're fine," Dr. Abdulov assures us with a sheepish smile. "Both perfectly healthy. But it seems there was a slight misreading in previous scans." Dr. Abdulov hands the baby boy over to one of the nurses. "You are now the proud parents of a healthy baby girl *and* a healthy baby boy."

"Andrey," Natalia trills, "did you hear that?"

"I heard." I drop my lips to her forehead to hide my shock. "You did amazing."

Two nurses approach us with identical little bundles in their arms. One is wrapped in a pink blanket and the other in blue. They place our daughter on Natalia and our son on me.

The second the weight of my son is in my grasp, something shifts inside me—something cosmic, otherworldly, something larger than I am.

And I feel whole.

44

NATALIA

The moment my eyes open, I'm looking for my babies. *Does Grigory need a new diaper? Is Sarra hungry?*

For a week now, they are all I've been able to think about. I've had dreams of rocking them to sleep and warming bottles.

"They're still asleep." Andrey's voice is a warm whisper against the back of my ear. His arms are banded around me, and my head is pillowed on his chest.

I follow his finger to the bassinet rocking next to our bed. Sure enough, two little swaddles are tucked inside, safe and peaceful.

"Then I should be asleep, too." I let my eyes fall closed.

"But I want to talk to you."

I angle my head back, and the second I see his full lips pulled into a smile and his icy gray eyes on me, I can't find it in me to be annoyed that my nap was interrupted. "I can't believe you woke a new mother up. That has to be a felony."

"It's not. Trust me. I'm familiar with most of the felonies."

I laugh, but he's not exactly kidding. I had children with a dangerous man. Though it's been easy to forget the last week—being a father has softened Andrey's edges in ways I never expected. If someone had told me a month ago that I'd get a front row seat to Andrey Kuznetsov learning nursery rhymes on YouTube, I would've told them they were crazy. But he's working so hard to be a good father to our babies.

"What was so important you had to wake me up?"

He holds a finger to his lips and tips his head towards the corner of the room. Before my eyes can focus in the shadowy corner, I hear the soft snoring.

"Again?" Slowly, I make out the shape of Misha curled into the cushy nursing chair.

"Mr. Nanny is always reporting for duty."

I swat Andrey's arm. "He's great with the kids. He got Sarra down for her nap today."

"Yeah, but we have an actual nanny. An expensive one."

"That was your choice. Everyone reasonably priced wasn't good enough for our babies," I remind him. Misha shifts in the chair, and I can't help but smile. "He wants to be involved. And I love the company."

"At this rate, we'll have to add another bed in here. A whole mansion, and we're all going to sleep in the same room."

"Did you just wake me up to grouch about sleeping arrangements?"

He slides a palm down my arm, twirling our fingers together. Slowly, he lifts my hand into the air. "I guess I didn't need to wake you up. I've just been carrying this ring around for a while now, and I wanted to make sure it would fit."

I stare at my raised hand for several long seconds before I can even begin to process the massive solitaire diamond glimmering on my ring finger.

"Andrey!" I screech.

He quiets me with his lips, pressing a kiss to my mouth while I continue to gape at my hand.

"Do you like it?" he whispers.

"Do I like— How did you even lift my hand?" I test my hand in the air, feeling the weight of the ring. "This thing is enormous. It's— Is it mine?"

"If you're asking if I put someone else's ring on your finger, the answer is no."

"But it must have cost a fortune."

"Far less than what you're worth." He brings my hand to his lips for a kiss. "I would have had it on your hand sooner, but I wanted the band engraved."

I turn my hand over to read the inscription etched into the fine platinum. ***Forever started with you.***

The words blur behind a veil of tears that I can't control. "This is perfect. The ring. You. It all means so much to me."

"*You* mean so much to me."

My heart flutters. "I like this new Andrey. The Andrey who wears his heart on his sleeve and gets all sappy."

He smirks. "Now, I'm sappy?"

"In the best possible way."

Andrey smiles, taking it like the compliment I intended. He looks towards the bassinet where Sarra has a little arm nestled over her brother. "These children, this family... You all brought me back to life. And I will spend the rest of our lives trying to repay you for what you've given me."

"I don't need you to repay me for anything, Andrey. The only thing I need—the only thing I've ever needed—is you. Only you."

"Then that will be my vow to you. I'll always be there for you and our children. No matter what." He arches a brow. "If you'll have me, that is."

A shiver races down my spine. "I'd be honored to be your wife, Andrey Kuznetsov."

He kisses me long and hard, sealing our promise in a private moment that is all ours. When we break apart, I stare down at the ring on my finger like it might disappear.

Andrey pokes my side. "Your little sentinel is waking up."

Misha stirs in the chair. He's too long for it—I swear he's shot up a foot in the last six months—so as he stretches out his legs and arches his back, he fumbles off-center and the chair dumps him forward onto the floor.

As soon as he hits the ground, he jolts up, his hair mussed and his eyes puffy with sleep, looking around for the evil culprit who upended him.

I have to slap a hand over my mouth so I don't burst out laughing.

Misha blushes as he rubs the sleep from my eyes. "Sorry. I didn't mean to fall asleep." He stands with a stretch and then walks over to the bassinet. "Are they almost ready for bottles?"

"Misha," Andrey says, gesturing for him to sit down, "you realize you're not their nanny, right?"

"I know. I just wanna be useful."

"You don't have to be useful," I tell him. "You're a teenager. Go outside, get in the pool, play some soccer. I feel like I'm holding you back."

Misha sinks down onto the edge of the bed. "You're not. I enjoy spending time with you and the twins."

"And we love having the company. I just don't want you missing out on anything because you think you have to be here with us."

Misha just shrugs. "We're family. Where else would I be?"

He says it so matter-of-factly, and I'm less than two minutes out from a marriage proposal, so there's not a chance of my eyes staying dry. I swipe at my cheeks, and Misha eyes the ring on my finger.

He whistles. "He finally gave it to you."

I look from Misha to Andrey and back again. "You knew?"

Misha shrugs. "I am a spy, remember?" He laughs and pulls me in for a hug. "Congrats, Nat. I'm happy for you."

"I hope you haven't already heard about the other exciting news," Andrey says.

Misha's searching gaze tells me he has no idea what Andrey is about to say.

"I haven't even discussed this with Natalia yet, but only because I knew she'd agree."

Misha stiffens, his Adam's apple bobbing up and down slowly. "Okay…?" He looks as nervous as I feel.

"When Natalia and I get married, she'll carry my name. And the twins were born with my name. So it seems only fair that you should have the same name, too."

"You… you want me to be a Kuznetsov?"

I hold my breath. My heart really can't take these big emotional reveals.

"You just said it yourself: we're family," Andrey says simply. "But it's your choice. Whether you want to take my name or not, it doesn't change how I feel. This would just be a formality."

"What kind of formality?"

"Legally," Andrey explains. "Since Natalia and I would adopt you."

Andrey was so right. I agree. I absolutely, undoubtedly agree.

I reach for Misha's hand, my chest hitching with emotion. "You already feel like mine, Misha. But like Andrey said, no pressure. It's up to you."

Misha's eyes are glassy. He looks down at the twins. "But you already have the perfect family. You have two brand new babies—a boy and a girl. What would you want with a fourteen-year-old whose dad is…?"

His voice trails off, and I grab his chin, forcing his eyes to mine. "You're brave and loyal. You're kind and thoughtful and smart. What parents wouldn't want a child like that? Our family is only complete with you in it, Misha."

A tear rolls down his cheek as he turns slowly to Andrey.

"I feel the same way, Misha. We would love to make you an official part of this family—if you'll have us."

Misha opens his mouth, but he collapses into tears and I grab him and hold him against my shoulder as he cries freely.

"We're gonna take that as a yes," I whisper into his ear.

He laughs through his sobs, and I meet Andrey's eyes over the top of Misha's head.

We have our answer.

45

ANDREY

Sarra, like her mother, is still asleep when Grigory starts to stir. The girl sleeps like the dead. Remi can be barking at a squirrel outside the window while Grigory wails his little head off, and Sarra won't wake up.

Grigory, on the other hand, takes after me. He's restless once the sun falls, which is how we find ourselves wandering through the moonlit gardens together night after night. He seems to like the sound of my voice, though, so I've told him about how his grandmother designed the gardens. How she adored them as much as he seems to.

"You would've loved her," I tell him, kissing his head as we meander between trees and around flower beds.

Ivan successfully moved my mother to a new care facility three states over. I don't want to believe my father would really attack her, but I know better than to underestimate him. She has a full-scale security team and around-the-clock care.

The daily updates from the staff aren't exactly uplifting, though. They're full of temper tantrums, refusals to take her medications, long bouts of confusion. The transfer has her on edge, and she's been asking for her own mother a lot.

I understand the impulse. As the world around me gets messier, I want my family closer—Natalia, the twins, Misha. Hell, I get antsy when the dog is out of sight for too long. If I thought there was any chance it would work, I'd build hundred-foot tall walls and never leave this property.

But the danger has a way of slipping through the cracks. The only way to keep them safe is to root it out.

I walk Grigory through the corner of the garden where my mother spent most of her time. It looks different now than it did back then. The gardeners keep things trimmed and weeded, but I preferred the wildness of my mother's gardening. Regardless, I can still feel her here on quiet nights like these.

"Hopefully, one day, you'll get to meet her," I tell him. "She should be here with all of us. She's part of the family."

I point out different flowers to him and talk about constellations I know nothing about until Grigory lets out a whimper I recognize immediately.

"Hungry already?" I kiss the top of his head and walk back to the house. "Papa's got you."

We trudge back inside and into my office, and I prepare a bottle of formula. Then we settle back onto the couch as he feeds.

He's halfway through his milk when his hand flutters against my chest, curling into my t-shirt as his eyes start to get heavy. Nothing ever feels quite so pure.

I used to spend sleepless nights in this office, worrying over territories and enemies. It feels like a different life. A different man.

Not for long, though.

Grigory's eyes are almost closed when my phone lights up, vibrating on the coffee table. Shura's name appears on the screen, and that old life comes flooding back.

Trying not to bother my son, I answer quietly. "It's late, which means this can't be good."

"It's Nikolai," he explains sharply. "He's hit a few of our places. Two of the clubs, a restaurant."

"How bad is it?"

"Three dead, seven injured. Some damage to the properties themselves."

"Motherfucker."

"He left a note." Is it my imagination or is Shura's voice shaking with anger? "The same one at all three locations. I'll be at the manor soon, and I can show it to—"

"Tell me now." I snuggle a sleeping Grigory onto the sofa, building a dam of pillows around him before I stand up. Suddenly, I'm thrumming with untapped energy.

Shura sighs, then starts to read. "***Congratulations on the baby, Andrey. Fatherhood must be exhausting. No wonder you've been MIA lately. Enjoy the paternity leave; wish I had the luxury. My best—Nikolai.***"

"Fuck."

"I'm turning into the drive," Shura says. "I'll be in the office shortly."

A few minutes later, Shura sweeps into the office. He's red-faced and angry, but when he sees Grigory on the couch, he softens. "Is he okay?"

"I just got him to go down." I gesture for Shura to follow me to the opposite side of the room. "Where's the note?"

I read it again, not surprised by the contents, but surprised by how angry seeing it in writing makes me.

"*Mudak*," I hiss, tearing the paper to shreds. "He put a lot of effort into making sure my men would see this message."

"They're just cheap tactics."

"And they might actually work." I let the shredded pieces of Nikolai's message fall like snowflakes and then I stomp over them as I start pacing again.

"Your men will stick by you, 'Drey."

"Efrem was proof that that isn't true. It looks bad, Shura. Nikolai managed to hit me again while I was busy doing what? Changing diapers and playing Mr. Mom?"

The vein in Shura's jaw is twitching. "You're not 'playing' at anything. These are your children you're raising."

I stop short, my gaze turning on the sleeping baby on the couch. I can only see the apple of his cheek turned up towards the ceiling. Instantly, the guilt sweeps in on the heels of anger. "You're right." I shake my head. "You're fucking right. And I don't have to apologize to anyone for wanting to be there for them."

"I know you want to sort out shit with your father first—but we can't let Nikolai run wild, either."

"If only Slavik had been considerate enough to pick out a more convenient time for a takeover. It's the least he could have done." I stride over to my son and sit down beside him. "Having kids has shown me how little I know my own father. No matter what happens between Grigory and me, I could never raise a hand against my boy."

"That's because you're capable of something that Slavik was never capable of." He winces like he already regrets what he's about to say, but he plows ahead anyway. "Love."

I just laugh bitterly.

Shura drops down into a chair. "Blame Kat for the sentimentality. I wasn't like this before her."

"Our women have changed us," I agree. "I don't think that's a bad thing."

He tucks his hand into his pants pocket and withdraws a packet of unopened cigarettes. "Except now, we have something to lose."

"How long you been carrying those around?"

"Since Katya started fraternizing with the enemy," he replies darkly.

"She's doing it for the greater good."

"No offense, brother, but that thought doesn't keep me warm at night. Not when I know that *my* woman is keeping that stinking pile of horseshit warm at night instead. And yeah, I know she's not actually doing the warming herself," he snaps before I can interrupt. "But it doesn't make it any better."

I match Shura's scowl with one of my own. "If I thought she was in any real danger, I'd pull her out of there in a heartbeat. You know that, right?"

Shura nods slowly. "Still, there are factors that are out of your control. And that includes Viktor."

He looks exhausted. Gaunt and hollow. I start to wonder why I didn't notice sooner, but then Grigory hiccups in his sleep.

Oh, right.

I've been wrestling with sleepless nights of my own. Just in a totally different context. I bounce onto my feet, a lightbulb flashing suddenly over my head. "We have to start thinking outside the box if we're going to take down these bastards quickly. The sooner this is over, the sooner Katya's free from Viktor's clutches, the sooner Misha gets some closure, the sooner Nat and I can concentrate on our family."

Shura's eyebrows arch hopefully. "What do you have in mind?"

"A certain somebody who was on that jet with Slavik on his swan song out of here. The only one who never made it back."

The hope withers on Shura's face. "You're not serious?"

"Why the fuck not? We know she's still alive."

"Doesn't mean she knows shit."

"And what if she does?"

Shura rises to his feet to meet me, still frowning. My enthusiasm isn't catching, apparently. "Brother, if she knows anything of importance, she'll be closely watched. What if Slavik is expecting you to go to her?"

I snort. "Have you met my father? He thinks she's beneath him, which means he'll underestimate her."

Shura straightens up. "Okay, so we get her Stateside and talk to her. What if she knows nothing?"

I shrug. "Then it's back to the drawing board."

Though I pray it doesn't come to that.

46

NATALIA

I sit bolt upright. "Sarra?" I gasp. "Grigory?"

But the room is empty. The bed is cold. Even Remi is gone.

I shove the blankets to the end of the bed and grab my robe. I tiptoe through the silent house, expecting danger at every turn.

My thoughts feel wild and uncontrollable. *What if they aren't here? What if someone took them?*

I'm halfway down the stairs when I hear a cry.

"Sarra!" I sprint down the stairs, following the sound out to the patio.

Then I freeze in the doorway, taking in the scene in front of me.

Andrey is kneeling next to the baby bathtub, suds up to his elbows, no shirt on, and our daughter nestled along his forearm. Misha is cross-legged next to them, petting Remi.

Mila and Aunt Annie are on the swing, cooing at a freshly-swaddled Grigory. The air smells like lavender soap and powder.

The dog is the first one to notice me. Remi perks up and then pads over, tongue lolling happily.

"Natalia!" Andrey says when he sees me. "What are you doing out of bed? You were supposed to text if you needed anything."

He straightens up, and I'm thinking about getting back into bed right now. But not in the way he means. He may be a father, but there's no dad bod in sight for my man.

I walk over to him and reach for my freshly washed daughter. "I'm postpartum, not an invalid."

"That doesn't matter." He wraps Sarra in a fresh towel and deposits her into my arms. "You should still be resting."

"I had a full night of sleep, thanks to you." I reach up and stroke the dark circles under his eyes. "How about you sleep tonight and I'll take the night shift?"

"I can handle it," he says dismissively. "Why don't you sit down? I'll get you something to drink."

"Andrey, you don't have to—"

But he's already on his way to the kitchen in search of refreshments. Misha follows him. "I'll go help."

Sighing, I walk Sarra over to one of the lounge chairs and sink into it. "I'm capable of getting myself a drink."

"But you don't have to," Mila points out. "I wouldn't complain if a man wanted to wait on me hand and foot."

"I'm not complaining. I just—"

"Don't know how to let yourself be taken care of," Aunt Annie jumps in. "Let that man dote on you, sweetheart. It's good for you both."

"You hit the jackpot," Mila agrees. "Enjoy it."

"I know I'm lucky. I just feel a little useless. He's done all the midnight feedings this week."

"Well, you pushed two human beings out of your vagina," Mila drawls. "You're entitled to a little pampering. If Kat were here, she'd say—"

"Where has Kat been lately?" I interrupt. "I called her three times yesterday and she texted that she'd call back, but she never did."

Mila looks away from me quickly—a bit *too* quickly, in my opinion. "She's been busy at work."

"There's no way she's that busy. Something's going on with her."

Mila opens and closes her mouth a few times before she suddenly jumps out of her chair. "The boys are back with drinks. I'll take Sarra."

She plucks my daughter from my arms before I can protest. Then Andrey sits down next to me.

"Do you know what's happening with Katya?" I ask.

"You'd have to ask Shura."

"I would, but Shura's never around anymore, either. Same with Leonty and Olaf. Is there a game of hide-and-seek going on that I'm unaware of?"

"Missing them?"

I narrow my eyes. "No, but I feel like I'm missing something."

"You don't have to sit around and wait for the other shoe to drop, Nat."

I freeze, caught between his arms and my wild thoughts. Isn't that the exact reason I rolled out of bed this morning, wondering where my children were? Wondering why it was so quiet? Scared that everyone had disappeared on me?

I take a deep breath. "Sorry. I'm being irrational."

He kisses my temple. "I don't blame you. I haven't exactly given you a stress-free environment this past year."

"It's not your fault."

"It is." His silver eyes turn steely. "But I intend to change that. Soon."

Despite the warmth of his body nestled against mine, I feel cold. "What does that mean?"

He kisses me again. "Don't you worry about that."

My fingers curl around the shirt he must've tugged on when he was inside. "Andrey, I don't want you taking any unnecessary risks for my benefit. I know you need to deal with Slavik and Nikolai, but don't rush anything."

"I'm handling it."

"Andrey…"

He hushes me, placing a finger against my lips. "Don't worry, little bird. Remember my promise to you. I've got you. I've got this family."

I believe him, but I don't feel any less cold.

The only thing I can do is scoot my way into Andrey's embrace and hope that at some point, the feeling passes.

47

ANDREY

"Fair warning," Shura whispers, cracking the door open, "she's a viper."

"She survived Slavik," I say. "She has to be."

Shura shrugs and then ushers in the guest of honor. Ola struts through the door, her heels clicking along the hard woods. As she passes Shura, she slides her manicured nails right over his stubbled jaw. "Thank you, handsome."

He recoils with a scowl. "I'll be right outside if you need me, 'Drey."

She chuckles, hitching a thumb towards my second. "He's scared of me."

"That's because he's smart." I gesture to the chair across from me. "Sit down, Ola."

Despite it being three in the afternoon, Ola is dressed in a shimmering party dress that leaves little to the imagination. She smirks as she settles into the seat and crosses her legs, baring a long expanse of thigh. "Right down to business, per usual. When was the last time we saw each other?"

"I believe it was at Raya, a few weeks before you flew the coop with my father."

"Ah, yes," she titters. "Raya. What a shithole. You walked in on me giving your father a lap dance."

I grimace. "You were always my father's type. Like attracts like."

"And apples don't fall far from the tree. Is that why I'm here? Finally ready to scratch that itch?" She's looking at me through lowered lids as she leans forward, placing her hand on my thigh and slowly snaking it upwards.

I push her hand away. "I'm a married man."

She throws her head back and cackles. Apparently, in addition to the boob job, my father also bought her a new set of pearly whites. "That certainly never stopped your daddy."

"My father and I are very different men."

"Hopefully, that means you can keep a woman satisfied in bed." She flicks her tongue along her bottom lip. "Slavik was a selfish lover."

"I'm not remotely interested in my father's sloppy seconds, Ola."

Her manufactured smile slips for a fraction of a second. "Then why am I here?

"This club is where I do business. This right here—" I gesture between her and myself. "—is business."

"Well, consider me intrigued."

"Don't be. You won't like what I have to say."

She wipes her sweaty palms on her thighs, but tries to pass it off as an itch. "Honey, if the price is right, I will like everything you have to say."

I promised myself I'd remain calm, but my face twists into a sneer. "Once a hooker, always a hooker, huh, Ola?"

"I'm no hooker," she hisses. "I haven't been for over a decade now. I'm your father's woman. His wife in everything but name."

This time, it's my turn to laugh. "Cut the shit. You may use Kuznetsov as your last name whenever you can get away with it, but you're no longer Slavik's number one. In fact, you're not his at all anymore, are you?"

Her heavily lined eyes pinch together. "He still provides for—"

"He gives you a small stipend monthly in exchange for what?" I ask. "Your silence?"

She lets out a panicked breath. Then she clears her throat, runs a hand through her long blonde locks, and rises to her feet. Two steps and she's forced herself between my legs, her hand draping through the open collar of my shirt.

"You know, I always found you incredibly attractive, Andrey," she purrs. "Sometimes, when your father was on top of me, I used to close my eyes and imagine it was you instead."

She starts to slide her hand lower, but I grab her wrist and twist until she cries out. "I thought I made myself clear," I growl, staring directly into her wide, terrified eyes. "I'm married. Touch me again and you'll regret it. Try giving your clients a handjob with no fingers."

I push her away, causing her to stumble back. She sinks back down without a word, still massaging her wrist.

"Now, let's skip the bullshit and cut straight to the chase, shall we?"

Glowering, Ola drops the whole seductress routine altogether. Her shoulders hunch and her legs and hands hang limply at her sides. "If I tell you anything, he'll know it was me. He'll hunt me down and kill me for betraying him."

"And your alternative is what? Refusing me now and dying on the spot?"

"I thought you were a different man than your father."

"I am. In purpose, if not in methods. I will do whatever it takes to protect my family. But I will do *whatever* it takes. Do you understand what I'm saying?"

The flush on her chest rises to her cheeks. "I'll tell you anything you want to know," she agrees. "But I have conditions."

"I never expected anything less. What do you want?"

"Freedom, money, and safety," she ticks off on her fingers. "I want to disappear from Slavik's radar. If he finds me, he'll—"

"You have my word. Tell me what you know and you'll have all three."

She raises her eyebrows. "Just like that?"

"I didn't build my reputation on nothing. The question is, do you have any information that's worth my while?"

She crosses her legs. "Nikolai and Slavik are working together."

It takes some effort to keep my face from betraying any emotion. "Since when?"

"Years now. Around the time Slavik started to grow restless." Her face pinches. "Around the time he started to get bored with me."

"Life in Russia wasn't what he expected?"

"Russia had changed since Slavik was last there. He was no longer the top dog and he hated it. He used to be—I wouldn't call him a gentleman… but charming, maybe? But those last few years with him…" She pulls up the large gold cuff on her wrist and shows me a thin, winding scar. "He got pretty brutal."

"I have to admit, I was surprised to learn that you were still alive."

"I may have lost my appeal to him, but I didn't lose my wits. I convinced him I was in love with him, that my loyalty was absolute. He believed me."

"Stroking his ego is always a good idea."

"Among other things." Her brows jump suggestively. "He started monitoring the situation over here, following your movements. When he realized how far you'd expanded on Kuznetsov territory, he was livid. Then he sensed an opportunity."

"He wanted to take what I'd built. Is that when he contacted Nikolai?"

She nods. "He was careful about how he approached the Rostov boy. But eventually, the two had a meeting. He flew Nikolai into Moscow on a private jet. He really rolled out the red carpet."

"How did he manage to bring Nikolai to the table?"

She shrugs. "I have no idea. I wasn't privy to the meetings. I just heard snippets of what happened afterwards. Even then, it wasn't much."

Silence falls between us. I push myself to my feet and saunter over to the tinted window. The street below is quiet. Apart from a few New Yorkers walking their dogs, there's nothing amiss. No sign of my enemies.

But they're out there.

They're always out there.

"So did I deliver?" Ola asks, unable to hide the tremor in her voice.

I glance at her over my shoulder. She's my age, no older than thirty-four or thirty-five, but she looks so much older. Wearier.

"Go back to your room and wait there. I'll have Shura bring you what you need."

"How do I know he won't just bust in and slit my throat?"

"You don't. I guess you'll just have to trust me."

Realizing she doesn't have another option, she turns and leaves. For once, she does so without a parting quip.

As soon as she's gone, Shura slips through the door. "She could be lying."

I'm not surprised he was listening in. I'd be more shocked if he wasn't. "Maybe," I agree. "But it doesn't change anything."

Nikolai and Slavik. Slavik and Nikolai. At the end of the day, they both need to go.

It doesn't matter to me which one dies first.

48

ANDREY

The door to my office flies open and Katya hurtles inside. She's teetering on her heels, a leopard-print dress and thick fur coat drowning out her small frame.

Shura reaches to steady her, but she barrels past him and dives into my bathroom. The sound of her retching answers the questions neither of us have had the time to ask.

Shura rushes to the door, but before he can knock or go in, I stop him. "Natalia never wanted me around when she was throwing up. I doubt Kat will be any different."

Shura sighs and retraces his steps back to my desk. "If he's touched her, so help me God, I'm going to end the fucker's life today."

"Let's wait for Katya to tell us what's going on, shall we?"

A few minutes later, Katya emerges, pink in the face as she dabs her lips with a paper towel. "Sorry about that, boys. I'm feeling a little rundown." Sinking into a seat, she lets out an exhausted sigh. "So, anyway. Info. Nikolai is working with Slavik."

"There's the corroboration you wanted," Shura mumbles.

Katya spins to me. "You already knew?"

"We found out a few hours ago."

Her eyes are wide and curious. "How?"

"Ola, Slavik's former mistress. I flew her down from Russia and she sang like a canary."

"Well, she wasn't lying," Kat confirms. "Apparently, Slavik's been planning this takeover for years. He got Nikolai on board and it accelerated everything."

"Viktor told you all this?"

"Just before I left him. I doubt he'll remember what he said to me when he wakes up, though. He was pretty drunk."

"It's not even five o'clock," Shura spits. Then he eyes her obnoxious dress. "Did he buy you that monstrosity?"

She shifts uncomfortably in place. "I've gotten away with not having sex with him, Shura. I can't refuse his gifts, too."

"You've really got him convinced, haven't you?"

"Easy, brother," I warn. "She's just doing her job."

"Who knew she'd be so damn good at it?" he mutters.

Kat whirls on him. "Are you accusing me of something? Don't be a coward. Spit it out. Say it to my fucking—"

I insert myself between them before Kat can get her manicured claws within striking range of my second-in-command. "He's not accusing you of anything, Kat. Shura's just—"

"Don't fucking speak for me!" Shura bellows. "I'm perfectly capable of explaining what I mean on my own."

"Go ahead then!" Katya replies. "Tell me what you really think of me!"

I meet Shura's eyes, silently advising him. *Don't say something you'll regret later.*

He promptly ignores my silent warning. "I think you're enjoying playing Viktor's whore."

Something you'll regret...

Like that.

Cringing, I close my eyes as Katya's breathing hitches. "You... you... *asshole!*"

Then she bursts into tears.

Far from doubling down on his rage, Shura looks panicked. "Kat—"

She holds up her hand, nearly face-palming Shura. "Don't talk to me. From now on, I'm addressing Andrey only." She turns her back on Shura and looks at me, tears still running unchecked down her cheeks. "There's one more thing you should know. The hit on Mila is still active."

"Yeah, I didn't expect that to disappear overnight," I admit. "My brother doesn't forgive a slight easily."

"It's more than that." Kat tugs on the hem of her dress. "He doesn't just want payback; he wants Mila out of the picture altogether."

"What is my brother's plan, Kat?" I ask gently, holding up a hand to stop Shura from butting in.

"He wants to... remarry."

"Oh, *fuck* no!" Shura explodes. "He wants to marry you, doesn't he?"

Katya winces and it's clear that Shura's right. "Has he asked you yet, Katya?"

She nods. "Pretty much."

"And what did you say?" Shura grits.

"I had to say yes!" Still, she refuses to meet his eyes. "Why do you think he told me about Nikolai and Slavik in the first place?"

Shura kicks the side of my desk hard enough that the entire thing slides a few inches to the left. "How much longer are we going to keep this up? Until you're married? Until you have his first child?"

"Shura..." Kat's eyes are still glistening with tears. But the anger has vanished from her face, her voice. She just looks broken now.

That's when I get it. When the pieces click.

Unfortunately, Shura doesn't seem to have reached the same conclusion.

"Katya, I know you feel you need to do this for Nat's sake, but trust me: she wouldn't want you putting yourself in this position for her." He gets on one knee in front of her and grabs her hands. "Please, I'm begging you—this has gone on long enough. You need to get out while you still can."

There's a beat of silence.

Then: "Okay."

Shura's jaw drops. "E-excuse me?"

Another tear falls down Katya's cheek. She turns to me. "Andrey, I think it's best for me to get out now. Is that okay?"

I can only nod. "Yes. Especially now."

Shura turns to me with a frown. "What does that mean? 'Especially now'?"

Katya touches his face, drawing his eyes back to her. "Shura… I'm pregnant."

If the man wasn't already on his knees, he would be now. He's speechless.

"Things have been so hectic lately that I didn't even notice that my period was late. But then the last few days… the morning sickness…"

His jaw tightens. "Is it—"

"If you ask me if the baby is yours, I will kick you in the nuts so hard that this will be your first and last child. Do you understand me, Shura Federov?"

A dumbfounded smile spreads slowly across his lips. He rises, grabs Kat with a hand on either side of her face, and smashes his lips against hers.

I turn away to give them some privacy.

"Idiot," Kat murmurs through a bubble of laughter.

Shura hugs her close, grinning like a fool over the top of her head.

But the second his eyes meet mine, his smile melts away. His eyes are cold and hard. "I'm going to be a father, 'Drey. I'm going to... *Fuck.* We have to end this," he breathes. "For all of our children."

49

NATALIA

"I cannot wait for my doctor's appointment."

"That's not something I ever thought I'd hear from you," Kat teases.

I pull myself out of the pool and slip onto the empty chair between the girls. "It's been six weeks and this might be the day I get cleared to start working out as normal."

"Oh. Of course. *'Working out.'*" Kat bites back a giggle as she nods not-at-all seriously. "I know how serious you are about *working out.*"

Mila cackles. "Yes, I too get excited about healthy, vigorous physical exercise. Preferably of the horizontal variety."

"That's not what I meant, assholes." As both my friends throw me skeptical glares, I toss my hands up. "Oh, alright—that is what I meant. It's been almost two months of no sex and I'm ready—"

"To get plowed?" Katya offers.

"For the no-pants dance?"

I wrinkle my nose. "Crude, but... not inaccurate."

I felt ready to go a couple weeks ago, but Andrey is a stickler for the rules where my health is concerned. He won't lay a finger on me until the doctor gives us the green light. His concern for me was touching at first, but now, I'd prefer a very different kind of touching.

"I thought Andrey would be the one itching to get me to this appointment, but..." I stare down at my conservative swimsuit. It's a bodysuit more than anything. The three-quarter zip is open, revealing the cleavage nursing has given me, but otherwise, I'm covered from neck to wrist.

"But what?" Mila prods.

I eye her tiny red bikini with no small amount of envy before gesturing to my own body. "I don't exactly look my best."

"For God's sake, Nat!" Mila cries. "You just had *twins*!"

"Right. Which is why Andrey basically pushed me off of him two nights ago." I put on a new lingerie set, sure I'd be able to seduce him. But he barely looked at me.

Kat waves me off. "You're crazy, girl. He wants you; he just doesn't want to impose on your body before it's ready."

"But it's ready. I'm ready!" I frown down at the pooch of my stomach. "Well, mentally, I'm ready."

"You're being ridiculous." Mila reaches for the sunscreen. "You're sexy as hell. Say the word and *I'll* take you to bed."

"Get rid of this tent you're calling a swimsuit and break out the cheeky bikinis. Andrey won't be able to help himself."

"You're one to talk. Why aren't *you* in a bikini?"

Katya never misses an opportunity to jump in the pool. But today, she's opted for sitting in the shade with her shorts and an oversized t-shirt I assume is Shura's.

She gives me a secretive smile. "Ah, well, funny you should ask… I have a little something to tell you two."

She continues smiling at us until I shake her shoulders. "Now is not the time to get good at secrets, Kat. Spit it out."

"I'm pregnant!"

I'm still dripping wet, but that doesn't stop me from throwing myself into her chair and bear-hugging the hell out of her while I scream.

"You're dripping on me," she gripes, though I can hear the smile in her voice.

Mila joins us in the huddle, squeezing us both. "I can't believe this!"

Katya finally manages to push us back to our own chairs. "I'm almost three months along. I didn't find out right away. I thought some of the symptoms were because of—" She cuts herself off. "Whatever, it doesn't matter. I'm so happy!"

"Why wouldn't you be?" Mila sighs. "You're having a baby with the man you love. What could be better?"

Katya shrugs. "I just never saw myself with a family. I fantasized about promotions and Stella McCartney suits. Not babies and white picket fences."

"Our kids won't be that far apart in age." I squeeze her hand. "This is gonna be so much fun!"

She laughs nervously. "I just hope I don't ruin this kid."

"You'll be fine. And if you need help, I'm here for you."

"We all are," Mila adds. "How does Shura feel about this?"

"He was thrilled. You know him—he's already drawing up the next twenty years of our lives." I hold my heart and Mila starts to get all misty-eyed. "Apparently, we're going to have a ton more kids. He wants a baseball team."

"And I'm sticking by it," Shura interrupts.

The three of us whip around to see our men coming down the stairs. I rush over and give Shura a huge hug. "I'm so happy for you two."

Gentleman that he is, Shura makes no mention of his damp shirtfront as he sits down beside Katya and drapes an arm around her shoulders.

Leonty nudges Mila. "We should get started. I want competing baseball teams."

Mila chokes on her orange juice. "Excuse me, but this body can't handle a baseball team. It's gonna be one and done for me."

Leonty just winks. "We'll see about that."

Their playful banter is like music to my ears. Is it possible that life can be like this? My friends happy? My family together? Everyone safe and thriving?

"What's going on in that pretty little head of yours, *lastochka*?" Andrey slides a hand up my thigh, but stops a few inches short of where I really want it.

"Oh, nothing," I say coyly. "Just peeking into the future."

"And? What do you see?"

"Exactly this," I say. "But with a lot more children."

He raises his eyebrows. "Ours or theirs?"

"A mix." I blush. "Maybe not a whole baseball team, but I do want a few more."

"Sounds like a plan."

Those silver eyes of his are so bright, but the clouds hanging over our heads are never far away.

"I'm not in a rush, though," I add. "We both need time."

One eyebrow notches higher on his forehead. "Why do I need time?"

"Well…" I clear my throat self-consciously. "Slavik and Nikolai, for one."

His mouth turns down instantly. He knows how I feel about putting down roots with those threats out there, but I still hate having to bring it up. I want to live in this perfect little bubble.

"Of course. I understand." He squeezes my thigh and gets to his feet.

"Where are you going?"

"I have a little work to take care of before your appointment this evening."

Without warning, he strolls across the lawn. Even the others look taken back by his sudden departure. Grabbing my cover-up, I pull it on and run after him.

"Andrey! Wait."

He stops at the staircase. "Don't run. I don't want you exerting yourself."

"I'm not the one running." I cross my arms over my chest. "I didn't mean to upset you, but—"

"You didn't upset me."

"Then why did you take off like a swarm of locusts were coming after you?"

He sighs, his face softening. "My reaction had nothing to do with you. It's Nikolai and Slavik. I want them gone."

"So do I, but we can't let them steal the little moments. We have to try to enjoy ourselves."

"It's hard when you can't even sleep at night," he bites out. When he sees my confusion, he drags a hand through his hair. "You've been having nightmares. You said his name."

I don't have to ask whose name I said. I remember the nightmare plenty well.

"Shit… I'm sorry."

"What are you apologizing for, Natalia? It's my fault."

"No, it's not. Don't say that."

With a sigh, he leans in and presses a kiss to my forehead. "I know you've only wanted to do therapy once a week since the twins arrived, but I think it might help to see her twice a week like you used to."

I'm so determined to throw him some sort of bone that I find myself nodding. "Okay, I will."

"Good." He grazes my cheek with the tips of his fingers. "I'll pick you up in an hour."

With that, he turns and walks off, leaving my skin tingling, my heart aching, and my core throbbing.

50

NATALIA

"Thank fuck that's over," Andrey rumbles the moment we pull out of the parking lot. "It's unnatural to force a man to watch his wife with another man between her legs."

"Oh, for God's sake," I scoff. Secretly, I'm kinda flattered by the chest-banging, *she's-my-woman* vibe he's got going. "He's my doctor. You didn't mind when he was pulling the twins out of me."

"Totally different situation."

"Well, whatever. I'm just glad I can start working out again."

His head swivels in my direction, eyebrows raised. "Have you been pounding pre-workout lately or something? I've had a gym on the property since we met, and I've never seen you use it once."

"That was before."

"Before what?" He looks over at me like he doesn't know. Like it's not painfully obvious exactly what I mean.

I shift uncomfortably in my seat. "I want my pre-baby body back. I'm sure you do, too."

He arches those dark eyebrows higher. "I like your body exactly the way it is."

"Yeah, I'm sure the stretch marks are a real turn-on," I snort. "The stuff fantasies are made of."

Andrey isn't laughing, though. "I have a woman who carried my children, gave birth to them, and has spent the last six weeks nursing and nurturing them. That is absolutely what fantasies are made of, Natalia."

I purse my lips. "Yeah. Sure. Totally."

Suddenly, the car swerves.

I grip the door, biting back a scream as Andrey parks on a deserted side street. "Andrey!" I shriek. "What are you doing?"

He turns to me after throwing the car in park. "I'm trying to figure out where I failed." He turns to me. "Because somehow, you're under the impression that I don't find you attractive."

My cheeks are burning red. "Well, we haven't exactly had sex recently."

"Because up until a few minutes ago, you weren't medically cleared for sex."

"I've been fine for the last two weeks and I... You know what? Never mind. This is so not a big deal. Let's just go home, okay?"

Andrey takes his hands off the wheel. "The night you wore that pink thing to bed, I had to sneak off in the middle of the night to jerk off before I could get any sleep. I nearly rubbed myself raw."

"You *what?*"

"Natalia, you have no fucking clue just how sexy you are. Right now, exactly the way you are." He curls a hand around my waist and suddenly, I find myself flying over the center console, landing right on Andrey's lap. He grabs my hand and places it on his crotch. "What do you feel?"

My eyes go wide. "You're hard."

He smiles, leaning his seat back so that my spine isn't hitting the steering wheel anymore. His hands glide down my back and squeeze my hips.

"Andrey," I squeal as he raises my skirt, hiking it around my waist. "What are you— We can't! Not here."

"Why the hell not?"

"Because…" I look around. This street appears deserted, but that doesn't mean it'll stay that way. "We're out in the open! Anyone who passes by will be able to see us."

His fingers drift up my thighs and push aside my panties. "Then let's give them a show."

"Let's just wait." I try to push him away even as I grind myself against his cock. "When we get home, we can—"

"I've waited long enough, *lastochka*," he growls, nipping at my ear as his fingers slip inside me. "I'm done waiting."

I stop caring about passersby around the same time I plant my palms on the roof of the car and roll myself onto Andrey's fingers. Dr. Abdulov and the Pope himself could be in the backseat, and I wouldn't be able to stop.

He circles his thumb over my center, and I cry out. It's embarrassing how close I already am. How much I've been waiting for this.

But Andrey doesn't seem to mind. His lips brush against the shell of my ear. "I've missed the way you respond to me."

He strokes his fingers out and back in, and I arch my back until my shoulder blades hit the horn. I'm only vaguely aware of the sound. It's nothing more than white noise to me now.

I'm too consumed with Andrey—his intense eyes, his perfect lips.

I scramble to unbutton his pants, and if there was any doubt about his attraction to me, it's gone the second he springs free. When I wrap my hand around his length, he growls. He's strung so tight that he can barely move as I press him to my entrance and slide down, down, *down*.

We sink together with a mutual sigh of relief, and I press my forehead to his. "I've missed you."

"I'm right here, *lastochka*." He folds his fingers through mine, wrapping our arms around my lower back so he can work into me deeper. "I'll always be right here."

We move together until the car is rocking back and forth. Until our panting fogs the windows.

"How could you have any doubt that I wanted you, baby?" Andrey snarls as he slams into me from below. "This is what I want. You and me, always…"

The orgasm robs me of an answer. For a long time, all I can do is moan and give into it. Until, finally, it sets me back down, breathless and sweaty and spent.

"This is what I want, too," I whisper to him. "Always."

51

ANDREY

Leonty fills the screen of the video call at a low angle, giving me a view of his chin and straight up his nostrils.

"Where's Mila?" I ask.

"I've got eyes on her." Leonty twists the phone around so that I can see Mila's silhouette through the glass windows. "She's sorting out the gift for Nat. Apparently, I have horrible taste and my suggestions weren't helpful, so I've been relegated to idling in the car along the curb."

"Have you spotted any suspicious activity?"

"It's New York," Leonty retorts. "Everyone here looks suspicious."

There are times when I admire my cousin's lighthearted, easygoing nature. There are times when I do not.

"Are you sure she's okay in there alone?"

"If I didn't think she was, I'd be in there with her." He sighs. "I've been a bit overprotective this week because of Viktor's hit out on her. She says I need to give her space, so that's what I'm trying to do."

"Give her space when she's back in the manor," I reply. "Not when you're out in the open."

"Don't let Mila hear you or she'll gripe at you about being overprotective, too." He runs a hand through his stubble. Ironically, it only makes him look more boyish. "Ah, here she comes."

Instead of getting into the passenger seat, Mila stops outside Leonty's door and pokes her head into the window to share the screen.

"I placed the order," she informs me. "It should be ready in about a week."

"Good. Now, why don't the two of you get back to the manor?"

Mila frowns. "Are you kidding? This is the first time I've been out of the house in weeks!"

Before I can tell her to stop taking unnecessary risks, Leonty beats me to the punch. "Baby, there's an active hit hanging over your head, remember? We've tempted fate enough by coming out at all today. Let's just get home."

Her lips jut out in a pout. "What's one more hour?"

"Mila," Leonty grits, his tone harder than I've ever heard it.

"Oh, alright. I'll come home like a good girl." Jabbing a finger at me, she adds, "But you can at least give me five minutes to grab something from the chocolate shop next door. Kat's been craving cocoa lately. I want to surprise her with something sweet."

Before either one of us can say anything, she's turned and swept into the store.

"Women," Leonty sighs, unbuckling his seatbelt. "I'll go in with—"

The unmistakable sound of gunshots blast through the air. Leonty nearly drops the phone, leaving me staring at a tumbling whorl of color.

"Fuck!" he screams. "Mila!"

The screen flashes before he dumps the phone somewhere. All I see is darkness, but I can hear every word.

"Motherfuckers!" Leonty screams under a torrent of splintering sound.

I hear glass breaking, more gunshots, and the panic of terrified screams. "Mila! Mila, stay with me, baby. Please."

I end the call and dial 911.

Shura, Kat, and Natalia come barreling around the corner just as I'm giving the emergency dispatcher Mila and Leonty's location.

"What happened?" Natalia asks, her face pale.

"There was an attack on Mila," I rasp. "I'm heading there now."

"I'll come with you," Shura says before darting out of the manor to fire up the Escalade. Katya follows behind him without a word.

"I'm coming, too!" Natalia insists.

"Natalia, I think it's better if—"

"Mila's my friend!" she explodes in my face. "And I will not sit here and wait for news when I could be with her. I'm coming."

I briefly consider tying her down and forcing her to stay, but we don't have the time. "Fine, but you're to stay by my side the entire time. Is that clear?"

She nods. "Always."

Leonty is slumped on the floor of the emergency ward when we get to the hospital. Elbows resting on his knees, his head hanging between his shoulder blades.

He looks up, eyes red-rimmed, dried tears etched onto his cheeks. "Shit, you all came."

"Of course we all came." Natalia grabs his arm, holding on like she's afraid to lose him, too. "Where is she?"

"They wheeled her in twenty minutes ago for emergency surgery." Leonty hiccups. "Fuck... there was so much blood..."

"Mila's strong, Leonty," Kat chimes in. "She'll make it."

Leonty looks past Kat to me. "You were right, Andrey. I should never have let her out of my sight. Not even for a second. This is all my fault."

I squat down in front of my broken cousin and clasp him by the shoulders. "Stop this, man. Mila needs you to be strong for her. Blaming yourself won't solve anything."

His eyes are locked on mine, but it's like he's looking through me. "If she dies... what will I do?"

Natalia wraps her arm around him and he sobs against her shoulder. Katya sits on his opposite side, patting his arm. I join Shura in the corner.

"Thank fuck for the girls," Shura rasps. "I wouldn't know what to do."

I don't say a word. I just nod in agreement.

Every minute that ticks by feels like an eternity. I pace the corridor, willing the emergency door to open. Willing some nurse to come offer us some kind of update about Mila's condition.

Two minutes pass.

Five.

Ten.

Twenty.

After a while, Natalia leaves Leonty with Katya and walks over to me. I pull her into my arms and kiss the top of her head.

"I hate that he has to go through this," she whispers, nuzzling into my chest. "I'm so worried for Mila. Terrified for the both of them. But I'm so relieved that it isn't you and me in their position." She chokes on her own words. "Does that make me a horrible person?"

"Not in the slightest," I assure her. "Tragedy makes you grateful for what you have left, even if you lose something."

Natalia bites her lip. "Do you think she'll survive?"

"All we can do now is hope."

Finally, the doors swing open and Mila's doctor steps out.

Leonty beats us all there. "Is she okay? Is she alive?"

There's a pregnant pause. "She's alive and stable."

"Oh, thank God!" Natalia mumbles, bending over as though she can't stand the relief. "Can we see her?"

"Soon. She's being wheeled into a private room as we speak. She lost a lot of blood, but she was extremely lucky. The bullet missed her major organs…"

As the doctor drones on about the details of the procedure, I grasp Natalia tightly, savoring the solid feel of her. The warmth of her. Her pulse, softness, smell.

A few minutes later, Leonty goes off with the doctor to see Mila. The rest of us congregate outside her room.

Shura meets my eyes above the women's heads. Silently, I gesture for him to follow me down the corridor. "Do you think it's possible to keep this quiet?" he murmurs.

"I think it's too late for that already," I admit. "Viktor's thugs will have spread the word by now."

Our conversation is cut short when Leonty reappears, gesturing the girls forward. "You can see her if you want. She's still unconscious, but I think she'd appreciate you being there all the same."

I'm about to follow them in when my phone starts to ring. When I see who's calling, I curse under my breath.

"Is it him?" Shura asks.

I nod. "You go in. I'll handle this."

The moment the door swings shut, I answer the call.

"Is it fucking true?" he yells. "Is my daughter dead?"

"Your daughter is still very much alive, Ivan," I assure him.

"I heard there was an attack. That Mila was the target—"

"There was an attack, yes, and yes, Mila was the target. She's just out of surgery. She's unconscious, but stable. The doctor expects her to make a full recovery."

"Surgery," Ivan croaks. "They tried to kill her…"

"But they didn't. She's still alive, Ivan."

"You promised me. You vowed that you would keep her safe."

"Listen—"

"No, *you* listen. My daughter was hurt under your watch. What good is your protection if it lands you in the fucking hospital?"

"Calm down, Ivan—"

"A *pakhan* who can't keep his own safe is no *pakhan* at all."

My hand clenches into a fist. "Careful now."

"No, I think you should be the one to be careful. The others should know exactly what they're risking, allying themselves with the likes of you."

"Don't forget who you're speaking to, Ivan."

The pause on the other side of the line is rife with tension, laced with fear. "I haven't forgotten a goddamn thing."

"Good. Viktor will be dealt with. That's a promise."

He hangs up without bothering to reply, leaving dead air ringing in my ears.

52

ANDREY

It's like shooting fish in a barrel.

Viktor has one arm chained to the bedframe by a pair of fuzzy red handcuffs, but that's about all of him I can see. Two naked women make up the rest of the picture. One of them seems to have lost her tongue down his throat. The other must've lost hers somewhere between his legs.

Before I can gag, I pull out my gun and aim at the bedpost looming over Viktor's head. Even with the silencer screwed on, the *pop* of the discharge is enough to make both women scream.

Neither one screams as loud as Viktor, though. I suspect that has something to do with the second woman reacting to the unexpected noise by clamping her jaw closed.

Poor bastard.

He's cursing up a storm and clutching himself as the women scurry in search of their clothes.

"Looks like you're bleeding, brother," I remark.

"Pity. I was hoping she'd bite it clean off," Leonty mutters.

The women are quivering from head to toe. When I incline my head to the door, they bolt without a backward glance at Viktor.

"I-I have security here with—"

"Bullshit." Spit flies from Leonty's mouth as he paces along the foot of the bed.

Shura drags a chair from the corner and sits like he's anxious for the show.

I'm eager myself.

"There's no one here with you because you're not important enough to require security, you fucking *mudak*." Without warning, Leonty lunges forward and lands a solid blow to Viktor's jaw.

"Fuuuck!" Viktor bellows, straining against his handcuffs. Despite how cheap the cuffs look, they're holding up just fine. The zip-ties I brought might not be necessary after all. "When Slavik finds out about this—"

"He'll send us all gift baskets for taking you off his hands," Leonty growls.

I only agreed to let him come on the condition that he controlled himself and followed orders. I'm not sure this qualifies.

He towers over my brother, top lip curled back. "I should put a bullet through your fucking mouth."

"Leonty," I caution. "Breathe."

With a snarl, he backs away to the furthest corner of the room. Shura is handling himself somewhat better, but even he's white-knuckling the back of the chair like he wishes it was Viktor's neck.

"I only did what any one of you would have done in my place!" Viktor cries out, his voice cracking. "My honor was at stake—"

"What fucking honor does a worthless rat like you have?" Shura seethes.

Viktor ignores Shura and focuses on me. "Can you let me out of these things?" he begs, pulling at the cuffs.

"You got yourself into them," I say. "You get yourself out. It's time you learned that lesson."

"Brother—"

"Oh, *now*, I'm your brother?"

He tries to push himself upright, but the cuffs have him chained in place. "Listen, you've humiliated me, I've humiliated you—"

"Don't flatter yourself. You don't have the power to humiliate me."

He flinches before his face hardens into that cruel, arrogant mask I know so well. "I heard you're a father now. Boy or girl?"

"Boy," I say on impulse.

Viktor's eyes dull. "An heir, then."

"Not if you have anything to say about it. Isn't that right, *brother*?"

"Don't be ridiculous," Viktor mumbles. "I would never wish harm on your son."

"That's the thing about you, Viktor," I sigh, turning my back on him and heading towards the door. "I can't believe a word you say anymore."

Shura gets to his feet. Only Leonty stays where he is. He cracks his knuckles. "Now?"

"What are you doing? What is he—" Viktor looks from me to Leonty. "Andrey! Brother!"

"You have fifteen minutes." I ignore Viktor and address only Leonty before I walk out. "But don't get too carried away. I need him alive."

When Viktor splutters awake again, he's naked and shivered, caked in blood. All of my *vory* surround him, but his eyes dart wildly around the room.

I know what he's looking for.

He won't find it here.

"Welcome, *brat*," I greet, ignoring the gnawing in my gut as I step forward. "This is judgment day."

I pull a scalpel from behind my back and it winks in the lights. I tap it against the heel of my hand as I approach him.

"Andrey," Viktor pleads, "you can't do this to me. I'm your brother!"

I raise my arm and circle in place, pointing the scalpel at the dark-eyed men forming the loose circle around us. "*These* are my brothers, Viktor. You are simply a traitor."

"I'm no traitor!" he yelps. "I always had your back—"

I laugh—a dark, cold laugh that has Viktor cringing back into silence. "I suppose you did have my back. All the better to stab me in it, right? Then again, I shouldn't have expected anything less from a coward."

Viktor's mouth curls down. "I'm not a coward—"

"No?" I turn around as the crowd of men part. Ivan strides between them, stopping where Viktor is restrained, his face twisted into an ugly grimace. "What do you call a man who orders his own wife's death?"

"Ivan…" Blood drips down Viktor's jaw and over his chest. The mark of the Kuznetsov Bratva is barely visible on his chest beneath the crusted grime. He smells like a slaughterhouse. The next few minutes will do him no favors in that department.

"You have the audacity to look me in the face? To call me by my name?" Ivan roars, drawing himself up to his full height. "After what you did to my daughter?"

There's a moment where I wonder if Viktor will beg for his life. Maybe, for once, he'll find some humility.

Then he sneers, and I can only sigh. Tigers never change their stripes, I suppose.

"Your daughter is a *whore*!" he spits. "She deserved what she got!"

Before Ivan can do him any damage, Leonty beats him to the punch—literally. He flies from the outer rim of the circle and cracks Viktor across the face with a wicked backhand, as if he didn't get enough of that when I left them alone in the whorehouse.

Viktor's teeth clack together and his eyes roll in their sockets.

Leonty looms over him, ready to deal out more. "Say another word about her, and I will cut out your damn tongue."

Ivan nods approvingly and rejoins his men, all of whom are wearing satisfied smirks.

"This is ridiculous," Viktor blanches as the circle reforms. "You've really brought me here to punish me over a *woman*?"

"It's a weak man that arranges a hit on his wife," I say. "It's an even weaker man that turns his back on his family."

"You're no family of mine. Not anymore."

"Those may just be the truest words you've ever spoken."

I know what I have to do. I'm prepared to do it. But when I look in my brother's eyes, I see the little boy who came to me wailing when he had nightmares.

That boy is long gone, though.

And he's never coming back.

I twist my scalpel in my hands. "Since we're both in agreement, it's time to make the parting official."

Viktor spasms, trying to free himself from his restraints. "No! Let me go. Let me the fuck out of here! If you kill me—"

"Kill you? As if I care whether you live or die. No, Viktor. I've brought you here to sever you from my Bratva once and for all." I place the tip of my blade against the tattoo on his chest. "This is *my* mark. You've worn it with *my* permission. As of this moment, consider that permission withdrawn."

I press the blade to his skin and do what I must.

Viktor screams and thrashes at first, but his energy wanes quickly. By the end, he's a pale, shivering mess. He's barely even conscious. And the tattoo is no longer a part of him.

"Unchain him and leave him naked on Slavik's doorstep," I order. "Viktor is his problem from now on."

My men move to do my bidding, but Ivan stands. "Every man in this room is depending on the Kuznetsov Bratva to retain power and influence. Viktor was meant to be your successor. With him gone—"

"Nothing has changed," I finish for him. "Do you have no faith in my victory, Ivan?"

"Of course I do," he splutters. "I am simply being practical. You need a successor."

Shura's jaw is a hard line. He holds my gaze, and I can hear the words he can't voice. *You promised Natalia.*

What I promised her was to keep our children safe.

Which is what I intend to do.

"I'm winning this war, brothers," I proclaim, addressing all the men standing around me. "And I also plan on living a very long time. But since this seems to be a matter of some concern, let me clear your minds…"

The room goes silent.

"I have a successor. My son, Grigory Kuznetsov."

53

NATALIA

Andrey is like a physical shield against all my worst thoughts and all my scariest nightmares. I've gotten used to his weight and warmth beside me. Come to depend on it, really.

So when I reach for his side of the bed and find cold sheets, my heart drops. My drowsiness fades as I bolt up, my eyes slowly adjusting to the darkness.

The twins' cribs are a few feet away in a pool of moonlight slanting through a crack in the blinds. There are patches of shadow here, there—and then one that moves.

"Andrey," I whisper.

He raises his head. "*Lastochka*. Did I wake you?"

I slip out of bed and pad across the carpet. I wrap my arms around his shoulders, leaning over the chair he's slouched in. "No, I was just missing you." He presses a kiss to my wrist but there's something about the distracted flutter of his lips that gets to me.

"Why aren't you in bed? It's late."

"I just got home." His voice is tired, somber.

I grip his shoulders a little tighter. "Is it done, then?"

Andrey's head drops lower. "I disowned him in front of the entire Bratva."

"Are you okay?"

"It had to be done."

I walk around him so I can see his face. "That's not what I asked."

He takes a deep breath. "It was harder than I expected it to be. Despite everything…"

"He's still your brother."

"Not anymore." His gaze slides to mine. Shadows have carved out hollows in his face. He looks haunted. "Natalia, there's something I have to tell you."

The tone of his voice has me taking a step back. "What?"

"Disowning Viktor has… consequences. The Bratva—my allies—they wanted stability. They needed it after what they saw."

I frown. "Things are more stable without Viktor. You gave them that."

He shakes his head. "It's not enough. They needed… They wanted… I had to tell them about Grigory."

I swivel towards the crib, half-expecting to see Grigory's side of it empty. "You didn't."

"I didn't have any other choice."

"You always have a choice," I snap. "And you chose your Bratva over our family!"

Something flickers in his eyes. "*Lastochka—*"

"Don't!" I rear back. "Don't touch me."

He freezes with his hand halfway towards me. Then it drops.

"You promised me you would keep them out of this until they were older. Look at them." I jab a finger towards the crib. "They're babies, Andrey! And now, they've got targets on their backs."

"I will keep them safe—"

"Like you kept Annie safe? Like you kept Mila safe?"

The words are out of my mouth before I can stop them. His face twists, but I'm too preoccupied with my own complicated emotions to regret it.

"You say you'll keep them safe, but you can't control everything. And you certainly can't control everyone!"

I'm talking too loud and Grigory fusses from his crib. I rush over, patting his back until he settles into sleep again. As soon as he's calm, I gesture for Andrey to follow me and storm into the nursery.

"I didn't make the decisions that led us here," Andrey rumbles, closing the door behind him. "I just did the best I could with the hand I was dealt."

"You promised me."

"I didn't break my promise to you, Natalia. I told you I would keep our children safe. I didn't promise that I would keep them out of the Bratva. That is not something I could promise you."

I play the moment back. Cool dread curls around my spine when I realize he's right. Andrey worded his vow to me carefully.

He runs a hand through his hair as he steps towards me. I back away and he freezes again, his eyes clouding over. "Baby—"

"After everything that we've been through… how could you expose our children to this world?"

"The men only know about Grigory. They don't know about Sarra."

"And you think that makes it better?" I don't recognize my own voice right now. "How lovely—only one of my children is in danger. What a relief. If one of them dies, at least I'll have a backup." The idea of it pierces my chest. My heart physically aches.

"That's not what I meant and you know it."

"Maybe I don't know you as well as I thought I did."

This time, when I back away from him, he follows. He drags me into his arms even when I struggle. "I hope one day you'll understand that everything I do is for this family."

I look up at his hypnotic silver eyes and my fight wavers. It would be so damn easy to sink into his chest and let him comfort me. But where would that leave me? Where would that leave my children?

I shove against his chest, and he finally lets me go.

"You made a choice for our family without thinking about my feelings or our children's safety. And it can't be undone."

"I never meant to hurt you."

"And yet you did." I turn away from him. The silence between us is charged. If he reaches for me again, I just might crumble. "I need space, okay? I need time to wrap my head around this."

"I can give you space," he agrees. "But just so we're clear, I'm not letting you go."

Gritting my teeth, I wipe away my tears and turn to face him. "I'm not leaving you, Andrey. I made a promise to you when I accepted this ring—and unlike you, I keep my promises."

54

NATALIA

Andrey,

I couldn't find you before I left—hence the note. I'm taking the kids to Aunt Annie's old place for a few days. I just need a breather in a different environment. Misha and Remi are with me, plus my six-man security team. So there's no reason to worry.

We'll talk when I get back home.

For the record, I'm still mad. I'll probably still be mad when I get home in three days.

But I love you. That's not going anywhere. And neither am I.

—Nat

I leave the note on our bed and then head downstairs with my duffel. The twins are already in their car seats by the door. Misha has Remi's leash and is blowing raspberries at his baby sister.

"Ready for our little adventure?" I ask.

"Adventure" might be overstating things. I'm running—I know that. Aunt Annie knew it, too, when she came to see me last night. Andrey sent her so I'd have someone to talk to, but there's nothing to say. I'm not interested in hearing his side of the story, and I'm not interested in staying in this house another second.

"The car seats are locked and loaded." Misha takes the bag from my shoulder. "Let me get the stroller."

The twins are wide awake for now, but they just ate, and I have a feeling they'll sleep on the drive over.

Leif is waiting outside for us, flanked by two jeeps loaded down with equipment. "Don't you think this is a little overkill, Leif?"

"No," he answers flatly, "I don't."

Rolling my eyes, I decide to pick my battles. "Things okay at the house?"

"Everything looks good. We did a thorough check."

"Perfect." I give him what I hope is my most charming smile and hurry through the next sentence. "By the way, I'd like to drive today."

Leif purses his lips. "I don't know if that's a good idea, Nat."

Of course, it's not. Because giving Natalia a little independence is never a good idea in this house.

But I save my complaints and jump straight to the begging. "Please, Leif? Preeeetty please? Just this once? Don't make me break out the sugar on top.'"

He groans. "Fine. Just today. But you're driving between the two jeeps, got it?"

I salute him. "Aye-aye, captain."

Misha gives me a fist pump and a high-five, and then we load the twins into the back of the armored SUV.

The moment we leave the gates of the manor behind, I take a deep breath, my hands relaxing on the wheel.

It feels good to drive myself.

It feels good to take control.

It feels good to spend some time alone—just me and my kids. Remi nudges my shoulder like he can read my mind and knows I almost forgot him, so I mentally add him to the list of my current blessings.

This is nice.

"Are you and Andrey fighting again?" Misha pipes up from the back seat.

Just like that, the rosy sheen of the moment fades. I don't want to talk about this, but Misha won't drop it until I do.

"We had a disagreement," I admit. "It'll blow over. I just needed a little space."

Misha nods, but I can see him chewing his bottom lip to bits. His brow is creased with worry.

"Misha, nothing has changed," I assure him. "We're still a family. We still love each other. But that's the other thing about families: they fight."

"But they don't *leave*."

Guilt twists inside me, but I ignore it. "I'm not leaving forever. This is just a temporary timeout."

"For you or for Andrey?"

"Both of us."

"Nothing changes?" he checks again after a long silence.

I smile, catching his face again in the mirror. "Nothing changes."

Apart from seeing his relieved smile, I notice something else in the reflection: a black car swerving around in the background.

Come to think of it, I saw that same car ten minutes ago.

Something in my stomach churns.

"Hey, Misha? Call Olaf for me, please." I'm too nervous to take my hands off the wheel. As I predicted, both babies are sleeping soundly, and I don't want to jostle the car and wake them.

Misha fumbles with my cell phone and then puts the call on speaker, holding it next to my head so I can talk hands-free.

"Natalia, now isn't a good—"

"Have you noticed the black car?" I interrupt. "I feel like it's tailing us."

Misha immediately spins around, and I hate that he has to be aware of this at all.

Olaf sighs. "Yes. We noticed. Just keep driving. We'll stay between—"

A thundering crash drowns out whatever Olaf was saying. I hear it from the road behind me and through the speaker, the sheer volume making my phone crackle.

"*Prygat!*" someone yells from inside Olaf's jeep as I watch it veer violently to the side in my rearview mirror.

"Oh my God!" Misha yelps, almost dropping my phone. "They just rammed into Olaf's—holy hell—they just did it again!"

The sound of crunching metal is deafening. I want to plug my ears, close my eyes, but I keep a firm grip on the steering wheel.

My babies are in this car.

"Keep driving, Natalia!" Olaf bellows. "Try to catch up with Leif. He shouldn't be that far ahead of you!"

Then the line goes dead.

"Hold on!" With my heart pounding like a jackhammer, I mash the accelerator. We rip forward, but I've completely lost sight of Leif.

This can't be happening... This can't be happening...

The babies are crying and Misha is trying to comfort them, but he keeps turning around the same way I keep checking the rearview mirror.

Olaf is doing his best to block the car from overtaking him, but for all his heft, the smaller, sleeker car is just plain fast. Engines scream as they vie for position.

"It's okay, babies!" I croak, swerving through the narrowing roads. "We're gonna be okay."

As the words leave my mouth, Olaf's jeep is knocked into a tailspin. He careens off the road, diving nose-first into a ditch.

The black car accelerates.

Closer.

Closer.

Closer.

Misha is shushing the twins, but I can hear his voice hitching. He sees what's going to happen.

"Hold on!" I scream, just as the car rams into us.

Everyone else is strapped in and buckled, but Remi is flung against the dashboard. He hits hard and falls under the dash, caught in the footwell, whining in pain.

"Nat, they're coming!" Misha's panicked words are the last thing I hear before the car rear-ends us for the second time.

Except this time, I lose control of the wheel.

The car swerves off in a sharp left, and we slam into a tree.

My ears ring. My body is heavy and numb. As I give in to the blissful oblivion of darkness, a comforting thought takes hold.

It will all be okay when I wake up.

This is just another nightmare.

∼

"Mom! Mom!"

There's a poke to my side. My face.

"Mom!"

I'm still dreaming.

"Mom!" someone sobs. "Please wake up. Please."

A nightmare. This is a nightmare.

Something warm and wet slides down my face. I inhale and cough, my lungs protesting against the smoke.

"MOM!"

It's like an electric shock straight to the heart. I jolt upright, already reaching for my son. "Misha?"

There's blood drying on his forehead and tears streaking down his dirty cheeks. Remi is limp in the passenger seat, but my eyes slip down to the single bundle Misha is clutching to his chest.

Not two…

Just one.

"No!" I choke, twisting around in my seat. Pain shoots down my side, but I ignore it and search the backseat.

"I've got Sarra," he says weakly.

"Grigory," I gasp. "Where's Grigory?"

But my son's car seat is empty.

"I… don't know. He's…." His breath catches. "He's gone."

55

ANDREY

"She left?" I storm into Annie's room, waving the note Natalia left on her pillow for me. "She fucking left?!"

Annie just sighs. "What did you expect her to do? She told you she needed space."

"I thought she'd move into another room. Or the pool house, even. I didn't think she'd disappear and take the kids with her."

Annie looks at me over the rim of her glasses. "The only thing she's concerned about right now is keeping her children safe. As far as she's concerned, that means keeping them as far from your world as possible."

My fists unfurl as I drop into the chair next to Annie's bed. "Fuck!" I bellow, spewing out a fraction of my pent-up frustration. "What do I do now?" I finally release the crumpled letter, letting it float to the floor like the last withered leaf of autumn.

"You could try giving her what she wants," Annie suggests softly. "Misha and Remi are with her—they'd never let anything happen to her. Not to mention the security detail she took. She'll be fine."

I glance out the window and the lawn looks painfully empty. Misha would be out on a morning walk with Remi by now. It's a nice morning, so Natalie might've taken the twins out to the grass, spread a blanket beneath a shade tree.

But there's no teenager running around with a ball. No dog barking. No sounds of chatter or laughter or infants crying.

I inhale sharply and let it out slowly, trying to soothe the restlessness in my bones. It doesn't do a damn bit of good.

Nothing does, and I'd know—I've tried it all.

Screaming at the ceiling. Pacing the empty hallways. Hefting around the weight of my useless phone in my pocket, trying to pretend there's a chance Natalia might change her mind and call me to come pick her up.

When my willpower snaps, I pull my phone from my pocket, except… it won't turn on.

I jog to the kitchen for a charger. Maybe Natalia did call. Maybe she wants me to come pick her up, but my stupid phone was dead.

I jostle from foot to foot, waiting for the screen to light up. Before it does, Shura strolls into the kitchen. "I heard Mila's out of the hospital. Is she around?"

"She's with Leonty." It's good news, but I wave him off, smashing the home button on my phone. "My fucking phone died."

"You expecting an important call or something?"

I shoot him a glare. "Natalia could have tried to call. I don't even know how long it's been dead."

When was the last time I used it? I've barely touched it since last night. Did she try to text me? Did she want to talk, but I missed it? Is that why she left?

"I'm sure she's fine," Shura offers.

But I don't hear a word as my phone lights up, and... *Fuck.* Seventeen missed calls.

None of them are from Natalia, but Leif called. And called. And called. The last one was only six minutes ago.

"What is it?" Shura leans closer. "Is everything okay?"

I'm about to call Leif back when my phone buzzes with a text.

LEIF: *attacked 8e/##s inju8r#ed*

"*PRYGAT!*" I roar, resisting the urge to fling my phone across the kitchen.

Instead, I fling it at Shura. A second after reading it, his eyes zip to mine. "We have to move fast."

I'm already halfway out the door.

Shura catches up in the driveway, and we leap into the car. He cues up the locations of the cars that Natalia and her security detail took.

Every minute of driving without finding them is agony. I rip around corners and scream down the straightaways, my only thoughts for my family.

And then we find it.

The wreckage.

"Shit," Shura curses. "I think that Jeep is Olaf's."

But I'm looking past the Jeep to the car wrapped around a huge oak further down the road.

I slam to a stop and shoot out of the vehicle. Shura yells something about backup, but I don't need backup. All I need is to get to the scrap metal that once held my family.

"Natalia!" I roar. "Natalia!"

As I approach, I hear the whine of an engine. And the wail of an infant.

My heart is lodged in my throat as I round the car and nearly drop to my knees with relief. Misha and Natalia are huddled on the ground. Natalia is holding the babies, her head dipped over them. They're dirty and bleeding and shaking, but alive. So fucking alive.

This time, I do drop to my knees. But only Misha and Remi look up at me. Natalia doesn't lift her head. She's too busy sobbing into Sarra's pink blanket that is now brown with dust and grease.

That's when I realize...

The blue bundle is empty.

Where is Grigory?

Where is my son?

Natalia is still sobbing, her arms shaking.

I look to Misha. "What happened?"

"They came after us," he rasps. His face is a mess of dry blood and wet tears. "They rammed into our car... They took Grigory..."

It's too horrible to be true. Too much to process.

"Natalia," I whisper. It's a plea. A question.

Is it true?

Is he okay?

Natalia just sobs harder, squeezing Sarra to her chest. That's all the answer I need.

"We're going to sort this all out, I promise you. We're going to get him back."

We have to.

There's no other choice.

I wave Misha and Remi back towards my car and scoop Natalia into my arms, baby and all. She doesn't fight me. I'm not sure she's capable of it right now.

"Are you okay?" I ask as we walk.

She doesn't answer, but I try to assess her for injuries. There are scrapes across her forehead. A bruise on her cheek. But otherwise, she seems okay. Physically, at least.

I place her in the back seat of my car and Remi jumps in after her, sticking to her like glue, licking away her tears.

It hurts even to look at her distraught face. So I turn away and Misha is standing behind me, his eyes locked on the dirt at our feet. "I should've protected them. I shouldn't have let him take Grigory."

I grab his shoulders, hauling him close. "You saw who it was?"

"I recognized him," he admits. "We crashed and I was dizzy,

confused. But the door opened. I thought maybe it was... you."

My chest aches. It should've been me. I should've found them. But I shove that thought aside and focus on Misha. "Who was it?"

"I don't know his name. He used to visit the compound sometimes, but I... I never met him, so I don't know—"

"Is this him?" I hold out my phone, a picture of the devil himself on the screen.

Misha's eyes go wide as he nods slowly. "Who is he?"

"My father," I answer. "Now, tell me exactly what happened. He opened the door, and then...?"

"He picked Grigory up, and I actually thought he was there to help us." Fresh tears flow down his cheeks. "Then he looked me in the eye and said..."

His voice breaks, and I clasp his neck, reassuring him with what little strength I have left.

He clears his throat. "He said, *'An heir for an heir.'*"

56

NATALIA

"It's going to be alright, Natalia. I swear it."

Andrey's face hovers in front of me. He cups my cheeks, wipes away my tears. But nothing soothes the ache in my chest. The soul-crushing weight of wrongness that permeates every second.

As if he realizes that, Andrey drops his hands. "Kat, Mila, and Misha will stay with you. I'm going to go get our boy back."

His lips press hard against my forehead; it has the seal of a promise. Then he's gone, and my room is empty, and the promise feels like nothing but words.

I stand up and walk to Sarra's crib because I'm supposed to. I'm supposed to take care of my daughter, and move, and breathe.

But it all feels so hard. My limbs are heavy, and my thoughts are lost to a dense fog.

"Nat?"

I turn to see Katya in the doorway. Mila and Misha are just behind her, watching me like I'm a house of cards at risk of collapse.

"Are you okay?"

For the first time in a long time, I respond. "How can I be okay? He has my son."

Mila sighs in what looks like relief. "You can talk. We were worried. We thought…"

"That I was having one of my episodes?" I finish for her. "I wanted Andrey to think I was."

"Why?" Katya breathes.

"So he wouldn't be expecting me to break into Nikolai's compound and get my son back."

Misha is the only one who doesn't gasp with shock. Instead, his jaw squares. He nods as though he understands exactly where I'm coming from.

"Nat, that's insane." Katya grabs my hand. "It's too dangerous."

If it's too dangerous for me, then how much worse is it for Grigory?

I pull my hand back. "Which is why no one will be expecting me. While Nikolai is preoccupied with Andrey and his men, I can sneak in, find Grigory, and get him out of there."

I look past Katya and Mila's horrified faces and turn to Misha. "You know the compound, Misha. Can you tell me how to get in and out without being seen?"

"On one condition," Misha says immediately. "I want to come, too."

I squeeze my eyes closed, running the math. Trying to decide if there's any way I can go in there alone and guarantee I can get Grigory out. Any way I can keep Misha safe and also keep my family whole.

"No. *No.*" Mila looks from Misha to me like she's not sure who to lay into first. "You can't. Either of you. This is—"

I open my eyes and hold out a hand to Misha. "Deal."

Katya swats the hand out of the air. "Nat! Misha can't go and neither can you."

"I want to go!" Misha argues. "I want to help."

"This is a literal war zone," Mila tells him.

"A war zone my infant son is in the middle of," I interject quietly. "Andrey wants to get him back, but Andrey is the target. He's the reason they took Grigory in the first place. Everyone will be on the lookout for him. While they are, Misha and I can sneak in."

"You're not thinking clearly," Katya insists.

My gaze flickers between Mila and Katya. "This is my family, my *son*. If you were in my place, wouldn't you do the same?"

Their eyes meet, and I know they understand.

"You're right," Katya admits. Mila starts to argue, but Kat shakes her head. "No, she is right, Mila. If it was my child, I'd want to be there. You would, too."

Mila opens her mouth, but this time, she says, "I'll come with you."

"Not a chance," I snap. "You're still recovering from major surgery." I turn to Katya and stop her before she can offer to come as well. "And you are pregnant."

"Nat—"

"I know how to handle a gun now," I charge ahead, growing more and more confident in my plan. "I know how to use it. And what's more, I'm not afraid to."

Misha slinks a little closer to me. "Neither am I."

I clasp his hand. "Go scope out the jeeps, Misha. We'll need to find one to hide in before the men drive out."

He slips out of the room, leaving me behind with Kat and Mila.

"It's going to be okay," I tell them, knowing I can't be sure. "Everything's going to be alright."

Katya's eyes are brimming with tears. I take her hand and give it a squeeze. "Our roles have reversed. Usually, you're the one with the crazy plan, and I'm the crying mess."

"You were never a mess, Nat. I could always see your strength, even when you couldn't." She hugs me tightly, her hands digging into my back. "I have something to tell you," she whispers as we break apart. She takes a deep breath and holds up her wrist, the yellowing bruise still visible. "Viktor is the one who gave me this bruise."

I gawk at her, but she charges ahead before I can ask any of the dozen questions flitting around my head.

"Remember when I said I was 'busy' at work? I was really working undercover. I got back into Viktor's good graces and coaxed information out of him."

My jaw drops. "Andrey knew about this?"

"Don't be mad. We didn't want you to worry."

"I can't believe Shura agreed to—" I smack my palm against my forehead. "That's why you two were fighting all the time. How did you convince him? How did you con Viktor?"

She winces. "It's a long story and we don't have the time for it right now. But when you come back—*safe and sound*, specifically—I'll tell you all about it."

Misha bursts into the room with two guns in his waistband. He hands one to me. "There are two jeeps at the tail end of the convoy. We can hitch a ride on them."

I tuck the gun into my jeans and clasp Misha's neck, pulling his forehead against mine. "No matter what, you stay with me, is that clear?"

He nods.

"Good." I turn to the girls. Mila has an arm wrapped around Katya, who's still fighting back tears. Sarra is sleeping in her bassinet, and I can barely bring myself to look at her.

This isn't goodbye. I'll be back.

Still, I whisper, "Take care of my daughter for me."

Katya sniffs. "Always."

"Be safe," Mila pleads. "And come back to us."

57

NATALIA

I'm face-down in the back of the Jeep when the explosions start.

Then come the gunshots.

I poke my head through the back window to see the compound is on fire. Smoke rises into the sky in thick, dark pillars.

I don't let myself think about how my son and Andrey are in there. I take deep, calming breaths. And as the last men disappear over the flattened gates, I open the hatch and jump out.

A second later, Misha does the same. I tip my head towards the gnarled entrance. A smoking car blocks the path.

"Do you know another way in?"

He nods and pulls me along the compound, staying as close to the walls as we can. It feels like we're running for ages. The compound seems to stretch on for miles, its high walls keeping everything out but the vultures.

Misha finally stops in front of an ivy-covered section of the wall and starts rooting through the creepers.

"There's a gate here," he explains without stopping his search. "I didn't even know it existed until the night I left… the night I was sent to spy on Andrey."

His movements get more and more frantic as he tries and fails to find the gate. The sounds of gunfire and screaming getting closer aren't helping his concentration.

Finally, he shoves aside a thick bundle of ivy to reveal a black metal gate. "Got it!"

Misha has to shove hard, but it screeches open by about a quarter-inch. Thankfully, the noise is drowned out by a wave of fresh gunshots.

A few more pushes and the gate is open wide enough for us to squeeze through. Before Misha can walk through, I grab his elbow. "You don't have to come with me."

He glowers. "You said I could. And I want to. Grigory is my brother."

I wish he was too scared to go. I wish he would stay in the car. But if he did, he wouldn't be Misha.

"Just stay close to me," I order. "And let me go first."

I have to duck low and wade through more creepers to get inside. The other side of the wall is completely deserted. It looks like Andrey has drawn all Nikolai's men to the front of the compound.

Which is a good thing, considering we're completely exposed right now. The closest structures are about thirty yards away —a small cul-de-sac of sheds spaced a few meters apart from one another.

"I know where we are." Misha points towards one of the sheds in the far distance. "That's where the youngest children were kept."

I'm already running in that direction, kicking up a cloud of sand behind me. This part of the compound is eerily silent compared with the bedlam brewing on the other side.

My heart constricts when I think about Andrey in the thick of that violence. But I can't let myself dwell for long.

My son needs me.

"Here!" Misha calls quietly. "Over here."

I join him behind one of the sheds, all of which have doors but no windows. "What is it?"

"I thought I saw someone over there," he whispers, pointing to a small shed two doors down from where we're hiding.

Then, like a sign from God, I hear it: a high-pitched cry that I recognize immediately.

"Grigory."

His cries are coming from the shed that Misha just pointed out. My heart is thrumming hard against my chest, but I've never been so sure of anything in my life. Come hell or high water, I'm getting Grigory out of here. Or I'll die trying.

"Misha, get ready."

We pull out our guns together, our eyes meeting at the same time.

"So do we just go in there?" he asks, his skin blotchy from the heat of the sun.

"No. I do."

His eyes bulge. "You want to go in there alone?"

"No one will be expecting me," I assure him. "In any case, I'm going to need you to drive one of Andrey's jeeps back to the little gate. That way, when I get Grigory, we'll have an exit strategy in place."

Misha's eyes narrow. "You're trying to get rid of me."

"I'm trying to get us all out of here alive."

"We don't know how many men are in there!" Misha says. "You might need backup!"

I put my hand on his shoulder. "Honey, if we're both taken, no one will know that we're here until it's too late. You need to get out of here."

"I can't leave you alone."

"They won't hurt me," I assure him. "Worst case, I'll be used as leverage, and you'll be on the outside, able to tell Andrey what happened. He'll come for us." Misha opens his mouth to protest but I talk over him. "Please, Misha. This *is* helping."

He doesn't look convinced, but we don't have a lot of other options. "O-okay, I'll go…"

I grab his face and press my lips against his forehead. "I love you."

He stumbles back and starts running. I don't have the luxury of watching him go. Flicking off the safety of my gun, I inch closer to the cabin. Grigory has stopped crying, but I already know which one he's in.

"I'm coming, baby," I mutter under my breath. "Mommy's coming."

I inch towards the entrance, trying to suss out how many men I'm dealing with.

As it turns out… just one.

The man has his back to the door. He's bending over a large wooden crate resting on top of rotten table legs. He moves a few inches to the left, and I have to clap a hand over my mouth to keep from gasping.

My baby.

Through the tiny gaps in the slats of the crate, I see Grigory. And leaning over him…

Is his uncle.

Everything falls into hyper-focus. I've never felt steadier in my life. I raise my gun and point it right at Viktor.

One clean shot. That's all it would take.

My finger is on the trigger. I'm just about to squeeze when he whips around suddenly and hisses, "You."

Not so long ago, Katya introduced me to a handsome young man with a little more sleaze than charm.

Now, he's hardly human. His cheeks are hollow. His eyes have caved into their sockets, leaving nothing behind but dark, purpled circles. He's lost so much weight that the shirt on his back protrudes out in harsh points over his joints.

"Viktor."

"Come for the little brat, yeah?" he croaks, displaying a yellowing set of teeth. He reaches for Grigory, and I take my finger off the trigger.

"Don't touch him."

Ignoring me, he scoops my son up into his arms, almost upending the crate in the same move. I start to lunge forward.

"Stop!" he snarls. "Or I might accidentally drop the little fucker on his head."

"Don't do this," I beg with my heart in my throat.

"That's what I told my *mudak* of a brother when he was slicing my chest open!"

I can barely process what he's saying. My eyes are fastened on the bundle in his arms. Grigory gives a little gurgle as though he's trying to say hello.

"Shut up when I'm talking!" Viktor hisses at the baby.

I flinch. It's not just anger I can see on Viktor's face. It's something else entirely—something that borders on madness.

"Please, Viktor… don't hurt my baby."

He smiles with his teeth, though his eyes are empty of all emotion. "You're the one with the gun."

"I'll put it down."

But I don't move. There are options in front of me, but they're all bad.

"What are you waiting for?" he challenges.

I don't even try to negotiate. I set the gun down on the floor in front of me and kick it away. It spins into the corner of the shed, taking shelter in the shadows.

"There." I lift both hands in the air and show him my empty palms. "I'm unarmed. Now, please, put the baby down."

He runs his tongue over his bottom lip. "You know what? I will put the baby down. That'll leave my hands free for you."

I don't even register the threat. All I feel is relief as he turns and puts Grigory back in the crate. Finally, I can breathe.

Then Viktor steps in front of the crib, blocking Grigory from view as he approaches me, his lips curling with contempt. "My brother thinks he's won, but I'll get the last laugh. I always do."

He grabs me by the neck and walks me into the wall. Air whooshes out of me as my back hits the solid wood and his knee presses hard between my legs.

"You think this is winning?" I rasp, determined to keep him talking. "Forcing yourself on a defenseless woman?"

"No woman is defenseless," he growls scornfully. "Not you, not my useless dead wife, not—"

"She's not dead," I interrupt. "Mila's far from dead. She's safe at home, in Leonty's arms."

The distraction works. Viktor's eyes swell, the veins in them popping red.

"Face it, Viktor. Try as you might, you will always be a loser. Second to your brother in everything."

His hand tightens around my neck. "You stupid whore, you don't know what you're talking about."

"No woman would ever choose you. Mila chose Leonty over you. Katya chose Shura over you—"

His fingers leave my neck and he slams his hand over my mouth. His palms taste like sweat and ash and blood. "If

Katya chose Shura, why the fuck did she come crawling back to me?"

"She was playing you, you moron. She only wanted to get information out of you!"

He releases me as though I've suddenly caught on fire. I try to get out from under his arms, but with a cry of rage, he flings me back against the wall.

My head bounces off the wood and stars dance in my eyes, but I refuse to drop. Grigory's startled cry gives me the strength I need to stay standing.

Viktor, on the other hand, looks like he doesn't hear a thing. "I'm going to kill you first," he spews. "Then I'm going to hunt Katya down. I'll save Mila for last. I want to savor her death."

The gun is several feet away, shining in the shadows like a beacon of hope. But Viktor is far closer to Grigory than I am to the gun. I can't risk it.

"Viktor!" a harsh voice snaps. His perfectly formed shadow creeps into the shed first. "What the fuck are you—"

My eyes snap to Nikolai at the same time he notices me.

The grimace on his face twists into a sinister smile. "Well, well... What a surprise."

His hair is matted with sweat and blood soaks the front of his shirt. It's clear he's abandoned the fight to cash in his little insurance policy.

I'd make a run for Grigory, but there's a gun hanging casually in Nikolai's grasp. Viktor stands between us, his body hunched inward like he wants to disappear.

"I see you came for your son," Nikolai observes. "I thought we made ourselves clear: an heir for an heir."

"You have no heir, Nikolai," I goad.

He raises his eyebrows. "You're not aware then? The boy Andrey took months ago—Misha—"

"You're referring to *my* son."

Confusion flashes across his face, trailed by understanding. He suppresses his surprise in favor of a weak smile. "How touching. You've taken the boy in as your own?"

"He had no one else."

"Except that he does," Nikolai counters, striding further into the shed. He passes right by Viktor as though he doesn't exist. "He has *me*. I'm his father."

"We can't choose who we're born to, but Misha chose his family." I raise my hand to my heart. "*We* are his parents."

The gleam of my ring catches the miniscule light in the shed. No one can miss it. Nikolai stares at the diamond with his teeth bared.

"One big, happy family," he snarls sarcastically. "Except for one thing: some loyalties can't be bought. Not with money or with kindness."

My arms prickle with goosebumps. "What are you trying to say?"

He licks his lips, his eyes narrowing. "My boy played his part well, but Misha's loyalties have always been to me. He's been fooling you from the start."

58

ANDREY

"Where the fuck is Nikolai?" I roar through the pandemonium raging around us.

Leonty and Shura both reload as they back towards me, our tight circle drawing in even tighter as enemies press in around us. Leonty is bleeding and Shura is limping, but they look as feral as Remi.

The dog has proven himself to be a force of nature in the battle. His teeth are stained with the remains of Nikolai's men, fur stuck out in stiff, red peaks where they bled on him as he tore out their throats.

"I saw him," Leonty pants, raising his gun and firing as several more Rostov men run towards us. "He was here just a minute ago."

"Until he wasn't," Shura growls. "I saw him run."

I squint into the distance. I can just about make out a rickety, bronze gate through the smoke. It separates the front of the compound from the back.

"That has to be where they're keeping Grigory." I shoot two men in the head before racing forward with Shura and Leonty flanking me. "We have to breach those gates."

"Shouldn't be a problem," Shura coughs, wiping soot and ash off his face with his forearm. "All his forces are preoccupied—"

He cuts off suddenly, his body going rigid, his face narrowing into a furious scowl as he stares at one of the watchtowers along the front perimeter of the compound.

"What is it?" I squint, trying to follow his gaze.

"I thought I saw..."

"Vladimir," I growl, finally seeing the man I've known since I was a child. I don't expect a warm greeting since I just killed his son, Efrem, for wavering loyalties.

Wordlessly, we close in around the tower. Leonty raises his gun to blindly light it up from below, but I grab his wrist to stop him.

"I have an easier way of weeding out rats. Shura," I say without ever taking my eyes off the tower, "smoke them out."

Nodding, Shura kindles a fire at the base of the watchtower. The beautiful, orange flames rise, consuming the aged wood hungrily.

Vladimir emerges on the upper platform, his face contorted with rage and drenched in sweat as he attempts to take us out from above.

We duck, avoiding his bullets as a few desperate men leap from the tower. Their bones snap as they hit the ground, but they aren't in pain long. We slaughter them where they land.

"*Mudak!*" Vladimir bellows, ignoring the flames licking his boots. "I will have my vengeance for Efrem!"

"Your son was a traitor," I spit back, twisting around to take aim at the legs of the tower.

A few strategically placed shots are all it takes for one of the tower's supports to give way. Leonty, Shura, and I scramble out of range as it collapses in a pile of fiery ash, taking Vladimir out with it.

Good fucking riddance.

As the smoke clears, though, I notice two figures on the other side of the wreckage. The taller of the two men is staring right at me. Before I even see his face, I know who it is.

"SLAVIK!" I thunder, raising my gun.

My father flees like the coward he is, weaving in and out of the fiery remnants of the watchtower. He scrabbles out of sight as my bullets bury themselves in burning wood instead of in his beating heart.

I don't think—I just take off after him.

But I don't get far before a blur of motion pops up in my peripherals half a second before it barrels straight into me.

I crash to the ground in a tangle of limbs, the breath driven from my lungs. Against all odds, I keep hold of my gun. I'm a millisecond away from unloading a clip into this bastard's stomach when I hear something that freezes my trigger finger.

"Dad?"

"*Misha?*" I choke.

His teeth are chattering hard as he scrambles backwards on all fours, blinking furiously against the swirling smoke. "It's me! Don't shoot."

Rage I've never felt before rises up in me. I grab his arm and drag him behind a sheet of twisted metal so we're somewhat shielded from the fighting. My hands are shaking as badly as his. "What the fuck are you doing here?"

"Natalia is here," he blurts. "I came with her."

There's no time to discuss the depths of this nightmare or the fear squeezing my lungs. All I can do is ask the only question that matters: "Where is she?"

"She's in a shed around the back of the property. We found Grigory."

"Lead the way."

Turning on his heel, Misha runs in the direction of the bronze gate I spied earlier.

My heels pounding into the dirt hurt. Hell, just breathing hurts. Ignoring the hitch in my throat and the pain searing down my sides, I keep running until we're closing in on the bronze gate.

Misha slips through the thin opening of the gate, and I go to follow him, but before I can, a hail of bullets scythes through the air, missing my face by mere inches. My ears are ringing from the gunfire as I throw myself to the ground to avoid the second round.

Misha twists around, his eyes wide as he stares at me through the narrow bars of the bronze gate.

"Go!" I yell at him. "Protect them! I'm right behind you!"

Misha hesitates, but my concentration is stolen by the two men advancing on me with their weapons raised. The man in front has ice-blue eyes, burning bright amidst the swirling red ash. "Your head will fetch me a nice reward, Kuznetsov."

He doesn't wait for my response as he levels his gun at me.

Before he can pull the trigger, a furry rocket darts out of the smog. With a ferocious growl, Remi lands on the man's chest and sinks his canines into his face. There's a second of earsplitting shrieking before he goes silent.

Horrified by his comrade's half-eaten face, the other man tries to run. But I put two of my bullets in his back, not staying to watch what happens after he drops onto the sand.

I make a run for the bronze gates when more Rostov soldiers start materializing in the distance. I'm abandoning my own troops, and fuck only knows where Shura and Leonty are by now. It's just me and Misha, and I have no choice but to put all my faith in the boy.

With a grimace, I squeeze through the gates.

Don't let me down, son.

59

NATALIA

"You're lying."

Nikolai throws his head back and laughs. "Why would I lie now? I have you and your runt right where I want you."

He keeps moving closer, and I skitter back. It's not all in fear. Every step back I take, I'm one step closer to my son.

I can just about see over the worn edges of the crate. Grigory has thrown off his blanket and one chubby hand lifts into the air as though he's waving to me.

"Whatever he may have said to you, Misha has always been *my* man." Nikolai stands between me and the only exit out of this death shed. Viktor joins him, pale and sweaty. He looks like a parasite who's latched onto Nikolai. "Who do you think informed me that you were pregnant?"

It's not true. Misha wouldn't do that to me. He couldn't.

Despite the sweat trickling down my back, I feel cold. "Yelena was informing on me."

He snorts. "You really think she was my only plant?"

"Misha hated Yelena. He's the one who figured out she was spying."

"You idiot woman, it was all an act," Nikolai hisses. "I sacrificed one spy in favor of the other."

It doesn't make any sense… except it could. Couldn't it?

I'm teetering on the edge, clinging to the deep roots of my love for my son when I see a shadow in the tiny gap of the door. Misha's face appears in the space, his hair matted with sweat.

He looks me right in the eye… and winks.

That's all I need.

Keep them talking, that wink says. *Keep them distracted.*

Keep them here until Andrey can find us.

"You're after the wrong man, Nikolai," I tell him, raising my voice as Misha's shadow creeps out of sight.

Nikolai sighs. "You believed whatever bullshit story he fed you, I see. You're an easy mark."

"You told me that this whole war started because Andrey turned your parents in, but you chose to believe the wrong Kuznetsov."

Nikolai's gaze drifts to Viktor, lazy, uncaring. "What do you have to say about that, eh?"

But Viktor doesn't look capable of thinking on his own anymore. He barely looks capable of standing on his own.

"Speak, *mudak!*" Nikolai spits.

Viktor jolts. "She's lying. Sh…she's lying."

From the corner of my eye, I see dust being kicked up in the distance. Someone is approaching, but they're being quiet about it.

"Slavik fed you a convincing story and you believed him," I continue, suppressing the urge to look towards the door every few seconds. "*He* was the one who turned your parents in to the FBI. *He* was the one who gave the cops all the evidence they needed to try your parents."

Nikolai's smile drops. "Why would he do that and then run?"

"He wasn't trying to leave his son a legacy. He wanted Andrey to fail. He wanted to blow up the Kuznetsov Bratva and re-create it elsewhere. He never meant for Andrey to rebuild what he'd destroyed."

I'm grasping at straws here, pulling words out of thin air to weave a believable story. But the more I talk, the more it makes sense to me.

Something seems to be making sense to Nikolai, too.

"Tell him, Viktor," I demand. "Tell him it's true."

Viktor's jaw drops. "I… I…"

"Fucking *SPEAK*!" Nikolai bellows again, causing Grigory to hurl his fists in the air and scream with terror.

Instinctively, I move towards the crate, but Nikolai points his gun right at me. "Stay where you are!"

I'm forced to stand and watch helplessly as my baby cries. But so long as that gun is pointed at me, it's not aimed at Grigory.

Slowly, however, Nikolai turns. The muzzle of the gun slides from me… to Viktor. "Is she telling the truth?"

Viktor cowers from the gun, his eyes darting from side to side. "I… My father didn't tell—"

Nikolai shoots into the floor an inch from Viktor's boot. Viktor lets out a startled yelp and collapses against the wall, gibbering in fear. Grigory shrieks even louder. I risk moving another inch towards the crate. At least now, I can see my baby's pink, distressed face.

"Give me answers or I'll blow your useless fucking brains right out of your head. You have five seconds to tell me the truth." Nikolai threatens. "One. Two. Three—"

"It was him!" Viktor cries, spit flying from his mouth. His eyes stay fastened on the gun. "It was Slavik who ratted your parents out to the FBI!"

Nikolai's lips pull back in a dangerous jeer. "He was using me to get rid of Andrey."

"H-he respects you—"

Viktor tries to salvage this, but Nikolai isn't hearing it. "I've had enough of your lies. It appears that's all a Kuznetsov is good for: lies and fuel for my fires."

Nikolai pulls the trigger without warning.

And just like that, there is one less Kuznetsov on this planet.

Viktor slumps against the wall, his head falling to the side like a ragdoll as blood spreads across his chest. His eyes are glassy and empty.

Nikolai's, however, are full of fire. With Viktor dead, there's nothing to distract him from me or my son. He turns on me.

"Your fight is not with me, Nikolai," I rasp.

He spits on Viktor's cooling corpse. "This changes nothing. The history runs too deep."

"If you hurt me or this baby, he will hunt you down!" My voice is so shrill that I barely recognize it.

"He will hunt me down regardless." Nikolai raises his gun once more. "I might as well make it worth his while."

Cool dread pools in my veins. One second is all it would take to end my life and leave Grigory exposed. Through my panic, I see something.

Misha.

He edges through the door as stealthily as he can manage. I'm actually glad that Grigory is still crying, because the sound drowns out Misha's advance.

Unable to stop myself, my eyes slip to Misha. And Nikolai notices.

He turns just as Misha lunges forward, shoulder driving into his stomach. A gunshot ricochets, and I throw myself at the crate, shielding Grigory with my body.

Then I hear something clatter across the floor.

Misha has knocked the gun out of Nikolai's hand and they're rolling on the floor, grappling for position. But Nikolai has at least eighty pounds on the kid, and he knows how to use his weight.

"You little shit!" Nikolai roars, landing a vicious punch on Misha's jaw.

I feel the blow as if Nikolai hit me.

I have to do something. I have to help him.

Then I remember my own gun.

It slipped into the shadows, but now, I can reach it. I crawl to the corner and grab hold of the weapon just as Nikolai stands over Misha, one foot on my son's chest.

"You had so much fucking potential," he snarls in Misha's face. "But you came from a whore. I should've known you'd die like one."

All the lessons I learned, courtesy of Shura and Evangeline, run through my head. But in the end, I don't need any of them.

I raise my gun and aim it at Nikolai's back.

He's still talking. "Now, I'm going to—"

His last words are lost to the sudden bubble of air and blood in his lungs.

His legs buckle. Color drains from his face as he turns slowly, catching sight of me in the corner, gun raised.

As he crumbles to his knees, I clutch one son tight to my chest and walk over to the other.

"You are done hurting my children," I whisper as Nikolai dies. "You'll never touch them again."

60

ANDREY

I'm running as fast as I can.

Then I hear the gunshot, and I run faster.

I blow through the door of the shed, and there's too much happening to process.

Misha, bruised and battered on the floor, trapped underneath Nikolai's boot.

But Nikolai's eyes are fastened on the woman standing a few feet away in the shadows, her arm raised.

A gunshot cracks through the scene and Nikolai falls to his knees, eyes still locked on the woman I can't look away from, either.

Natalia steps forward, shattered light falling across her face. She's harsh and beautiful, an avenging angel with a babe clutched in one hand and a gun in the other.

"You are done hurting my children. You'll never touch them again."

Why did I think I needed to race over here and rescue her? This woman doesn't need rescuing.

Nikolai opens his mouth, but only blood spurts from his lips. Natalia stares at him in cold disgust.

But the second she looks away, her face softens. She drops to Misha's side and clutches his face.

He grabs her wrist. It takes him a few coughs to find his voice again, but when he does, he asks, "Are you okay?"

"I'm fine," she assures him. "And so is Grigory. Because of you."

"*Lastochka*," I murmur, stepping into the cool gloom of the shed.

Misha's face breaks into a relieved grin when he sees me, but Natalia eyes me carefully. "I had to come, Andrey, and I'm not apologizing for it."

Like she thinks I could be upset with her right now. After what I just saw. I cup her face in my palm and press a kiss to her forehead. "I'm not asking you to apologize. You did brilliantly, little bird."

Grigory cries, and I press a kiss to the top of his head, too.

Then there's a groan from behind us.

Together, we turn to face the man bleeding out on the floor.

"Misha," Nikolai mumbles. His eyes are apathetic despite the fact he's on death's door.

Misha sidles closer to my side.

"You'd side with the people who killed your father?" Blood colors Nikolai's teeth a ruby red.

Misha shakes his head. "You were never my father. A father is someone who chooses you. Like Andrey did."

Nikolai's eyes spark with anger. "You would take his name? The name of my enemy?"

Misha glances towards Natalia and me. "I already have."

"He's our boy, Nikolai," Natalia claims proudly.

It's as though the light drains right out of him. He looks like a living corpse. But through sheer force of will, he keeps breathing.

"Just answer one thing for me," he hisses through clenched teeth. "Will you kill Slavik?"

I pull out the knife I've sheathed within my boot and squat down in front of Nikolai. "He'll be next in line behind you to get into Hell."

Nikolai nods. "Then—"

Before he can get the words out, I slice the knife across his throat.

The moment I release him, he collapses onto the floor, ending a decade-long battle that cost me a mother, an unborn child, and a former lover.

As I straighten up, a strangled whimper reaches me from the opposite corner of the shed. Natalia clutches Grigory tighter to her chest, backing away as Misha snatches up Natalia's gun and points it at my brother.

Viktor is three-quarters of the way to death, and his hollow eyes barely even blink.

"Stand down, Misha. This is my fight." I carefully unwind the gun from the boy's fingers and walk over to Viktor. "You always were a stubborn bastard, *brat*."

He tries to say something back, but it's nothing but spits and gurgles. I squat down beside him and Viktor shudders, his eyes leaking salty tears.

"I didn't give Nikolai the dignity of last words, but we still share blood. So say what you need to say."

Viktor grabs weakly at the cuff of my shirt, his limp fingers barely able to take hold of me. Every word out of his bloody mouth costs him dearly. "L-let… me… live…"

I don't expect the gut twist that those words bring forth. For one tiny millisecond, I consider it.

Then I hear my son's raspy cry.

"I can't let you live, Viktor. You've gone too far."

"Please," he croaks. "You… know me. This is not… me. He did… this…"

I shake my head. "This is always who you have been, brother. A coward and a traitor, ready to backstab the people closest to you if it meant getting on top with the least effort."

"Brother… I beg… you…"

I wrap a hand around his neck and pull him towards me until we're practically nose to nose. I press the tip of my gun directly over Viktor's heart.

"You were dead to me the moment you came after my family —Grigory, Natalia, Mila, our own mother. Now, you're just dead."

I pull the trigger.

His last breath warms my face. And then he's gone.

It doesn't feel as momentous as I hoped, taking out two enemies in the span of minutes. It's all a waste, and I'm sorry to be part of it.

But the job isn't done yet.

"We have to get out of here." Natalia lays a hand on my shoulder. "Andrey, we need to go."

Grigory's weak cry is what pulls my focus from my brother's body. I kiss my son's chubby hand and turn to his mother. "You and Misha go. But I have to stay. Slavik needs to die."

We shuffle out of the shed just as Leonty and Shura lope towards us. They're limping and bloody, but alive.

"You guys okay?" Leonty asks.

"We're all fine." Natalia looks to a shed further down the road that my men have surrounded. "What's going on?"

Shura turns to me, his eyes blazing. "We managed to corner Slavik, but we wanted to wait for your call, Andrey."

"Let me come with you," Misha requests, stepping forward with his chest puffed out.

I clasp his shoulder. "I need to do this on my own. I'm leaving you in charge. Stay with your mother and protect your brother. I'm counting on you, son."

I press a kiss to Natalia's lips and stride towards the shed.

It's time for one last conversation with my father.

61

ANDREY

"Well, well, if it isn't my firstborn."

Slavik is more dried blood and soot than he is skin and bones. The whites of his teeth and his eyeballs are the only bits of color left in him.

There's a gun in his hand, but he can barely hold onto it, let alone lift it. "It's foolish for us to be fighting, son. We're on the same side, after all."

"Funny," I scoff. "It took your allies being killed and your men being defeated before you came to that conclusion."

"I always held that position. You were the one who stubbornly clung to my power."

"I built everything I have."

"From the Bratva I handed to you." His eyes narrow. "Sons are meant to respect their fathers."

"And fathers aren't meant to sacrifice their children's safety and happiness for their own benefits," I retort. "That's not the mark of a father; it's the mark of a coward."

His hands tighten on the gun. "Careful, son. Or I might just disinherit you. Viktor may not have your fortitude, but at least he knows how to heel when he's told."

I ignore the tightening in my chest at the thought of my brother. "Unfortunately for you, corpses don't do anything they're commanded to."

Shock bleaches the rest of his color. "You killed him?"

"I did what I had to do."

Ash falls around us like black snow, cinders from the fire I started at the watchtower.

Finally, he nods. "I would have done the same in your place. You're much more like me than I thought. Come back in the fold and we can build—"

"Spare me, old man," I spit. "I already built an empire, no thanks to you. Don't pretend you care about me now. You're still only trying to save your own damn skin."

Slavik shifts from one leg to the other, the muzzle of his gun roving slowly in my direction.

"How would it look," he muses, "killing your own father?"

"I don't concern myself with others' opinions. A true *pakhan* does what he must."

Slavik sneers. It suits him. His face was built for it—to sneer at the child he raised while his other son rots. While his sins rain down on him like ash until he's buried in it.

"I've been around a lot longer than you have, boy. Once I'm

done with you, I'm going to take that pretty little pet of yours and make her my whore."

My fingers spasm as I imagine what it would feel like to wrap my hands around his throat. To watch his eyes fade to darkness.

"But don't worry," he adds. "I'll make sure your son is provided for. After all, I need heirs. My supply of them is dwindling."

He shoots at the same time I do. My bullet buries itself in his arm while his barely grazes my shoulder. I get away with a flesh wound while Slavik roars in pain, stumbling backward until he collides with the exterior wall of the shed behind him.

But before I can finish what I came here to do, he turns and scampers up a nearby set of stairs.

Growling, I sprint after him.

The stairs are wooden, singed by the spreading fires and popping in the heat. Each step creaks under my weight as I go up, up, up…

And emerge onto a rickety rooftop.

It's like looking into the lowest circle of hell from up here. Fires rage on all sides, huge licks of black smoke and orange flames. On the far side of the scaffolding is my father. He's facing outward, hands clasped behind his back. I don't see his gun anywhere.

"Turn around," I order, leveling my own weapon at him. "I will not shoot a man in the back."

When I feel heat behind me, I turn to see that the flames have chewed up the stairs. Going back down that way is no longer an option.

I look back to my father as he turns slowly. My whole world is a kaleidoscope of red and black and my eyes sting.

"Why did you do it?" I rasp. "Why did you turn in the Rostovs and run? Why did you abandon us?"

Slavik's eyebrow floats upward. "You're asking now?"

"There won't be another chance." Heat sears my throat. Sweat trickles down my spine.

"Your mother used to tell me that I didn't have what it took to be a *pakhan* anywhere else." He's whispering, but somehow, his voice carries across the dozen or so yards between us. "I had to prove her wrong."

"And you decided to destroy what you built here first?"

"I couldn't let her enjoy what I had created," he snarls. "I wasn't going to let her reap the benefits of what was mine."

"You took her sanity. Why take her comfort, too?"

"Because she refused to bend. I had no choice but to break her."

The screams coming from beneath us are growing more and more audible. Through the frenzy of voices, I hear one raised above all the others. "Andrey!"

My father recognizes it, too.

"Your woman is already mourning your death." Slavik smiles through his sweat-drenched face as he sinks onto his knees. The wood groans beneath him. "Can you hear her cry?"

"I promised her I would come back to her. I intend to keep that promise."

Slavik clutches his heart sarcastically. "How touching. You're a sentimental one, aren't you?"

"What I am—" I raise my gun as the flames lick closer. "—is a man of my word."

Slavik pouts out a lip, still mocking me. "You would shoot a defenseless man?"

"No." I snort. "I don't intend to waste another bullet on you."

I raise my foot and slam it down on the wood plank beneath me. The same one Slavik is kneeling on.

The wood vibrates, absorbing the force… until it can't take anymore. And it splinters.

My father falls through the gap. The flames beneath swallow him before he even has a chance to scream.

"Goodbye, Slavik," I whisper to the entire space where he'd stood. "The flames can have you."

Then I turn and jump.

EPILOGUE: ANDREY
SIX MONTHS LATER

ANDREY: *You better not still be at work.*

NATALIA: *What if I am?*

ANDREY: *Then I'm gonna have words with Richard. And they won't be pleasant.*

NATALIA: *I just got back from six months of maternity leave. Richard has been accommodating enough.*

ANDREY: *Only because he's terrified of me. Sure you don't want to quit?*

NATALIA: *And do what?*

ANDREY: *I'd say it's about time I put another baby in you.*

NATALIA: *The twins are only seven months old.*

ANDREY: *My point exactly.*

NATALIA: *Andrey…*

ANDREY: *If you're not back in half an hour, I'm coming to*

Sunshield to fuck you on Richard's desk. We'll see how "accommodating" he is after that.

NATALIA: *There's no need to get saucy. I'm already home.*

I put my phone away and go in search of my wife. It doesn't take long.

She's in the gardens with my mother, the two of them sitting on a bench in front of my mother's favorite fountain. A pair of blue jays is eyeing a rival pair of cardinals across the water's surface.

"Isn't that bird pretty, Arina?" Natalia asks, pointing to the male who is prancing around for his mate.

Arina looks blankly where Natalia is pointing. "I like birds."

"I know you do," Natalia says gently. "Sarra loves them, too."

Arina tilts her head to the side. "Who?"

"My daughter." They've had this conversation a hundred times already, but you wouldn't know it from Natalia's face. Patient. Loving. Kind.

"You have a daughter?"

Natalia beams. "I do. I have a son, too."

"I always wanted a little girl."

"I have good news for you then," Natalia replies with an easy grin. "Sarra is your granddaughter."

"I'm a grandmother?" Her brow crinkles before she decides, "That's nice."

I step behind a hedge so they won't see me watching.

Epilogue: Andrey

"So, that would make you...?" My mother's lips press together when she can't find the right words.

"Your daughter-in-law," Natalia finishes. "I married your son four months ago. You were at the wedding, actually. We had it right here in the garden. You did such a good job designing it that we couldn't think of anywhere more beautiful."

My mother fidgets, her mind having a hard time accepting the reality Natalia is laying out for her. Natalia reaches out to squeeze her fingers, and just like that, she calms down.

Was it always that easy?

"I can't remember," Arina admits.

"That's okay. I forget things, too. But we made a video. I can show it to you if you want."

Arina is quiet for so long that I think she's zoned out again. "I'd like that," she says finally. "Maybe another day."

"Whenever you're ready." Natalia smiles, patting her hand.

"I never thought Andrey would get married," Arina blurts suddenly, just when I think the conversation is over. "He's not like his father, is he?"

I tense without realizing it, only relaxing when Natalia shakes her head. "No. He's not like his father at all."

"I'm glad." Arina pulls her hand from Natalia's and looks up at the sky. "It's getting dark."

Natalia rises to her feet and offers Arina a hand. "Let me take you back to your room."

My wife helps my mother to her feet, and the two of them turn towards the manor as I step onto the path. Arina stiffens, but Natalia winks.

"Hello, Andrey." She leads Arina over to me. Without letting go of my mother's hand, she stretches on her tiptoes and kisses me on the lips. "Arina and I were just going back inside, weren't we, Arina?"

My mother simply nods, but she doesn't make eye contact with me. "It's getting dark," is all she says.

We walk her to her room together. When I look back, the birds are gone.

"I can't believe our teenager is in bed before the babies," I sigh as we finally close the door to the nursery.

It was an hour of soothing one twin only for the other to start wailing, setting off the first. I know they're only seven months old, but I'm convinced they were doing it on purpose.

Natalia walks into my arms and rests her cheek on my chest. "Our teenager had a full day of school and then football practice. The twins spent most of the day in the same four square feet of blanket."

"If Katya and Mila have their way, the twins will be running track and field before too long."

As the twins' self-described "favorite aunts," Katya and Mila have taken it upon themselves to get the twins crawling as soon as possible. But I'm fine letting them be adorable potato sacks for another few weeks. Once they're mobile, life is going to get crazy.

"It was a great idea to make Misha join a team," Natalia says. "I think he's actually making friends."

Epilogue: Andrey

"I'm surprised he gave in so easily."

She rolls her eyes. "He'll do anything you suggest. He worships the ground you walk on."

I walk her into our bedroom, pressing fluttering kisses along her neck. "You're the one he worships. The kid is taking guitar lessons. That has 'Natalia Kuznetsov' written all over it."

"Guilty as charged. But he enjoys them! I checked."

She squeals as I push her onto the mattress and climb on top of her. "I know. I heard him playing for Kat yesterday."

"Oh! That reminds me: Kat and Shura can't watch the twins Saturday evening like normal. They're going on a babymoon."

I arch a brow. "What in the hell is a babymoon?"

"It's like a honeymoon before you have a baby. One last trip before they're drowning in the newborn stage."

"Forget them. What about us?" I taste the soft skin behind her ear, pressing my lips to her thundering pulse. "We have three kids. We need alone time more than they do."

Her cheeks turn a rosy pink. "I didn't think you'd mind."

"Ordinarily, I wouldn't," I admit, ghosting my lips over hers. "But I had plans this weekend."

"Oh?"

I pull at the shoulder ties of her dress. "It was going to be a magical weekend, but I guess I'll have to cancel the three-night stay I booked at Chateaux Arnaud."

She gasps. "You didn't!"

"We didn't have a proper honeymoon after the wedding. And I was thinking, since you're done breastfeeding, it was time we had a real honeymoon—no friends, no kids, no dog."

Her eyes shine brightly, but she bites her bottom lip all the same. "But what about the twins?"

"Luckily, we don't need Kat and Shura. Annie and Mila have already agreed to take them."

"Really?" There's still a shadow of doubt. "They're ready for that for three whole days?"

"Beatrice will be there to help, too. What's the point of having a five-star nanny if we don't make use of her?"

She's still chewing on her lower lip. "What about Misha?"

"You said it yourself: Misha's busy. He's got classes in the morning and football in the evenings. And Remi never leaves his side. He's not gonna miss us for a weekend."

"Okay, but—"

I pin her arms to the mattress over her head. "What's the point of moving every single one of our friends into this manor if we can't rely on them every so often?"

She gently pries a hand free so she can caress my face with her fingers. "It was your idea to have Kat, Leonty, and Shura move in, wise guy."

"Doesn't mean I don't miss the quiet every now and then." Our hips brush and I know she feels the electric jolt between our bodies. "Especially if that quiet involves you."

She takes a deep breath and nods. "You're right. We need a little break—just the two of us."

"Just the two of us, some good food, a lot of great sex…"

Natalia arches a brow. "All this sex we'll be having—do you have ulterior motives, Mr. Kuznetsov?"

I press a hand to her stomach, already imagining her filled with my child. I twitch at the very idea. "I gave you six months, Natalia."

She reaches between us to palm my hardness. "Some would argue that's not long enough."

"Fine. Then consider it practice for when you are ready to have another baby."

She strokes me over my boxes, a slow smile spreading across her face. "You have yourself a deal, sir."

Growling, I slip my tongue into her mouth as I relieve her of her clothes. Her body is unbelievably soft, unbearably supple under mine. She trembles as I slide home in her.

We rock together, fingers intertwined, breathing mingled. "Oh, fuck it," she moans. "Put another baby in me."

"You might regret that tomorrow, *lastochka*," I whisper in her ear as I sink in deeper

"When it comes to you, Andrey Kuznetsov," she sighs dreamily, "I regret nothing."

EXTENDED EPILOGUE: NATALIA
FIVE YEARS LATER

Check out the Extended Epilogue to EMERALD VICES:
https://dl.bookfunnel.com/4ja7ivg4w5

ALSO BY NICOLE FOX

Novikov Bratva
Ivory Ashes
Ivory Oath

Egorov Bratva
Tangled Innocence
Tangled Decadence

Zakrevsky Bratva
Requiem of Sin
Sonata of Lies
Rhapsody of Pain

Bugrov Bratva
Midnight Purgatory
Midnight Sanctuary

Oryolov Bratva
Cruel Paradise
Cruel Promise

Pushkin Bratva
Cognac Villain
Cognac Vixen

Viktorov Bratva
Whiskey Poison
Whiskey Pain

Orlov Bratva

Champagne Venom

Champagne Wrath

Uvarov Bratva

Sapphire Scars

Sapphire Tears

Vlasov Bratva

Arrogant Monster

Arrogant Mistake

Zhukova Bratva

Tarnished Tyrant

Tarnished Queen

Stepanov Bratva

Satin Sinner

Satin Princess

Makarova Bratva

Shattered Altar

Shattered Cradle

Solovev Bratva

Ravaged Crown

Ravaged Throne

Vorobev Bratva

Velvet Devil

Velvet Angel

Romanoff Bratva

Immaculate Deception
Immaculate Corruption

Kovalyov Bratva
Gilded Cage
Gilded Tears
Jaded Soul
Jaded Devil
Ripped Veil
Ripped Lace

Mazzeo Mafia Duet
Liar's Lullaby (Book 1)
Sinner's Lullaby (Book 2)

Bratva Crime Syndicate
Can be read in any order!
Lies He Told Me
Scars He Gave Me
Sins He Taught Me

Belluci Mafia Trilogy
Corrupted Angel (Book 1)
Corrupted Queen (Book 2)
Corrupted Empire (Book 3)

De Maggio Mafia Duet
Devil in a Suit (Book 1)
Devil at the Altar (Book 2)

Kornilov Bratva Duet
Married to the Don (Book 1)

Til Death Do Us Part (Book 2)

Heirs to the Bratva Empire

Can be read in any order!

Kostya

Maksim

Andrei

Princes of Ravenlake Academy (Bully Romance)

Can be read as standalones!

Cruel Prep

Cruel Academy

Cruel Elite

Tsezar Bratva

Nightfall (Book 1)

Daybreak (Book 2)

Russian Crime Brotherhood

Can be read in any order!

Owned by the Mob Boss

Unprotected with the Mob Boss

Knocked Up by the Mob Boss

Sold to the Mob Boss

Stolen by the Mob Boss

Trapped with the Mob Boss

Volkov Bratva

Broken Vows (Book 1)

Broken Hope (Book 2)

Broken Sins *(standalone)*

Other Standalones

Vin: A Mafia Romance

Box Sets

Bratva Mob Bosses (Russian Crime Brotherhood Books 1-6)

Tsezar Bratva (Tsezar Bratva Duet Books 1-2)

Heirs to the Bratva Empire

The Mafia Dons Collection

The Don's Corruption

Made in the USA
Columbia, SC
25 August 2024

41144318R00233